餐旅英文

English for Hospitality and Tourism

鄭寶菁 編著

Foreword

English for Hospitality and Tourism

As a Commissioner at the Trade and Investment Queensland (Australia) Office in Taiwan, I find that the topics and language content covered in English for Hospitality and Tourism to be extremely powerful for individuals who travel the world for business, pleasure or visiting friends and relatives.

English for Hospitality and Tourism provides the key essentials & tools to help a person to start a good dialogue, as well as helps you create strong and life-long impressions on people whom you meet within only a few minutes. English for Hospitality and Tourism also provides dialogue pieces that are rich in culture & information, helping you connect to other people from the English-speaking world in a snap, and prompt communications that provide long-lasting and memorable relationships.

English for Hospitality and Tourism provides a systematic way of learning communicative & listening English language learning skills. English for Hospitality and Tourism also provides an ultimate guide to"small talk", providing great conversation starters that helps you make small talk that leave everlasting impressions.

English for Hospitality and Tourism is filled with straightforward, easy-to-learn, yet essential English phrases and dialogues that can immediately help you boost international relationships. It also provides practical scenarios and simulations that one might encounter in the international world of business and tourism; when communicating with individuals from English-speaking backgrounds. English for Hospitality and Tourism would not only help you learn English language at ease, but also, enhance your international and cultural perspectives.

English for Hospitality and Tourism provides a great overview of the hospitality, food & beverage services, and travel & tourism industries in various aspects including language studies, culture and actual scenarios & settings in various industries and occupations. What is most interesting about this book is that it covers the most interesting hospitality, tourism and food & beverage topics that you, perhaps, could never have thought of, expanding your concepts in hospitality and tourism, bringing you innovative travel ideas either from the perspectives of a tourist, a learner of the English language or a businessman/woman.

- What I find to be the most interesting topics covered by English for Hospitality and Tourism include the following:
- Interesting ways to explore a city – balloon rides, helicopter rides;
- Different ways to drink whiskey – neat, water back (chaser), highball;
- The 6's of wine tasting→See–Swirl–Sniff–Sip–Savor–Spit;
- State-of-the-art self-service, check-in kiosks at airports
- This is also one of the latest technological developments in Australian airports, as well as other international airports. English for Hospitality and Tourism encompasses the latest developments including self-service kiosks, self-tagging and self-service bag drop, all of which I think are a "must-know" for all.

Thus, I strongly recommend English for Hospitality and Tourism to current and future practitioners in the international business and tourism world, from those intending to step into the hospitality and tourism industries to those who intend be at the forefront of the world of international trade, investment, tourism and business.

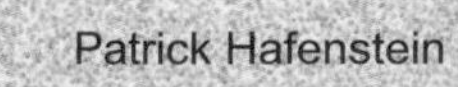

Patrick Hafenstein

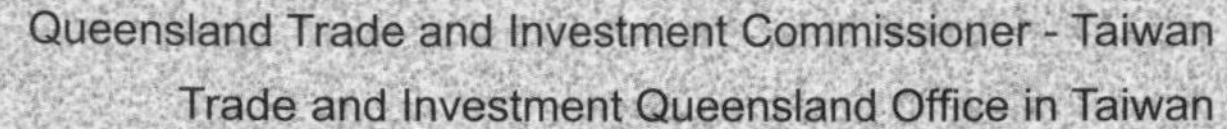

Queensland Trade and Investment Commissioner - Taiwan

Trade and Investment Queensland Office in Taiwan

Foreword

English for Hospitality and Tourism

When I flipped through the units of English for Hospitality and Tourism, I immediately felt that I was touched by a "magic wand" that allowed me to "travel" beautiful journeys, "view" fantastic sceneries, "glide" through the wonderful world of fantastic artists & artworks of Picasso, "see" the most wondrous Seven Wonders of the World at Stonehenge, and "watch" the amazing Auroras in Sweden.

I have no doubt that English for Hospitality and Tourism enriches one's English proficiency for professionals already in the field as well as those intending to step into the field. It also creates great excitement for a learner as it is filled with interesting adventures, hotspot destinations as well as things to eat, drink, see & do! English for Hospitality and Tourism empowers one with cross cultural information that have been neatly embedded in the main conversation contents of each unit. The book is designed like a fairy-tale like story book, traveling from Taiwan across Europe to all these bucket list destinations.

What makes English for Hospitality and Tourism interesting is that the book brings its learners through a beautiful, dream-like journey, whilst learning English with a great sense of ease. English for Hospitality and Tourism also provides rich and great insights into cultural, artistic, smart tourism concepts (E-tourism), at the same time, making its learners feel that English language learning is never too difficult for a non-native speaker.

As I went through each unit, I felt I was slowly being immersed in a European dream tour - understanding Michelin restaurants; sightseeing in beautiful London city; watching a Broadway show; visiting one of the Seven Wonders of the World; passing by beautiful lavender & sunflower fields on my way to a vineyard tour to Provence, France; watching the amazing Northern Lights in Sweden; and drinking exotic wines and Scottish whiskey.

When I went through the book, I immediately knew that English for Hospitality and Tourism is THE BOOK for those in our industry. With Taiwan growing in its hospitality, tourism, food & beverage industries, this is a MUST HAVE book for those intending to step into the industry, or for those who are already in the industry. Taiwan is growing more and more international by the day. Thus, English for Hospitality and Tourism is a definite must learn, must have book for students, teachers and professionals in the industry.

I can confidently state that English for Hospitality and Tourism can help any learner become a more confident, very well-informed, more international, and definitely more communicative in the English language. I'd strongly recommend English for Hospitality and Tourism to managers and employees for in/out company training programs as well as for employee training programs, and for those in the hotel, hospitality, tourism, food & beverage industries intending to internationalize their work environment and prepare for tomorrow's increasingly competitive international market.

Lee Yuting

Yu-Ting, Lee
Chief Executive Officer (CEO)
King Car Group

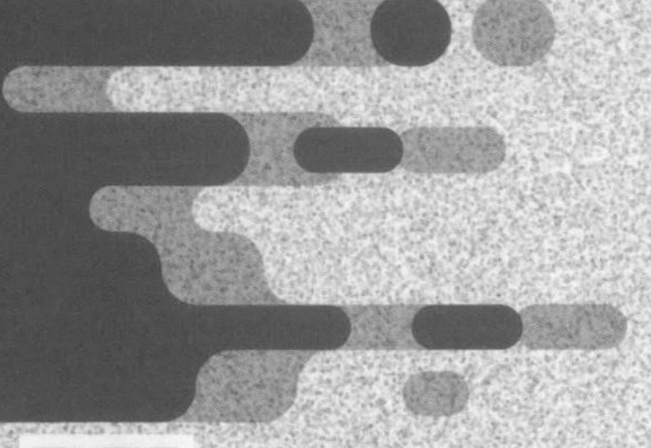

Foreword

English for Hospitality and Tourism

English for Hospitality and Tourism provides a great international perspective of the hospitality, tourism and food & beverage service industries. In addition, the book on English for Hospitality and Tourism makes you feel as if you were literally journeying your way across Europe, learning about culture, art, and the English language at the same time.

When you go through each unit, you will literally feel as if you were enjoying a shot of exquisite whiskey, a glass of great wine or even drinking a shot of great Italian espresso. You will also literally feel as if you were sledging through the cold wintery snow in Sweden, luxury shopping in Vienna, looking into the wilderness in Kiruna, Sweden; sightseeing in the famous London city, and sleeping on an ice bed in Sweden. All these magical and amazing experiences are made to "come true" in this book. What's even more amazing about the book is that without you noticing, you are already immersed and day-dreaming away in the scenarios of each unit of the book, and forgetting that you are naturally learning the English language at the same time.

In addition to offering good coverage of concepts, skills and knowledge of the English language, English for Hospitality and Tourism explores and beautifully covers all the essential industry knowledge including some of the following:

- Communication & interactional English communication skills
- Culture — famous artists(Picasso, Van Gogh, Matisse and Renoir) and Italian coffee drinking culture.
- Smart tourism — online ticket reservation for Broadway musicals, self-service check-in kiosk at the airport.
- Food & Beverages — Michelin restaurants, whiskey, rose wine, wine tasting, vineyard tours and coffee drinking culture.
- Unique forms of hospitality services — ice hotels and nature & wilderness tours in Sweden such as Husky sledging.

Although English for Hospitality and Food & Beverage Service is filled with lots of fun-filled topics, it does not forget the realities and settings that those in the industry today might encounter. For example, it covers air-ticket reservation, hotel reservation, foreign currency exchange and self-service check-in kiosk. It is definitely an up-to-date book that takes into consideration the fast-changing technological aspects of the industry. For example, keywords, vocabulary and phrases involved in airline reservations such as e-bookings, e-reservations, e-tickets, e-itineraries, e-receipts, amongst many other smart tourism concepts have been beautifully blended into the main contents of the dialogue of each unit. English for Hospitality and Tourism also introduces a "futuristic" perspective of self-service check-in which expects every passenger to check-in 100% by himself/herself at the airport. This aspect is actually already happening in airports in developed countries, and is one simulation that is a must-know for everyone.

All the procedures, simulation of the scenarios of each unit are very real, tactful and practical. There is plenty to learn from each unit, as each unit is so condensed with rich and powerful information that one might expect in a real-life scenario. English for Hospitality and Tourism is a great book that has been carefully researched and adapted for non-native speakers of English in Taiwan, ·and understands extremely well the handicaps & gaps in English language for Taiwanese learners.

Whatever your identity may be — from a world traveler; a professional in the tourism and hospitality, an educator in the College of Food & Beverages, College of Eeisure Management, Hospitality Management, College of Business; to a student or self-learner-English for Hospitality and Tourism is definitely a must-have, must-teach and must-learn great book!

Professor Jinn-Yang Uang
Dean of Business School
College of Business
Chinese Culture University
Taipei, Taiwan

Foreword

English for Hospitality and Tourism

English for Hospitality and Tourism is one of the most practical, yet fun-filled books I have ever come across! I would highly recommend it to all non-native speakers of English in the hospitality, food & beverage service, travel & tourism industries. English for Hospitality and Tourism provides a great spoken & listening training guide towards those intending to step into, or for those already in the hospitality, tourism and food & beverage industries.

English for Hospitality and Tourism covers a good mix of the hospitality, tourism and food & beverage industries. It consists of a wide, yet smartly narrowed-down range of topics including E-tourism, ethnic cultures, art, food & beverages, miracles of nature, nature & wilderness, international brand names that no one should ever miss out! The contents of the book have been so carefully blended with such rich information and language learning that one does not feel the pressure of learning the English language at all. The topics and contents are so lively, life-like and catchy that it seems like such an interesting "story-book" rather than an English language book to start off with!

English for Hospitality and Tourism provides a learner with a great overview of hospitality, food & beverage service, travel & tourism industries using a European context, and covers the most interesting travel destinations in the world that one could ever imagine. London (UK) is one of the most visited cities in the world. Stonehenge in Wiltshire, the United Kingdom is one of the most famous and recognizable sites in the world, and also considered one of the Seven Wonders of the World. Edinburgh (Scotland) is widely known for its great Scottish whiskies. Vienna (Austria) is well-known for its many flagship stores & premium luxury goods, and is a shopping haven. Provence (France) is a wine heaven. Rome (Italy) is famous for its great coffee, coffee culture and coffee history. Malaga (Spain) is the birthplace of Picasso, one of the most influential artists of the 20th century. Jukkasjärvi in Sweden is the best spot in the world nearest to the North Pole to experience the wondrous Northern lights.

English for Hospitality and Tourism is a great book for a non-native speaker of English as it has many interesting exercises that are easy to follow, filled with so many fantastic and eye-catching photos that attract one's attention that makes one want to flip the pages. It is also a very informative book and I could immediately tell that the author has done a great amount of research in order to create such an innovative, well-informed, structured, yet fun-filled book.

English for Hospitality and Tourism provides an invaluable reference for learners, current & future practitioners and anyone working towards professional qualifications in the hospitality, tourism and food & beverage industries. This book strongly supports a range of professionals and is a "must-have" whatever your identity may be – from professionals in the tourism & hospitality business; educators in the College of Food & Beverages, College of Leisure Management, College of Hospitality Management, College of Business, College of English Language; teachers Teaching English as a Second Language (TESL), students, self-learners, to world travelers.

TiChih Chen Steven

Senior Consultant, United Daily News Group
Former General Manager Education Department, United Daily News Group

Preface

English for Hospitality and Tourism

English for Hospitality and Tourism is designed to give learners the most essential English communication and listening skills necessary for those in the hospitality, tourism, and Food & Beverage Service industries. English for Hospitality and Tourism is entirely based on the communicative language approach. Its primary goal is to enable learners to communicate effectively based on an array of typical hospitality, tourism and food & beverage scenarios and situations. English for Hospitality and Tourism also helps learners develop the English language skills necessary to step into the industry, or for those already in the industry.

English for Hospitality and Tourism provides a perfect mirror view of a tourist/customer and roles played by those in the industry including Michelin restaurant staff 米其林餐廳服務員, travel agents 旅行代辦人 / 旅行代理人, sommeliers 侍酒師, vintners 釀酒師 / 葡萄酒商, baristas 咖啡師, duty-free shopping service attendants 免稅店服務員, museum attendants 博物館服務員, box office clerks 百老匯劇院售票員工, airport ground staff 機場地勤服務員 ,bank clerks at a foreign exchange counter 兌換外幣銀行專員 ,customs officers 海關, hotel receptionists 飯店接待員, hotel bellboy 旅館的服務生 and customer representatives 客戶服務代表。

Christina

鄭寶菁

Content

STRUCTURE OF THIS BOOK

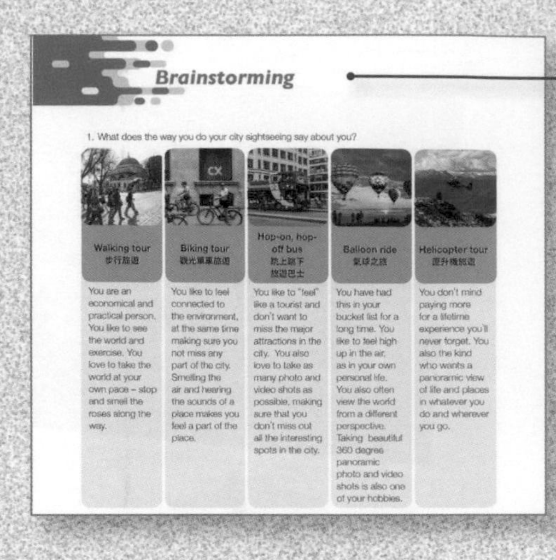
Brainstorming

1. What does the way you do your city sightseeing say about you?

Walking tour 步行旅遊	Biking tour 騎單車旅遊	Hop-on, hop-off bus 跳上跳下旅遊巴士	Balloon ride 氣球之旅	Helicopter tour 直升機旅遊
You are an economical and practical person. You like to see the world and exercise. You love to take the world at your own pace – stop and smell the roses along the way.	You like to feel connected to the environment, at the same time making sure you not miss any part of the city. Smelling the air and hearing the sounds of a place makes you feel a part of the place.	You like to "feel" like a tourist and don't want to miss the major attractions in the city. You also love to take as many photo and video shots as possible, making sure that you don't miss out all the interesting spots in the city.	You have had this in your bucket list for a long time. You like to feel high up in the air, as in your own personal life. You also often view the world from a different perspective. Taking beautiful 360 degree panoramic photo and video shots is also one of your hobbies.	You don't mind paying more for a lifetime experience you'll never forget. You also the kind who wants a panoramic view of life and places in whatever you do and wherever you go.

Brainstorming
腦力激盪
運用照片及簡單文字呈現，配合常用問句激發學習想像力。

Conversation
會話
模擬飯店、旅遊和餐飲行業之實境會話，增進英語溝通能力。

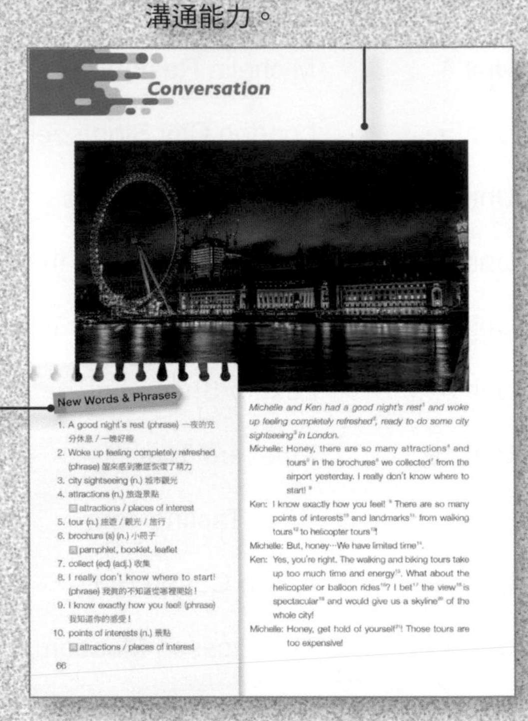
Conversation

New Words & Phrases

1. A good night's rest (phrase) 一夜的充分休息／一晚好眠
2. Woke up feeling completely refreshed (phrase) 醒來感到徹底恢復了精力
3. city sightseeing (n.) 城市觀光
4. attractions (n.) 旅遊景點
   attractions / places of interest
5. tour (n.) 旅遊／觀光／旅行
6. brochure (s) (n.) 小冊子
   pamphlet, booklet, leaflet
7. collect (ed) (adj.) 收集
8. I really don't know where to start! (phrase) 我真的不知道從哪裡開始！
9. I know exactly how you feel! (phrase) 我知道你的感受！
10. points of interests (n.) 景點
    attractions / places of interest

Michelle and Ken had a good night's rest[1] and woke up feeling completely refreshed[2], ready to do some city sightseeing[3] in London.

Michelle: Honey, there are so many attractions[4] and tours[5] in the brochures[6] we collected[7] from the airport yesterday. I really don't know where to start![8]

Ken: I know exactly how you feel![9] There are so many points of interests[10] and landmarks[11] from walking tours[12] to helicopter tours[13]!

Michelle: But, honey—We have limited time[14].

Ken: Yes, you're right. The walking and biking tours take up too much time and energy[15]. What about the helicopter or balloon rides[16]? I bet[17] the view[18] is spectacular[19] and would give us a skyline[20] of the whole city!

Michelle: Honey, get hold of yourself[21]! Those tours are too expensive!

66

New Words & Phrases
單字及片語
補充大量單字及片語，每頁皆與會話內容互相對應，使學生可隨時查閱相關單字。

Basic Words
基礎單字
圖像記憶學習法，輔以圖片增加印象，讓枯燥的背誦單字更簡單。

Conversation Preview
會話預習
會話前的預習加速進入學習狀況，有效提升上課之學習成效。

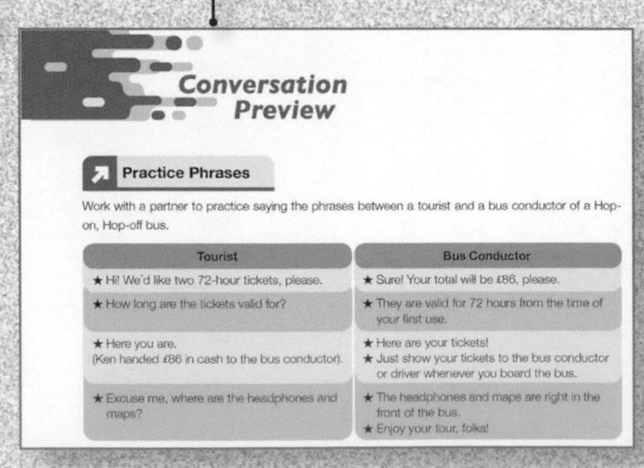
Conversation Preview

Practice Phrases

Work with a partner to practice saying the phrases between a tourist and a bus conductor of a Hop-on, Hop-off bus.

Tourist	Bus Conductor
★ Hi! We'd like two 72-hour tickets, please.	★ Sure! Your total will be £86, please.
★ How long are the tickets valid for?	★ They are valid for 72 hours from the time of your first use.
★ Here you are. (Ken handed £86 in cash to the bus conductor).	★ Here are your tickets! ★ Just show your tickets to the bus conductor or driver whenever you board the bus.
★ Excuse me, where are the headphones and maps?	★ The headphones and maps are right in the front of the bus. ★ Enjoy your tour, folks!

STRUCTURE OF THIS BOOK

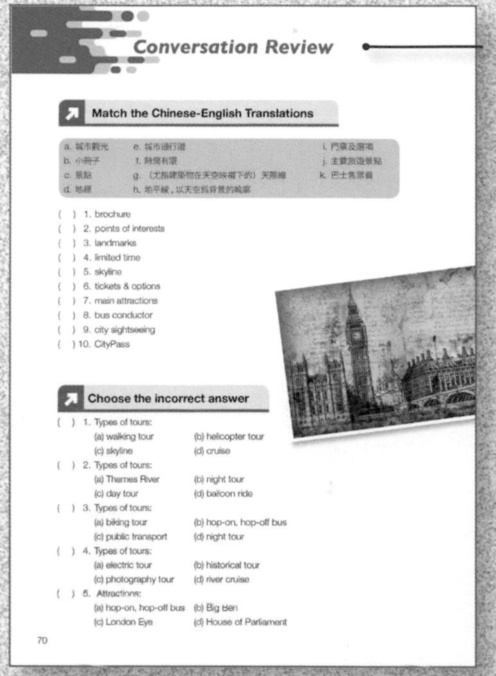

Conversation Review

Match the Chinese-English Translations

a. 城市觀光	e. 城市通行證	i. 門票及選項
b. 小冊子	f. 時間有限	j. 主要旅遊景點
c. 景點	g. （尤指建築物在天空映襯下的）天際線	k. 巴士售票員
d. 地標	h. 地平線，以天空為背景的輪廓	

( ) 1. brochure
( ) 2. points of interests
( ) 3. landmarks
( ) 4. limited time
( ) 5. skyline
( ) 6. tickets & options
( ) 7. main attractions
( ) 8. bus conductor
( ) 9. city sightseeing
( ) 10. CityPass

Choose the incorrect answer

( ) 1. Types of tours:
(a) walking tour (b) helicopter tour
(c) skyline (d) cruise

( ) 2. Types of tours:
(a) Thames River (b) night tour
(c) day tour (d) balloon ride

( ) 3. Types of tours:
(a) biking tour (b) hop-on, hop-off bus
(c) public transport (d) night tour

( ) 4. Types of tours:
(a) electric tour (b) historical tour
(c) photography tour (d) river cruise

( ) 5. Attractions:
(a) hop-on, hop-off bus (b) Big Ben
(c) London Eye (d) House of Parliament

70

Conversation Review
會話複習

藉由練習題不斷強化及反覆練習前面所學習之大量口說英語、聽力內容、關鍵詞彙、重要句子和行業關鍵詞，以達到事半功倍之學習效果。

Listen and Pronounce
聽力及發音練習

大量聽力及發音練習，有助於提升聽力及口說能力，並應用於飯店、旅遊及餐飲等相關行業。

Listen and Pronounce

Listen to the audio first. Then, try pronouncing each one of the following:

1. Balloon tour	氣球旅遊
2. Biking tour	單車旅遊
3. Cultural tour	文化旅遊
4. Food tour	美食旅遊
5. Helicopter tour	直升機旅遊
6. Historical tour	歷史古蹟旅遊
7. Hop-on, hop-off bus tour	隨上隨下觀光巴士
8. Photography tour	攝影旅遊
9. Running tour	跑步旅遊
10. Speedboat tour	高速遊艇旅遊

Listen and fill in the blanks

Listen to the conversation and fill in the blanks.

1. The couple is looking at attractions and tours from the brochures they collected at the airport, and is planning to do some London city s __________.
2. There are many points of interests and landmarks, from walking tours to __________, but the couple has limited time.
3. Ken suggests the helicopter and balloon rides would give them a spectacular v __________ and s __________ of the London city!
4. Looks like the couple decided to catch the h ________-________, h ________-________ bus where they can visit the House of Parliament, Tower of London, Big Ben, and London Eye!
5. The couple bought two __________ for a total of £ __________.

Photographs
圖片配對題

藉由彩色圖片來引導學生選出正確之單字，以加深學習記憶。

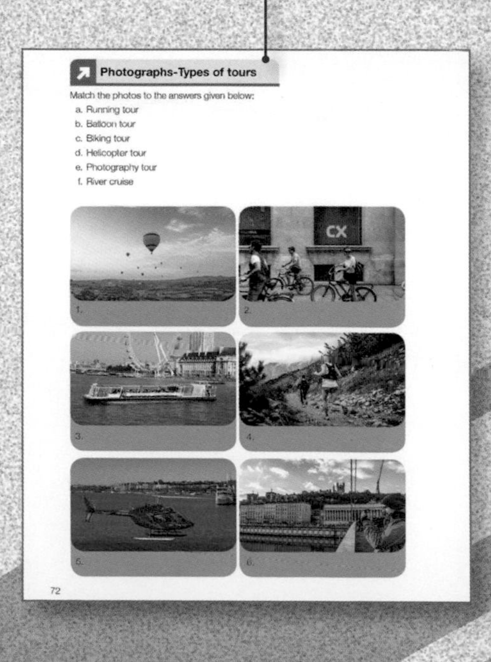

Photographs-Types of tours

Match the photos to the answers given below:

a. Running tour
b. Balloon tour
c. Biking tour
d. Helicopter tour
e. Photography tour
f. River cruise

1. 2. 3. 4. 5. 6.

72

AIR-TICKET RESERVATION

Unit 01

Learning Objectives

What you will learn in this unit...

- How to make an air-ticket reservation?
- How to take an air-ticket reservation?
- Names of major airlines.
- Names of some countries and their capital cities.
- Types of air-tickets.
- What is on a flight itinerary?
- Procedures involved in making an air-ticket reservation.
- Procedures involved in confirming an air-ticket reservation.
- Air-ticket reservation related keyword verbs, phrases and idioms.

Brainstorming

1. What airline you choose says about you?

Singapore Airlines 新加坡航空

Your desired level of service is very high. You also love a comfortable life and highly value courtesy & efficient service.

Qatar Airways 卡塔爾航空

You are the type who makes sure that you get the most value out of the money you spend. You also enjoy excellent food, great service and good in-flight entertainment. And, you know that you can request for a seat change if there's one available!

Eva Air 長榮航空

You enjoy good food, comfortable seating and accessories. You know that this airline can provide you with services that exceed your expectations in every way.

Emirates 阿聯酋航空

You have traveled a lot on many other airlines, and finally found "the" airline that best satisfies you. You also enjoy the extra leg room that is more than what you get on some premium economy flights elsewhere.

Qantas Airways 澳洲航空

You believe that your inflight experience should be as exciting as your destination. You also value service quality, spacious cabins, seasonal cuisines and a good of inflight entertainment.

2. What are the names of some major airlines?
   Examples: Qantas Airways, Cathay Pacific, American Airlines, etc.
3. Name some popular countries and their capital cities.
   Example: Australia, Canberra (capital city).
4. Ask your partner what is his/her favorite airlines.
5. Ask your partner what is his/her favorite country.
6. Ask your partner what is his/her favorite city.

BASIC WORDS

travel agent 旅行代辦人

travel agency 旅行社

Airlines 航空公司

CROATIA AIRLINES
EGYPTAIR
AEGEAN
TURKISH AIRLINES
Ethiopian
Avianca
ADRIA
AIR CHINA
TAP PORTUGAL
AIR CANADA
Blue1
AIR NEW ZEALAND
ASIANA AIRLINES
QANTAS
Lufthansa
ANA
SAS Scandinavian Airlines
UNITED
LOT
BRITISH AIRWAYS
SINGAPORE AIRLINES
THAI

One-way / Single trip air-ticket 單程機票

Round trip / Return air-ticket 來回機票

Multiple destinations / Stopovers 中途停留

Departure date / Departing 出發日期 / 出發

Return date / Returning 回程日期 / 回程

8,699 miles

San Francisco, USA

Bengaluru, In

direct / non-stop flight 直飛

stopover 中途停留

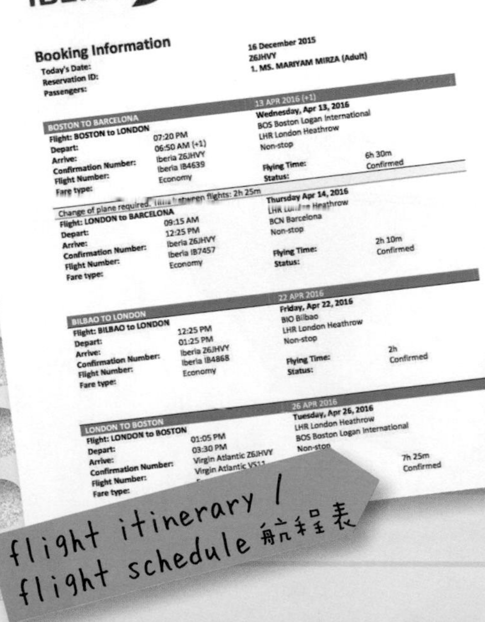

IBERIA

Booking Information

Today's Date: 16 December 2015
Reservation ID: Z6JHVY
Passengers: 1. MS. MARIYAM MIRZA (Adult)

BOSTON TO BARCELONA — 13 APR 2016 (+1)

Flight: BOSTON to LONDON		Wednesday, Apr 13, 2016	
Depart:	07:20 PM	BOS Boston Logan International	
Arrive:	06:50 AM (+1)	LHR London Heathrow	
Confirmation Number:	Iberia Z6JHVY	Non-stop	
Flight Number:	Iberia IB4639	Flying Time:	6h 30m
Fare type:	Economy	Status:	Confirmed

Change of plane required. Time between flights: 2h 25m

Flight: LONDON to BARCELONA		Thursday Apr 14, 2016	
Depart:	09:15 AM	LHR London Heathrow	
Arrive:	12:25 PM	BCN Barcelona	
Confirmation Number:	Iberia Z6JHVY	Non-stop	
Flight Number:	Iberia IB7457	Flying Time:	2h 10m
Fare type:	Economy	Status:	Confirmed

BILBAO TO LONDON — 22 APR 2016

Flight: BILBAO to LONDON		Friday, Apr 22, 2016	
Depart:	12:25 PM	BIO Bilbao	
Arrive:	01:25 PM	LHR London Heathrow	
Confirmation Number:	Iberia Z6JHVY	Non-stop	
Flight Number:	Iberia IB4868	Flying Time:	2h
Fare type:	Economy	Status:	Confirmed

LONDON TO BOSTON — 26 APR 2016

Flight: LONDON to BOSTON		Tuesday, Apr 26, 2016	
Depart:	01:05 PM	LHR London Heathrow	
Arrive:	03:30 PM	BOS Boston Logan International	
Confirmation Number:	Virgin Atlantic Z6JHVY	Non-stop	
Flight Number:	Virgin Atlantic VS11		7h 25m
Fare type:			Confirmed

flight itinerary / flight schedule 航程表

WikiAirlines

YOUR TICKET+ITINERARY

e-ticket itinerary receipt 電子機票之收據

Conversation Preview

Practice Phrases

Work with a partner to practice saying the phrases between a travel agent and a customer.

Travel Agent 旅行代辦人	Customer 客戶
★ Tiger Travel Agency. This is Ann. How may I help you?	★ Good morning! I'd like to make air-ticket reservations to London for two.
★ Will that be one-way or return air-tickets? ★ Will that be single or round trip tickets?	★ Return, please. ★ One way, please. ★ Single, please. ★ Round trip, please.
★ Is there any particular airlines that you prefer?	★ British Airways, please. ★ I prefer British Airways. ★ EVA Air, please. ★ I prefer EVA Air. ★ British Airways and EVA Air.
★ Can I have your departure date and return date? ★ Can I have your travel dates, please?	★ We plan to depart on July 1st and return on July 30th. ★ July 1st to July 30th.
★ Can I have your phone number? ★ Can I have your contact number?	★ Sure. It's 0987-654-321.

Travel Agent 旅行代辦人	Customer 客戶
★ Hi, Ken. I have checked out the flight schedules for both British Airways and EVA Air. ★ For EVA Air, there only one flight available every Thursday. There are two stopovers. The first stopover is in Bangkok and the second stopover is in Amsterdam. ★ The total flight time is 23 hours and 50 minutes.	★ Hmmm...Sounds like a really long flight.
★ British Airways has direct flights from Taipei to London. ★ And, the flight time for British Airways much shorter, around 14 hours.	★ I'd like to make a reservation on British Airways.
★ Can I have your email address, please?	★ It's ken1234@gmail.com
★ I'll e-mail you the flight price and flight itinerary. ★ Can you also e-mail me your first names and last names as shown in your passports?	★ Thank you. ★ Sure. ★ Of course.
★ Please note that you would need to pay within the next three days to lock in your flight price. ★ Otherwise, prices are subject to change without notice.	★ Got it! I'll let you know soon.
★ I will e-mail you your e-ticket a copy of your e-ticket itinerary receipt.	★ Thank you.

Listening Practice

track 01

Listen to the audio. Listen to the conversation between a travel agent and customer, and then choose the correct answer.

( ) 1. (a) Ken wishes to make two return air-ticket reservations to London for their honeymoon.
(b) Ken wishes to make two one-way air-ticket reservations to London for their honeymoon.

( ) 2. (a) Either British Airways or EVA Air would be fine for Ken.
(b) Ken prefers British Airways over EVA Air.

( ) 3. (a) The EVA Air flight to London is a non-stop flight and the total flight time is 23 hours and 50 minutes.
(b) The EVA Air flight to London includes two stopovers and the total flight time is 23 hours and 50 minutes.

( ) 4. (a) The British Airways flight to London is a direct flight, and the total flight time is 14 hours.
(b) The EVA Air flight to London includes two stopovers, and the total flight time is 14 hours.

Test Yourself

Fill in the blanks with the correct answers:

a. stopovers	c. direct flights	e. one-way
b. flight schedules	d. flight price	f. departure date

1. Travel agent: Tiger Travel Agency. This is Ann. How may I help you?
Ken: Good morning! I'd like to make air-ticket reservations to London for two.
Travel agent: Will that be ____________ or return air-tickets?
Ken: Return air-tickets, please.
2. Travel agent: Is there any particular airline that you prefer?
Ken: Either British Airways or EVA Air will be great.
Travel agent: Ok. Can I have your ____________ and return date?
Ken: We plan to depart on July 1st and return on July 30th.
3. About thirty minutes later, Ann from Tiger Travel Agency called back.
Travel agent: Hi, Ken. I have checked out the ____________ for both British Airways and EVA Air. For EVA Air, there only one flight available every Thursday. There are two ____________ . The first stopover is in Bangkok and the second stopover is in Amsterdam.
4. Ken: What is the flight schedule like for British Airways?
Travel agent: British Airways has ____________ from Taipei to London. And, the flight time for British Airways much shorter, around 14 hours.
5. Ken: I'd like to make a reservation on British Airways.
Travel agent: Sure. Can I have your email address, please?
Ken: It's ken1234@gmail.com
Travel agent: I'll e-mail you your ____________ and flight itinerary.

Conversation

track 02

Ken and Michelle plan to go to Europe for their honeymoon[1]. Ken calls up Tiger Travel Agency[2] to make their air-ticket reservations.

Travel agent[3]: Tiger Travel Agency. This is Ann. How may I help you?

Ken: Good morning! I'd like to make air-ticket reservations to London for two.

Travel agent: [a] Will that be one-way[4] or return[5] air-tickets?

Ken: Return air-tickets, please.

Travel agent: [b] Is there any particular[6] airline[7] that you prefer[8]?

Ken: Either British Airways[9] or EVA Air[10] will be great.

Travel agent: Ok. [c] Can I have your departure date[11] and return date[12]?

Ken: We plan to depart on July 1st and return on July 30th.

Travel agent: Sure. Can I have your phone number?

Ken: Sure. It's 0987-654-321.

Travel agent: [d] I'll call you back in a bit.

About thirty minutes later, Ann from Tiger Travel Agency called back.

Travel agent: Hi, Ken. [e] I have checked out the flight schedules[13] for both British Airways and EVA Air. For EVA Air, there only one flight available[14] every Thursday. There are two stopovers[15]. The first stopover is in Bangkok[16] and the second stopover is in Amsterdam[17].

Ken: Hmmm...Sounds like a really long flight.

Travel agent: Yes, it is. [f] The total flight time is 23 hours and 50 minutes.

Ken: What about British Airways?

Travel agent: British Airways has direct flights[18] from Taipei to London. And, the flight time for British Airways is much shorter, around 14 hours.

New Words & Phrases

track 03

1. honeymoon (n.) 度蜜月
2. travel agency (n.) 旅行社
3. travel agent (n.) 旅行代辦人 / 旅行代理人
4. one-way air-ticket (n.) 單程機票
   同 single trip 反 return air-ticket
5. return air-ticket (n.) 來回機票
   反 one-way ticket 同 round trip)
6. particular (adj.) 特別的 / 特定的
7. airline (n.) 航空公司 同 airway / Air
8. prefer (vi.) 更喜歡 / 較喜歡
9. British Airways (n.) 英國航空
10. EVA Air (Evergreen Airlines) (n.) 長榮航空
11. departure date (n.) 出發日期
    反 arrival date 同 travel date(s))
12. return date (n.) 回程日期
    反 departure date 同 travel date(s)
13. flight schedule (n.) 航班時間表
14. flight available (phrase) 有位置班機
15. stopover (flight) (n.) 中途停留
    同 multiple stops
    反 non-stop flight / direct flight)
16. Bangkok (n.) 曼谷〔泰國首都〕
17. Amsterdam (n.) 阿姆斯特丹〔荷蘭首都〕
18. direct flights (n.) 直飛
    同 non-stop flight 反 multiple destinations

New Words & Phrases

19. flight price (n.) 機票價格
    同 air-ticket price
20. flight itinerary (n.) 航班行程
    同 flight schedule
21. first name (n.) 名字 反 last name
22. last name (n.) 姓名 同 first name
23. lock in (price of air-ticket) (idiom) 鎖定價格
    同 keep / secure
24. otherwise (adv.) 否則
25. subject to change (phrase) 可以自行調整
    反 not subject to change
26. e-ticket itinerary receipt (n.)
    電子機票之收據

Ken: [g] What are the air-ticket prices for both airlines?

Travel agent: [h] The air-ticket price for EVA Air is $45,000 (forty-five thousand dollars). And, [i] the air-ticket price for British Airways is $60,000 (sixty thousand dollars).

Ken: I'd like to make a reservation on British Airways.

Travel agent: Sure. Can I have your email address, please?

Ken: It's ken1234@gmail.com

Travel agent: I'll e-mail you the flight price[19] and flight itinerary[20]. Can you also email me your first names[21] and last names[22] as shown in your passports?

Ken: Sure.

Travel agent: [j] Please note that you would need to pay within the next three days to lock in[23] your flight price. [k] Otherwise[24], prices are subject to change[25] without notice.

Ken: Got it! I'll let you know soon.

The next morning, Ken confirmed and paid for his air-tickets. The travel agent then e-mailed him a copy of his e-ticket itinerary receipt[26].

Q & A

1. What is the reason Ken is making air-ticket reservations?
2. What airlines does Ken wish to travel on?
3. What is the flight schedule like for EVA Air?
4. What is the air-ticket price for EVA Air?
5. What information did the travel agent e-mail Ken before he confirmed and paid for his air-tickets?

Important Sentences

a. Will that be one-way or return air-tickets?
你要單程還是來回機票呢？

b. Is there any particular airline that you prefer?
你有特別喜歡那一家航空公司嗎？

c. Can I have your departure date and return date?
你可以提供我你的出發日期及回程日期嗎？

d. I'll call you back in a bit. (同義詞：I'll call you back soon)
我會儘快回電。

e. I have checked out the flight schedules for both British Airways and EVA Air.
我查到英國航空及長榮航空班機時間。

f. The total flight time is 23 hours and 50 minutes.
飛行時間總共是二十三小時五十分鐘。

g. What are the air-ticket prices for both airlines?
這兩家航空公司機票價格是多少？

h. The air-ticket price for EVA Air is $45,000.
長榮航空票價是 $45,000.

i. The air-ticket price for British Airways is $60,000
英國航空票價是 $60,000.

j. Please note that you would need to pay within the next three days to lock in your flight price.
請注意如果你要鎖住目前機票價，你必須在三天內付款。

k. Otherwise, prices are subject to change without notice.
否則，這個價格可以不經通知自行調整。

Conversation Review

Mix and Match the Chinese-English Translations

a. 航班行程	d.旅行社	g.出發日期	j.機票價格
b. 回程日期	e.單程機票	h.中途停留	
c. 電子機票之收據	f.來回機票	i.直飛	

( ) 1. travel agency
( ) 2. one-way air-ticket
( ) 3. return air-ticket
( ) 4. departure date
( ) 5. return date
( ) 6. stopover (flight)
( ) 7. direct flights
( ) 8. flight price
( ) 9. flight itinerary
( ) 10. e-ticket itinerary receipt

track 04

Listen and fill in the blanks

Listen to the conversation and fill in the blanks.

1. The customer would like to purchase two __________ air-tickets.
2. The customer would like to travel on EVA __________.
3. The customer is planning to __________ on March 16th and __________ on March 30th.
4. There is one __________ in Bangkok on the way to London.
5. The air-ticket __________ for one person is $55,000 for EVA Air.

 Listen and Pronounce

I. Listen to the audio first. Then, try practice pronouncing each one of the cities and countries below.

City	Country
1. Athens 雅典	Greece 希臘
2. Auckland 奧克蘭	New Zealand 紐西蘭
3. Berlin 柏林	Germany 德國
4. Dublin 都柏林	Ireland 愛爾蘭
5. Edinburgh 愛丁堡	Scotland 蘇格蘭
6. Helsinki 赫爾辛基	Finland 芬蘭
7. London 倫敦	United Kingdom 英國
8. Madrid 馬德里	Spain 西班牙
9. Moscow 莫斯科	Russia 俄羅斯
10. Osaka 大阪	Japan 日本

II. Listen to the audio first. Then, try practice pronouncing each one of the airlines below:

1. Air Canada	加拿大航空公司
2. British Airways	英國航空公司
3. Cathay Pacific Airways	國泰航空公司
4. Delta Airlines	美國達美航空公司
5. KLM-Royal Dutch Airlines	荷蘭皇家航空公司
6. Lufthansa	德國漢莎航空公司
7. Qantas Airways	澳洲航空公司
8. Swissair	瑞士航空公司
9. Turkish Airlines	土耳其航空公司
10. United Airlines	美國聯合航空公司

Choose the incorrect answer

( ) 1. Types of flights:

(a) stopover flight

(b) multiple stops

(c) direct flight

(d) flight itinerary

( ) 2. Airlines:

(a) EVA Air

(b) London Airways

(c) British Airways

(d) Japan Airlines

( ) 3. Airlines:

(a) Cathay Pacific Airways

(b) United Airlines

(c) Alibaba Airways

(d) Singapore Airlines

( ) 4. Items on an e-ticket

(a) flight number

(b) city / airport

(c) booking reference number

(d) flight delay time

( ) 5. Items on an e-ticket:

(a) departure time

(b) arrival time

(c) pick-up time

(d) departure date

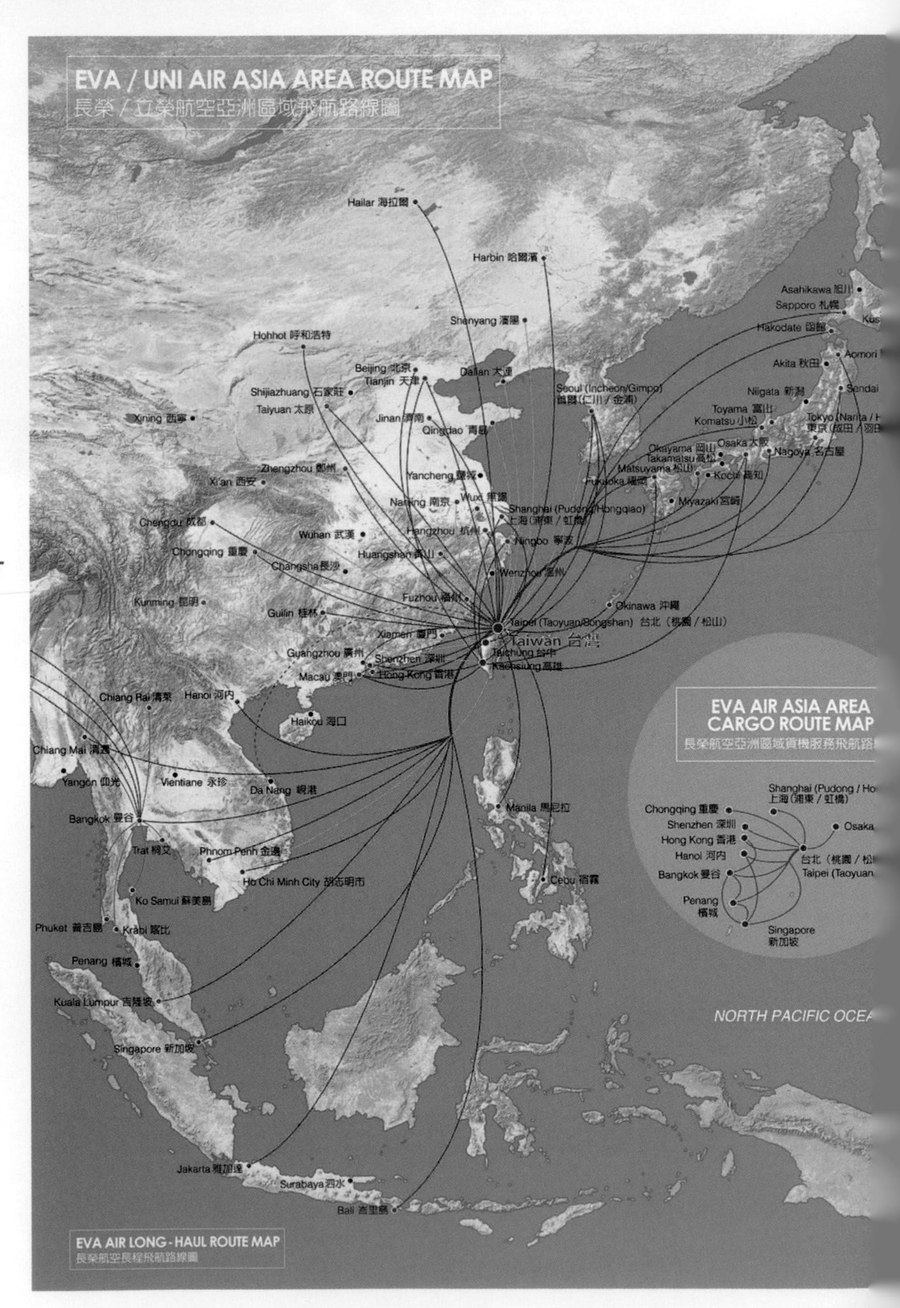

 Photographs - Flight Itinerary

Look at the electronic ticket (e-ticket) itinerary below and answer the following questions:

EVA Air Electronic Ticket Passenger Itinerary

ELECTRONIC TICKET

EVA AIRWAYS
INTERNET BOOKING
WWW.EVAAIR.COM
TAIPEI TAIWAN
IATA: 343 93155
TELEPHONE: +886 2 25011998

DATE: 27 NOV 2016
AGENT: 0001
NAME: KEN CHANG MR.
FQTV: 3325835052

ISSUING AIRLINE :EVA AIR
TICKET NUMBER :ETKT 695 2439646110
BOOKING REFERENCE: AMADEUS: 8HTWOR,AIRLINE: BR/8HTWOR

FROM/TO	FLIGHT	CL	DATE	DEP	FARE BASIS	NVB	NVA	BAG
TAIPEI TAIWAN TAOYUAN INTL TERMINAL 2	BR 225	W	17JAN	0740	WL1MIW	17JAN	17JAN	30K

FROM/TO	FLIGHT	CL	DATE	DEP	FARE BASIS	NVB	NVA	BAG
SINGAPORE CHANGI TERMINAL 3	BR 226	M	30JAN	1310	ML6MIW	30JAN	30JAN	30K

TAIPEI TAIWAN
TAOYUAN INTL
TERMINAL 2

ARRIVAL TIME: 1740 ARRIVALDATE: 30JAN

AT CHECK-IN, PLEASE SHOW A PHOTO IDENTIFICA TION AND THE DOCUMENT YOU GAVE FOR REFERENCE AT RESERVATION TIME.

Using the flight itinerary above, answer the below questions:

a. 695 2439646110
b. 8HTWOR
c. 07:40 or 7:40 am
d. 12:05 pm
e. Terminal 3
f. 13:10 or 1:10pm
g. direct flight
h. 17:40 or 5:40 pm
i. Terminal 2
j. EVA Airlines
k. January 30th
l. stopover flight

( ) 1. What airline is the traveler taking?
( ) 2. What is the ticket number?
( ) 3. What is the booking reference number?
( ) 4. What is the flight departure time from Taipei to Singapore?
( ) 5. What is the flight arrival time from Taipei to Singapore?
( ) 6. What terminal is the flight arriving at in Singapore on Jan 17th?
( ) 7. What is the flight departure time from Singapore to Taipei?
( ) 8. What is the flight arrival time from Singapore to Taipei?
( ) 9. What terminal is the flight arriving at in Taipei on January 30th?
( ) 10. Is this a direct flight or a flight with a stopover?

HOTEL RESERVATION

Unit 02

Learning Objectives

What you will learn in this unit...

- How to make a hotel reservation.
- How to take a hotel reservation.
- Procedures involvod in a hotel reservation.
- How to take notes during a hotel reservation.
- Names of different hotel room types according to type of beds.
- Names of different hotel room types according to type of view.
- Types of different hotel room amenities.
- Types of different hotel facilities.
- What priorities are there for a hotel guest when choosing a hotel?

Brainstorming

1. What type of hotel you choose says about you?

Airport hotel
機場飯店

You choose a hotel that is nearest to your destination. You seek convenience.

Resort & Spa
度假酒店及水療中心

You like a hotel that provides you relaxation and that has a romantic gist to it. You are also a sentimental and romantic person.

Villa
別墅

You only want the best of everything and would not sacrifice anything at the expense of your comfort.

Bed & Breakfast (B&B)
民宿

You love the feeling of being home away from home. You love the comforts of having breakfast ready when you wake up in the morning.

Capsule hotel
膠囊旅館

Price is everything to you. As long as you can save, it doesn't matter at what other expense it takes to get to where you want to go or even how long it takes for you to get there.

2. What are some of the most famous hotel chains in the world?
   Example: Hyatt Hotel.
3. What different types of hotels are there?
   Example: airport hotel.
4. What are the different types of rooms in a hotel?
   Example: standard room.
5. What are the names of different hotel room types according to type of view?
   Example: city-view room.
6. What are the list of amenities and facilities provided by a hotel?
   Example: room amenities include hair dryer.
   Example: hotel facilities include swimming pool.
7. What are your priorities when it comes to choosing a hotel?
   Example: 5 star hotel.
8. Can you name some common hospitality job titles?
   Example: hotel receptionist.

BASIC WORDS
Types of hotel rooms with different views
景觀客房
City view room
市景房
Lake view room
湖景房
Ocean / Sea view room
海景房
Mountain view room 山景房
Types of rooms
飯店房型
Single room
單人房
Double room
雙人房（兩張單人床）
Suite 套房
Quadruple room 四人房

Practice Phrases

Work with a partner to practice saying the phrases below between a hotel receptionist and a hotel guest.

Hotel Receptionist	Hotel Guest
★ London Bridge Hotel. May I help you?	★ Yes. I'd like to make a reservation for a room for two persons.
★ When would you like to check in?	★ July 1st.
★ When would you like to check out?	★ July 4th.
★ So, that's three nights from July 1st and checking out on July 4th.	★ That's correct.
★ What kind of room would you like?	★ A standard room with city view.
★ Just a moment. Please hold the line...	
★ I'm sorry. We are fully booked from the 2nd to the 3rd. ★ However, we have a room with a London Bridge view available. ★ It's an extra £30 (thirty pounds) per night. Is that alright with you?	★ Yes, that sounds great!
★ Would you like to include breakfast? It's £25 per person.	★ I'd like to include breakfast for two, please.
★ Can I have your last name and first name?	★ My last name is Lee. L as in love, E as in elephant and E as in elephant. ★ And, my first name is Michelle.
★ Do you have a contact number?	★ Certainly. It's +886-2-2700-2700.
★ Your total for three nights including breakfast for two is £1,500 (one thousand five hundred pounds) plus 15% tax.	★ Got it!
★ Can I have your email address?	★ Sure. It's michelle@gmail.com.
★ Looks like we are all set! ★ Just to remind you that you must cancel 48 hours in advance so as not to incur any cancellation charges.	★ Got it!
★ Look forward to seeing you!	★ Look forward to seeing you too !

Test Yourself

Fill in the blanks with the correct answers:

a. fully booked
b. check out
c. check in
d. last
e. first
f. city
g. cancellation charges
h. standard

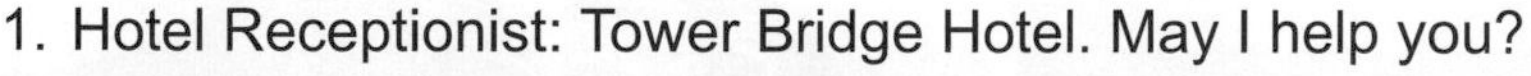

1. Hotel Receptionist: Tower Bridge Hotel. May I help you?
   Hotel Guest: Yes. I'd like to make a room reservation for two persons.
   Hotel Receptionist: Sure. When would you like to ____________?
   Hotel Guest: April 1st.
   Hotel Receptionist: When would you like to ____________?
   Hotel Guest: April 4th
2. Hotel Receptionist. What kind of room would you like?
   Hotel Guest: A ____________ room with a ____________ view.
   Hotel Receptionist: Just a moment. Please hold the line...
3. *The hotel guest waited on the line for a couple of minutes.*
   Hotel Receptionist: I'm sorry. All our standard rooms with a city view are fully-booked from April 1st to the 4th. However, we have a standard room with an ocean view available.
   Hotel Guest: Yes, that sounds great!
4. Hotel Receptionist: Sure. Can I have your ____________ name and ____________ name?
   Hotel Guest: My last name is Kim. And, my first name is Ken.
5. Hotel Receptionist: Looks like we are all set! Just to remind you that you must cancel 48 hours in advance so as not to incur any ____________ .
   Hotel Guest: Got it!

Listening Practice

track 06

Listen to the audio. Listen to the conversation between a hotel receptionist and a hotel guest, and then choose the correct answer.

(   ) 1. (a) The hotel guest would like one room at London Hotel for two persons from May 21st to May 24th.
(b) The hotel guest would like two rooms at London Hotel for one person from May 21st to May 24th.

(   ) 2. (a) The standard rooms with a city view are fully booked from May 21st to May 24th.
(b) The standard rooms with a London Bridge view are fully booked from May 21st to May 24th.

(   ) 3. (a) The hotel guest's last name is Window and her first name is Michelle.
(b) The hotel guest's last name is Wang and her first name is Michelle.

(   ) 4. (a) The total price for a standard room for two with a London Bridge view for three nights excluding breakfast for two is £800 plus 15% tax.
(b) The total price for a standard room for two with a London Bridge view for three nights including breakfast for two is £800 plus 15% tax.

Conversation

track 07

Michelle is about to call up London Bridge[1] Hotel to make a reservation for their upcoming[2] trip to London, UK.

Hotel Receptionist[3]: London Bridge Hotel. May I help you?

Michelle: Yes. [a] I'd like to make a room reservation for two persons.

Hotel Receptionist: Sure. [b] When would you like to check in[4]?

Michelle: July 1st (July first).

Hotel Receptionist: And, [c] when would you like to check out[5]?

Michelle: July 4th (July fourth).

Hotel Receptionist: So, that's three nights from July 1st and checking out on July 4th.

Michelle: That's correct.

Hotel Receptionist: [d] What kind of room would you like?

Michelle: A standard room[6] with a city view[7].

Hotel Receptionist: Just a moment. Please hold the line...

Michelle waited on the line for a couple of minutes...

Hotel Receptionist: [e] I'm sorry. All our standard rooms with a city view are fully booked[8] from July 1st to the 4th. However, we have a standard room with a London Bridge view available. It's an extra £30[9] (thirty pounds) per night. Is that alright with you?

Michelle: Yes, that sounds great!

Hotel Receptionist: [f] Would you like to include breakfast? It's £25 per person.

Michelle: I'd like to include breakfast for two, please.

New Words & Phrases

track 08

1. London Bridge (n.) 倫敦橋
2. upcoming (adj.) 即將來臨的 / 即將到來的
   同 forthcoming 反 later
3. hotel receptionist (n.) (旅館) 接待員
   反 hotel guest
4. check in (hotel) (phrasal verb) 入住旅館
   反 check out
5. check out (hotel) (phrasal verb) 退房
   反 check in
6. standard room (n.) 標準房
   同 regular room
7. city view (room) (adj.) 市景（房）
8. fully booked (adj.) 客滿 / 表示飯店客房已被訂完了
   同 no vacancy 反 vacancy
9. £30 (n.) 30 英鎊

Hotel Receptionist: Sure. Can I have your last name[10] and first name[11]?

Michelle: My last name is Lee. L as in love, E as in elephant and E as in elephant. And, my first name is Michelle.

Hotel Receptionist: Got it! Can I have your contact number[12]?

Michelle: It's +886-2-1234-5678.

Hotel Receptionist: Got it! Your total for three nights including breakfast for two is £1,500 (one thousand five hundred pounds) plus 15% tax.

Michelle: Got it!

Hotel Receptionist: Can I have your email address?

Michelle: Sure. It's michelle@gmail.com.

Hotel Receptionist: [g] Looks like we are all set! [h] Just to remind you that you must cancel[13] 48 hours in advance[14] so as not to incur[15] any cancellation charges[16].

Michelle: Got it!

Hotel Receptionist: [i] Look forward to seeing you!

New Words & Phrases

10. last name (n.) 姓名
    反 first name 同 surname / family name
11. first name (n.) 名字 反 last name
12. contact number (n.) 聯絡號碼
13. cancel (vt.) 取消
    同 abort 反 keep / reserve
14. 48 hours in advance (phrase)
    提前 48 小時
15. incur (charges) (vt.) 招致(費用) / 產生(費用)
16. cancellation charges (n.) 取消產生的費用
    同 cancellation fees

Q & A

1. On which dates did Michelle wish to check in and check out?

______

2. What kind of room did Michelle want to make a reservation for initially?

______

3. What is the extra cost of a standard room with a London Bridge view?

______

4. What is the hotel guest's last name and first name?

______

5. What is the total price of the hotel room including breakfast for two?

______

Important Sentences

a. I'd like to make a room reservation for two persons.
我想訂兩個人的房間。

b. When would you like to check in?
你想什麼時候入住？

c. When would you like to check out?
你什麼時候退房？

d. What kind of room would you like?
你喜歡什麼樣的房型？

e. I'm sorry. All our standard rooms with a city view are fully booked from July 1st to the 4th.
對不起。我們所有標準房型從七月一號到四號都全滿。

f. Would you like to include breakfast? It's £25 per person.
你要含早餐嗎？每人 25 英鎊。

g. Looks like we are all set!
看起來我們都安排好了！

h. Just to remind you that you must cancel 48 hours in advance so as not to incur any cancellation charges.
只是提醒您，您必須提前 48 小時取消，以免產生取消而產生的費用。

i. Look forward to seeing you!
我們期待見到你！

Conversation Review

Match the English-Chinese translations

a. 標準房	e. 取消產生的費用	i. 入住旅館
b. 市景 (房)	f. 聯絡號碼	j. 退房
c. 即將來臨的 / 即將到來的	g. 客滿 / 表示飯店客房已被訂完了	k. 取消
d. (旅館) 接待員	h. 招致 (費用) / 產生 (費用)	l. 提前 48 小時

( ) 1. check in (hotel)
( ) 2. check out (hotel)
( ) 3. upcoming
( ) 4. hotel receptionist
( ) 5. standard room
( ) 6. city view (room)
( ) 7. fully booked
( ) 8. incur (charges)
( ) 9. contact number
( ) 10. cancel
( ) 11. 48 hours in advance
( ) 12. cancellation charges

track 09

Listen and fill in the blanks

Listen to the conversation and fill in the blanks.

1. The customer would like to ___________ on July 1st.
2. The customer would like a standard room with a ___________ view.
3. The hotel has a standard room with a London Bridge view available for an extra ___________ per night.
4. The customer would like to include ___________ for two at £25 per person.
5. The customer must cancel 48 hours ___________ so as not to incur any cancellation charges

track 10

Listen and Pronounce

Listen to the audio first. Then, try practice pronouncing each of the below hotel chains.

1. Best Western	貝斯特酒店
2. Candlewood Suites	燭木套房酒店
3. Crown Plaza Hotels & Resorts	皇冠假日酒店及度假村
4. Hilton Hotel and Resorts	希爾頓酒店及度假村
5. Holiday Inn	假日酒店
6. Howard Johnson	霍華德・約翰遜
7. Hyatt Hotel	凱悅酒店
8. Ibis Hotels	宜畢斯酒店
9. InterContinental Hotels Group	洲際酒店集團
10. La Quinta Inns and Suites	拉金塔旅館及套房酒店

Photographs

1. Which of the following statements best describes the picture?
   (a) A hotel guest is taking notes for a hotel reservation over the phone.
   (b) A hotel receptionist is helping a hotel guest make a hotel reservation over the phone.
   (c) A hotel guest is making an online hotel reservation.
   (d) A hotel receptionist is helping a hotel guest make an online hotel reservation.

Your Answer: (   )

2. Which of the following statements best describes the picture?
   (a) A hotel guest is taking notes at a hotel.
   (b) A hotel guest is checking out at a hotel.
   (c) A hotel guest is checking in at a hotel.
   (d) A hotel guest is making a reservation at a hotel.

Your Answer: (   )

Unit 03

FOREIGN CURRENCY EXCHANGE

Learning Objectives

What you will learn in this unit...

- Learn where you can exchange foreign currency.
- Learn which countries use the Euro dollar.
- Learn about currency denominations of the Euro dollar.
- Learn about the major foreign currencies, their names and countries.
- Learn how to calculate exchange rates.
- Foreign currency exchange related keyword verbs, phrases and idioms.

Brainstorming

1 Where you choose to exchange foreign currency says about you?

Home country bank 國內銀行	**Home country airport 國內機場**	**Destination airport 目的地機場**	**Foreign exchange counter at your destination country 目的地兌換外幣中心**	**Credit Card 信用卡**
You are always well-prepared ahead of time, and don't like uncertainties in a foreign country.	You don't know much about how to manage your finances so long as it is convenient for you – exchange rates at the airport are not the best!	You are either forgetful or are not very good at managing your finances – exchange rates at the airport are not the best!	You are good at managing your finances and you have done your homework – exchanging foreign currency at your travel destination often gets you better rates than your home country.	You are extremely bad at managing your finances – credit card companies normally charge you extra for exchange rate differences.

2. Where can you exchange foreign currency?
   Example: at a bank, at the airport, etc.
3. What countries in Europe use the Euro dollar? Example: France.
4. Name five major foreign currencies, their names and countries.
   Example: Australian dollar (AUD$), Australian dollar.
5. Find out the foreign exchange rates for today between two currencies.

BASIC WORDS

bank clerk
at a foreign exchange
counter
兌換外幣銀行專員

currency 貨幣

foreign
exchange
counter
外匯櫃檯

commission fee
手續費

Euro Dollar
Currency
Denominations
歐元貨幣面值

€5 = 5 Euro dollars = €5 歐元
€10 = 10 Euro dollars = 10 歐元
€20 = 20 Euro dollars = €20 歐元
€50 = 50 Euro dollars = €50 歐元
€100 =100 Euro dollars=€100 歐元
€200=200 Euro dollars =€200 歐元
€500 =500 Euro dollars=€500 歐元

exchange rates 匯率

transaction receipt 交易收據

Conversation Preview

Practice Phrases

Practice the below phrases between a customer and a bank clerk.

Bank Clerk at a foreign exchange counter	Customer
★ What currency do you have?	★ New Taiwan dollars (NT$) ★ Euro dollars (歐元) ★ US dollars (US$) ★ Australian dollars (AUS$)
★ How much would you like to exchange?	★ €$1000, please. (one thousand Euro dollars) ★ €100, please. (One hundred Euro dollars) ★ €500, please. (five hundred Euro dollars) ★ €1000, please. (one thousand Euro dollars)
★ In what denomination would you like? ★ We have €20, €50, €100, €200 and €500 (twenty, fifty, one hundred, two hundred and five hundred)	★ Can I have five $100s, five $50s, ten $20s and five $10s? (five one hundred's, five fifties, ten twenties and five ten's)
★ Would you like your transaction receipt?	★ Yes, please. ★ No, thanks.
★ Is there anything else I can help you with?	★ No, that's all. ★ Thanks for your help.

Test Yourself

Fill in the blanks with the correct answers:

a. transaction receipt	d. commission
b. currency	e. denomination
c. exchange rate	

Amy is at the London Heathrow airport and would like to exchange some foreign currency.

1. Amy: Excuse me. I'd like to exchange some Euro dollars.
   Bank clerk: What ___________ do you have?
   Amy: New Taiwan dollars (NT$).
2. Bank clerk: The current ___________ is €1 to NTD34.71. How much do you want to exchange?
3. Amy: One thousand Euro dollars, please. How much is the ___________ fee?
   Bank clerk: There is no commission fee.
   Amy: That sounds great!
4. Bank clerk: Your total comes up to NT34,710.
   Amy: Here's NT$35,000.
   Bank clerk: In what ___________ would you like? We have €20s, €50s, €100s, €200s and €500s. (twenties, fifties, one hundred's, two hundred's and five hundred's)
   Amy: Can I have five $100s, five $50s, ten $20s and five $10s? (five one hundred's, five fifties, ten twenties and five ten's)

Listening Practice

track 11

Listen to the audio. Listen to the conversation between the bank clerk and customer, and then choose the correct answer.

( ) 1. (a) Ken is buying Euro dollars.
(b) Ken is selling Euro dollars.

( ) 2. (a) The customer will get one Euro dollar with 34.80 New Taiwan dollars.
(b) The customer will get one New Taiwan dollar with 34.80 Euro dollars.

( ) 3. (a) The customer will have to pay €$1000 (one thousand Euro dollars) and a commission fee.
(b) The customer will have to pay €$1000 (one thousand Euro dollars) and no commission fee.

( ) 4. (a) Ken paid $35,000 New Taiwan dollars in exchange for one thousand Euro dollars.
(b) Ken paid $34,800 New Taiwan dollars in exchange for one thousand Euro dollars.

Conversation

track 12

Ken and Michelle just arrived in London, and are the airport.

Ken: Honey, I think we should exchange some more Euro dollars. We already have some British pounds, but, we don't have any Euro dollars.

Michelle: But we have our credit cards, and our hotel & air-tickets have already been prepaid[1]?

Ken: Yes. But, we might need some petty cash[2] for transportation[3], souvenirs[4], and, maybe some gifts[5]?

Michelle: But, the exchange[6] rate[7] at the airport is really low.

Ken: We are not exchanging a lot of money. [a] Better be sure than sorry!

Michelle: I don't see any foreign exchangers on this floor.

Ken: [b] Let's check it out then!

Michelle: Oh! I see a sign that says currency exchange on the second floor.

Ken and Michelle went up the escalator[8] to the second floor.

Ken: Oh, there! I see it! It's right at the end on the left-hand side.

They walked towards a foreign currency exchange counter[9].

Ken: Excuse me. I'd like to exchange some Euro dollars.

Bank clerk[10]: [c] What currency[11] do you have?

Ken: New Taiwan dollars (NT$).

Bank clerk: [d] The current exchange rate is €1 to NTD34.89 (One Euro dollar to thirty-four point eight nine New Taiwan dollars) [e] How much do you want to exchange?

New Words & Phrases

track 13

1. prepaid (adj.) 預付 反 postpaid
2. petty cash (n.) 零用金
   同 pocket money / small change
   反 big bucks
3. transportation (n.) 交通
4. souvenirs (n.) 紀念品
5. gifts (n.) 禮物 同 presents
6. exchange (vt.) 兌換 / 交換
7. exchange rate (n.) 匯率
8. escalator (n.) 手扶梯 反 staircase
9. foreign currency exchange counter (n.)
   貨幣兌換櫃台 同 foreign exchange booth
10. bank clerk (n.) 銀行專員
11. currency (n.) 貨幣 同 money

Ken: €$1000 (one thousand Euro dollars), please.
[f] How much is the commission fee[12]?

Bank clerk: [g] There's no commission fee.

Ken: That sounds great.

Bank clerk: So, your total comes up to NT$34,890.

Ken: Here's NT$35,000 (thirty-five thousand New Taiwan dollars).

Bank clerk: [h] In what denomination[13] would you like? We have €20s, €50s, €100s, €200s and €500s. (twenties, fifties, one hundred's, two hundred's and five hundred's)

Ken then turned towards the bank clerk.

Ken: Can I have five $100s, five $50s, ten $20s and five $10s? (five one hundred's, five fifties, ten twenties and five ten's)

Bank clerk: Here you are. [i] Here's your transaction[14] receipt[15]? Is there anything else I can help you with?

Ken: No, that's all.

Bank clerk: Have a great flight!

Q & A

1. What are some reasons that Ken thinks they need to exchange some more Euro dollars?

 ______

2. What currency are Ken and Michelle using to exchange currency?

 ______

3. What is the exchange rate for one Euro dollar to the New Taiwan dollar?

 ______

4. How much is the commission fee?

 ______

5. In what Euro dollar denominations can the bank clerk offer?

 ______

New Words & Phrases

12. commission fee (n.) 手續費
 同 charges
13. denomination (n.) 貨幣等的面額
 同 unit
14. transaction (n.) 交易
15. receipt (n.) 收據 反 bill

Important Sentences

a. Better be sure than sorry!
有備無患！

b. Let's check it out then!
我們過去看一看吧！

c. What currency do you have?
你有什麼貨幣呢？

d. The current exchange rate is €1 to NTD34.89
(One Euro dollar to thirty-four point eight nine New Taiwan dollars)
目前的匯率是一塊歐元等於 34.89 新台幣。

e. How much do you want to exchange?
你要換多少錢？

f. How much is the commission fee?
手續費是多少？

g. There is no commission fee.
沒有手續費 .

h. In what denomination would you like?
你想要換什麼樣的面額？

i. Here's your transaction receipt.
這是你的交易收據。

Conversation Review

Match the English-Chinese translations

a. 零用金	f. 收據
b. 匯率	g. 預付
c. 手續費	h. 貨幣兌換中心
d. 交易	i. 銀行專員
e. 貨幣的面額	j. 貨幣

( ) 1. prepaid
( ) 2. petty cash
( ) 3. exchange rate
( ) 4. foreign currency exchange booth
( ) 5. bank clerk
( ) 6. currency
( ) 7. commission fee
( ) 8. denomination
( ) 9. transaction
( ) 10. receipt

Foreign Currencies: currency names, codes and symbols

Search the Internet to find out currencies of ten different countries. Then, fill out your answers including country, currency name, currency code and currency symbol in the box below.

Country 國別	Currency Name 幣別	Currency Code 代碼	Currency Symbol 代號
Example: Australia 澳洲	Australian Dollar 澳幣	AUD	$
1.			
2.			
3.			
4.			
5.			

Listen and fill in the blanks

track 14

Listen to the conversation and fill in the blanks.

1. The customer would like to exchange some ________ dollars using New Taiwan dollars.
2. The customer would like to exchange € ________ dollars.
3. There is no ________ fee.
4. The money exchanger has currencies in €20s, €50s, €100s, €200s and €500s ________ .

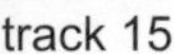

Listen and Pronounce

track 15

Listen to the audio first. Then, try practice pronouncing each one of the foreign currencies below:

Currency Name 幣別	Country 國別
Australian Dollar 澳幣	Australia 澳洲
British Pound 英鎊	United Kingdom (U.K.) 英國
Canadian Dollar 加拿大幣	Canada 加拿大
Euro Dollar 歐元	European Union 歐盟
Hong Kong Dollar 港幣	Hong Kong 香港
Japanese Yen 日圓	Japan 日本
Singapore Dollar 新加坡幣	Singapore 新加坡
South Korean Won 韓元	South Korea 南韓
New Taiwan Dollar 新台幣	Taiwan 台灣
US Dollar 美元	United States of America (U.S.A) 美國

Matching pictures with words

a. currency
b. commission fee
c. foreign exchange counter
d. currency denominations
e. exchange rates
f. bank clerk at a foreign exchange counter

1.

2.

3.

4.

5.

6.

Photographs

Look at the pictures and then answer the questions:

1. Choose the correct answer:

   (a) The woman is exchanging money at a foreign exchange counter.
   (b) The woman is asking how much the exchange rate is.
   (c) The woman is looking at some information on exchange rates.
   (d) The woman is calculating the foreign exchange rate.

   Your answer: (   )

2. Choose the correct answer:

   (a) Some people are at a bank.
   (b) Some people are at a currency exchange counter.
   (c) Some people are at an airport information counter.
   (d) Some people are at an ATM machine.

   Your answer: (   )

MICHELIN RESTAURANTS

Unit 04

Learning Objectives

What you will learn in this unit...

- How are Michelin stars defined?
- List of one, two and three-starred Michelin restaurants in London.
- Some ways to make a Michelin restaurant reservation.
- The top 15 countries with the most number of Michelin restaurants in the world
- How long in advance do you think it takes to make a reservation for a (a) 3-star, (b) 2-star, and (c) 1-star, Michelin restaurant?
- Understanding Michelin restaurant reservation systems.
- How to make a reservation at a Michelin restaurant?
- How to take a reservation at a Michelin restaurant?
- Michelin restaurant reservation related keyword verbs, phrases and idioms.

Brainstorming

1. How are Michelin stars defined?

The Michelin Plate 米其林 餐盤餐廳	Michelin Bib Gourmand 米其林必比登 超值餐廳	One Star Michelin Restaurants 米其林 一星餐廳	Two Star Michelin Restaurants 米其林 二星餐廳	Three Star Michelin Restaurants 米其林 三星餐廳
A simply good meal with no menu price standard 簡單好吃，沒有標準價格	Exceptionally good food at moderate prices 價位中等卻同時擁有美味料理與優質服務的「超值餐廳」	Very good cooking in its category, worth a stop 擁有高品質的料理，值得一試	Excellent cooking, worth a detour 料理傑出，就算要繞路才能到也值得	Exceptional cuisine, worth a special trip 餐點卓越，爲了它來場旅行也心甘情願
Simply a good meal and good cooking. There is no menu price standard in this rating.	A restaurant must offer menu items priced below a maximum determined by local economic standards.	A good place to stop on your journey, offering cuisine prepared to a consistently high standard.	A restaurant worth a detour, indicating excellent cuisine and skillfully and carefully crafted dishes of outstanding quality	A restaurant worth a special journey, indicating exceptional cuisine using superlative ingredients and where diners eat extremely well.

2. Find out the list of one, two and three -starred Michelin restaurants in London.
3. What are some ways to make a Michelin restaurant reservation?
   Example: make a phone call, etc.
4. What are the top 15 countries with the most number of Michelin restaurants in the world?
   Example: Italy, Spain, etc.
5. How long in advance do you think it takes to make a reservation for a (a) 3-star, (b) 2-star, and (c) 1-star, Michelin restaurant.

BASIC WORDS

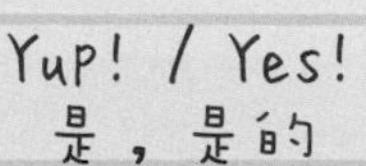

Yup! / Yes!
是，是的

Nope! / No!
不，不是

Restaurant Gordon Ramsay
161 reviews Details
££££ · French, British Edit

4.5 Star review
4.5 星評價

Some ways to make a Michelin restaurant reservation
訂米其林餐廳的方式：
上網訂位

OpenTable online booking
OpenTable 網站訂位

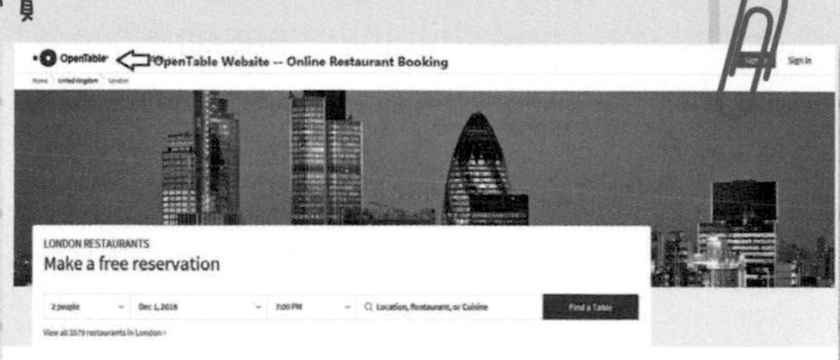

Reservation Genie booking website
Reservation Genie 網站訂位

Twitter account 推特帳戶
『透過【推特】帳戶，隨時能掌握最新米其林餐廳座位狀態』

American Express Platinum Card
美國運通白金卡

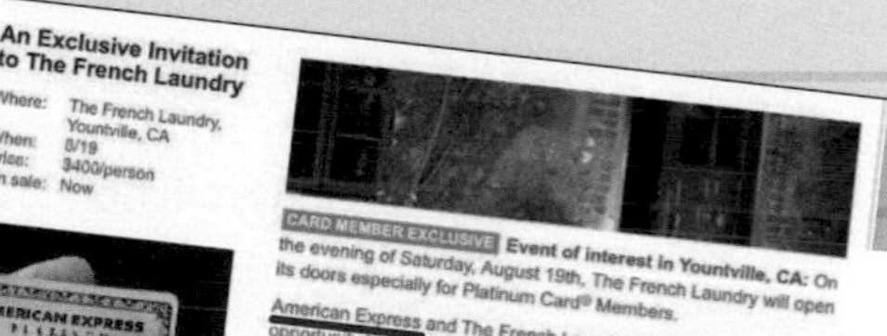

An Exclusive Invitation to The French Laundry

Where: The French Laundry, Yountville, CA
When: 8/19
Price: $400/person
On sale: Now

CARD MEMBER EXCLUSIVE Event of interest in Yountville, CA: On the evening of Saturday, August 19th, The French Laundry will open its doors especially for Platinum Card® Members.

American Express and The French Laundry offer you the special opportunity to reserve your seats right now for a memorable dinner at Chef Thomas Keller's spectacular three-Michelin-starred restaurant in the heart of Napa Valley. Enjoy a world of comfort and culinary imagination in a historic building constructed of river rock and timbers situated across from its culinary garden. Indulge, relax, and revel in a nine-course tasting menu.

To purchase: Call Platinum Card Concierge at 888-637-9517 and use your Platinum Card.

See terms and conditions below

credit card concierge services
信用卡禮賓服務

keep dialing / keep calling
一直重撥

busy signal
電話忙線 / 佔線信號

Conversation Preview

Practice Phrases

Work with a partner to practice saying the phrases below.

Partner A	Partner B
★ Did you know that there are only two 3-Star Michelin restaurants in London?	★ You must be kidding!
★ Which restaurant's review is better?	★ Alain Ducasse at the Dorchester has a 4.7 Star review. ★ Restaurant Gordon Ramsay has a 4.5 Star review. ★ Their reviews are pretty close.
★ What are some ways to make a Michelin restaurant reservation?	★ Well...for a start, we can try booking through the restaurant's website. ★ There are also other popular online booking websites for Michelin restaurants – OpenTable and Restaurant Genie.
★ Are there any other ways to make a reservation?	★ We can also log in a Twitter account for updates on cancellations. ★ We could use a credit card concierge service. ★ Ah! If only we had an American Express Platinum Card?! ★ Unfortunately, we don't have one. So, that's out of the question!
★ Why don't we just call the restaurant directly? ★ But, I heard that we have cannot easily give up when we get a busy signal. ★ We just have to keep dialing until we get a ringtone, especially if it's a 3-Star Michelin restaurant.	★ Yes, I agree. I heard that's the best bet for a 3-Star Michelin restaurant. ★ Let's give it a shot!

Listening Practice

track 16

A couple is discussing about making a reservation at a Michelin restaurant. Listen to the audio, and then choose the correct answer.

( ) 1. (a) There are only two 2-Star Michelin restaurants in London.
(b) There are only two 3-Star Michelin restaurants in London.

( ) 2. (a) They don't want to make a reservation for Restaurant Gordon Ramsay because it is very difficult to make a reservation for a 3-Star Michelin restaurant.
(b) They want to make a reservation for Restaurant Gordon Ramsay because they still have nine months before they leave for London.

( ) 3. (a) They are going to make a restaurant reservation online first.
(b) They are going to make a restaurant reservation by calling first.

( ) 4. (a) They are going to make a reservation using a credit card concierge service.
(b) They are not going to make a reservation using a credit card concierge service.

Test Yourself

Fill in the blanks with the correct answers:

a. OpenTable	d. concierge service
b. review	e. Restaurant Genie
c. log in	f. Michelin

1. Ken: Which restaurant's __________ is better?
Michelle: Alain Ducasse at the Dorchester has a 4.7 Star review and Restaurant Gordon Ramsay has a 4.5 Star review.
2. Ken: I heard that it's very difficult to make a reservation, especially for a 3-Star __________ restaurant.
3. Ken: What are some ways to make a Michelin restaurant reservation?
Michelle: We can try booking through the restaurant's website. There are also other popular online booking websites for Michelin restaurants __________ and __________.
Ken: Ok. Let me try to book online first.
4. Ken: Honey... Are there any other ways to make a reservation?
Michelle: We can __________ to a Twitter account. If there are any cancellations, we'll get an update.
5. Michelle: We could also use a credit card __________. Ah! If only we had an American Express Platinum Card?!

Conversation

track 17

It has been Michelle's honeymoon wish to dine in[1] a 3-Star Michelin restaurant since Ken and her got married two years ago...

Michelle: Honey, did you know that there are only two 3-Star Michelin restaurants in London?

Ken: You must be kidding![2]

Michelle: Nope![3] I'm not!

Ken: [a] Which restaurant's review[4] is better?

Michelle: [b] Alain Ducasse at the Dorchester has a 4.7 star review[5] and [c] Restaurant Gordon Ramsay[6] has a 4.5 Star review. Their reviews are pretty close.

Ken: Hmmm... I heard that it's very difficult to make a reservation, especially for a 3-Star Michelin restaurant.

Michelle: Well... we still have six months before we leave for London. Maybe, we should try Restaurant Gordon Ramsay which has a 4.5 Star review. What do you think?

Ken: I think it's a great idea. But, what are some ways to make a Michelin restaurant reservation?

Michelle: Well... [d] for a start[7], we can try booking through the restaurant's website[8]. There are also other popular online booking websites for Michelin restaurants - OpenTable[9] and Restaurant Genie[10].

Ken: Ok. Let me try to book online first.

Ken tried to book directly on the restaurant's and OpenTable websites, but there was no availability[11].

Ken: Honey... Are there any other ways to make a reservation?

Michelle: [e] We can also log in[12] to a Twitter account[13] for updates on cancellations.

Ken: Well, there's no guarantee[14] there.

New Words & Phrases

track 18

1. dine in (phrasal verb) 在餐廳用餐
2. You must be kidding! (phrase)
   你是在開玩笑嗎？
3. Nope! (adv.) 是 no 比較親切的說法
   同 No! 反 Yup! / Yes!
4. restaurant review (n.) 餐廳評價
5. 4.7 Star review (phrase) 4.7 星評價
6. Restaurant Gordon Ramsay(n.)
   戈登 · 拉姆齊餐廳
7. for a start (phrase) 首先 / 作爲開始
8. booking through the restaurant's website
   (phrase) 在餐廳網站訂位
9. OpenTable (n.) 網站訂位
10. Reservation Genie (n.) Reservation Genie
    網站訂位
11. availability (n.) 有位子的可能性
    同 open 反 unavailable
12. log in (n.) 注冊 / 登錄 反 log out
13. Twitter account (n.) 推特帳戶 『透過【推特】帳戶，隨時掌握最新米其林餐廳座位狀態』
14. guarantee (n.) 保證

Michelle: You're right! We could use a credit card[15] concierge service[16]. Ah! If only we had an American Express Platinum Card[17]?!

Ken: Unfortunately[18], we don't have one. So, that's out of the question! [19]

Michelle: Hmmm...[f] Why don't we just call the restaurant directly[20]?

Ken: Yes, I agree. I heard that's the best bet[21] for a 3-Star Michelin restaurant.

Michelle: Sure. But, I heard that we have cannot easily give up when we get a busy signal[22]. We just have to keep dialing[23] until we get a ringtone[24], especially if it's a 3-Star Michelin restaurant.

Ken: Sure! Let's give it a shot! [25]

New Words & Phrases

15. credit card (n.) 信用卡
16. concierge service (n.)
    禮賓服務『使用信用卡禮賓服務訂位』
17. American (AMEX) Express Platinum Card (n.) AMEX 美國運通白金卡
18. unfortunately (adv.) 不幸地 / 可惜
    反 fortunately
19. That's out of the question! (idiom)
    那是不可能的！同 beyond consideration / unthinkable
20. Call the restaurant directly (phrase)
    直接打電話到餐廳 反 book online
21. best bet (idiom) 上策 / 最安全可靠的辦法
    同 first choice
22. busy signal (n.) 電話忙線 / 佔線信號
    反 ringtone
23. keep dialing (idiom) 一直重撥
    同 keep on calling
24. ringtone (n.) 鈴聲 反 busy signal
25. Let's give it shot! (idiom) 就試一試吧！
    同 Let's give it a try!

Q & A

1. Why does Michelle wish to dine in a 3-Star Michelin restaurant?

   ____

2. Why do Ken and Michelle want to make restaurant reservations six months before they leave for London?

   ____

3. What does it mean by "that's out of the question"?

   ____

4. How did Ken first try to make a reservation at Restaurant Gordon Ramsay?

   ____

5. What did Michelle advise Ken about calling the restaurant directly?

   ____

Important Sentences

a. Which restaurant's review is better?
哪間餐廳的評價比較好？

b. Alain Ducasse at the Dorchester has a 4.7 Star review.
在多切斯特酒店的艾倫杜卡斯〔三星米其林餐廳〕有 4.7 星的評價。

c. Restaurant Gordon Ramsay has a 4.5 Star review.
戈登．拉姆齊餐廳〔三星米其林餐廳〕有 4.5 星的評價。

d. For a start, we can try booking through the restaurant's website.
首先，我們可以嘗試在餐廳網站訂位。

e. We can also log in to a Twitter account for updates on cancellations.
我們也可以註冊一個推特帳戶，隨時把握最新（米其林餐廳座位）狀態。

f. Why don't we just call the restaurant directly?
我們爲什麼不直接打電話到餐廳？

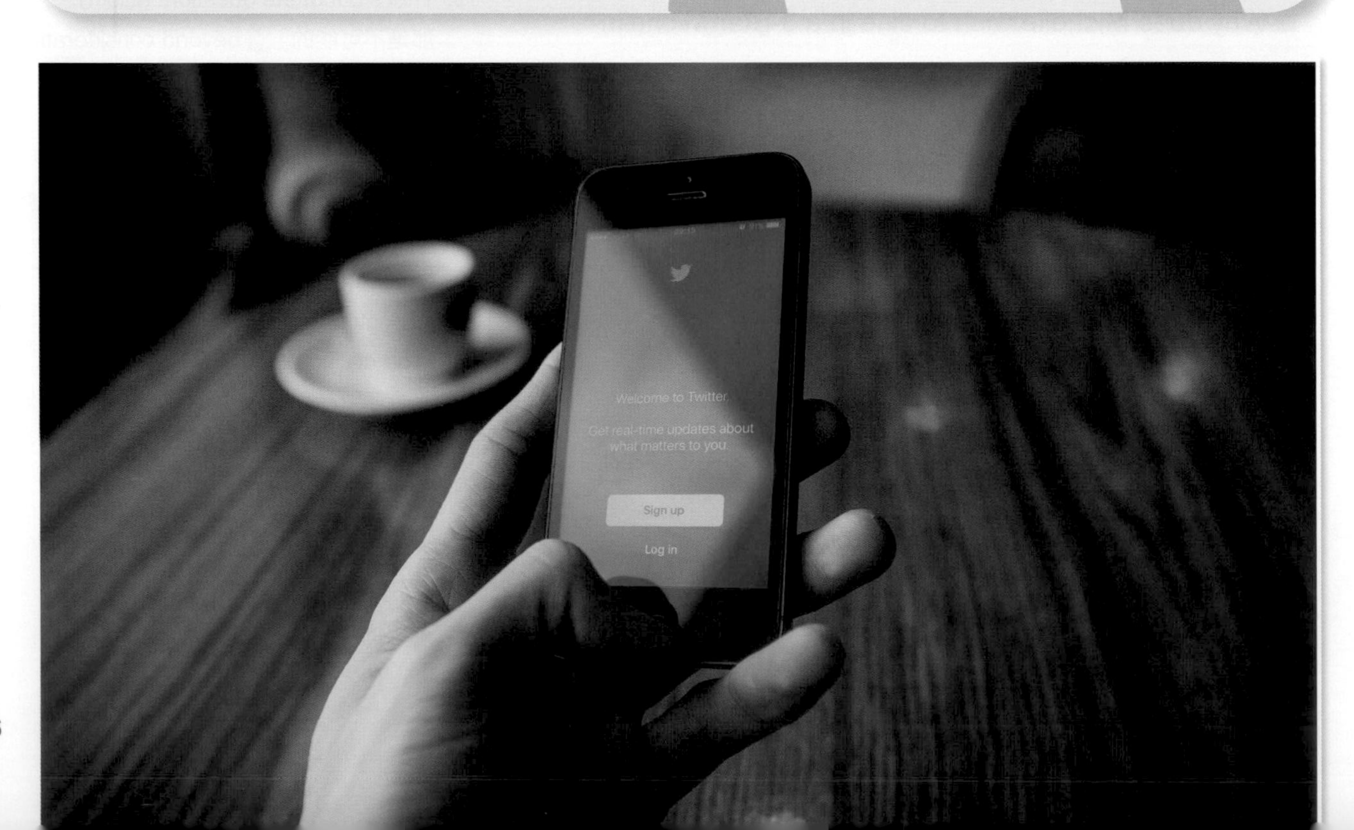

Conversation Review

What are some ways to make a Michelin restaurant reservation?

a. Use a credit card concierge service
b. Book online through the restaurant's website
c. Book online through the Restaurant Genie website
d. Call the restaurant directly
e. Log in to a Twitter account for updates on cancellations
f. Book online through the OpenTable website

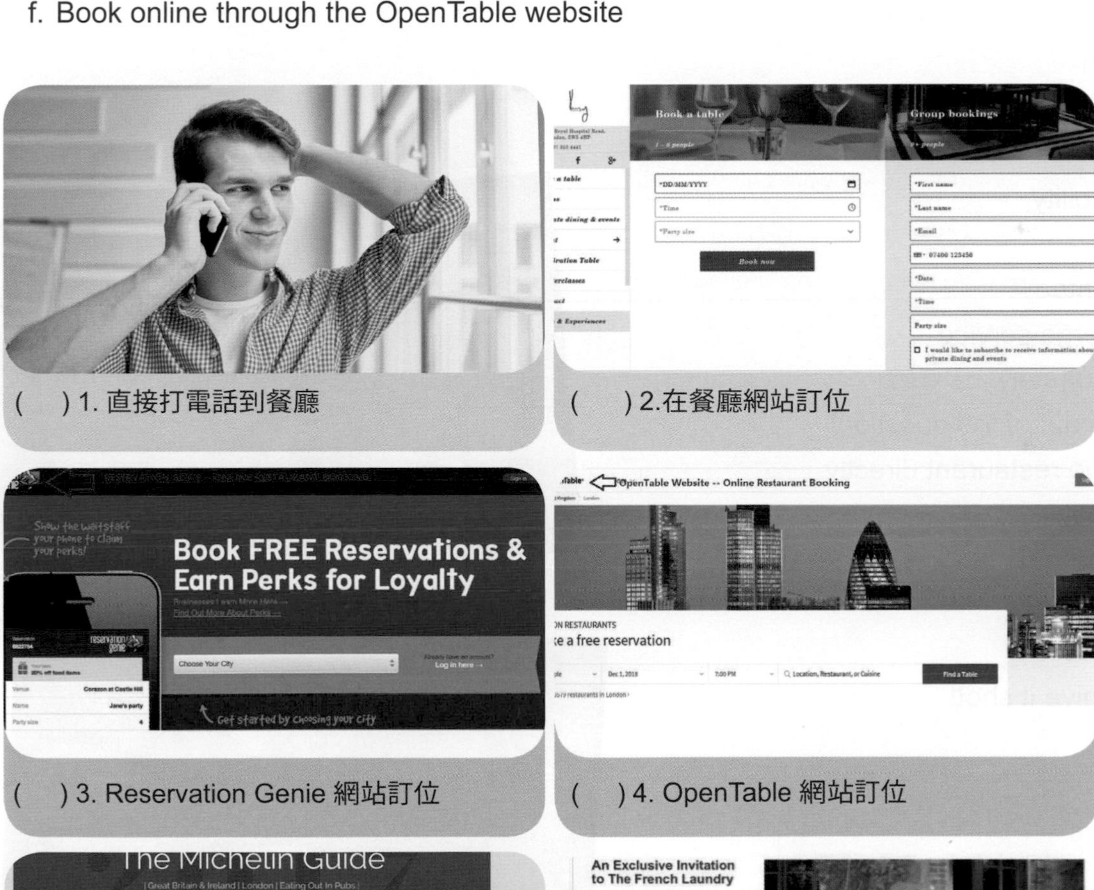

(　　) 1. 直接打電話到餐廳

(　　) 2.在餐廳網站訂位

(　　) 3. Reservation Genie 網站訂位

(　　) 4. OpenTable 網站訂位

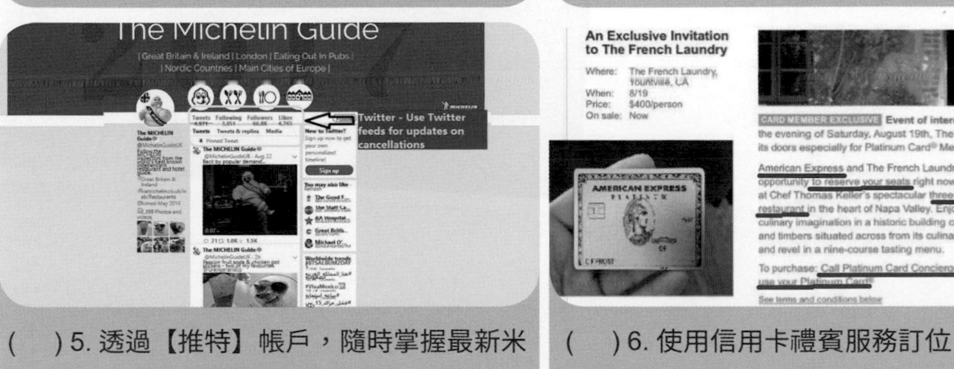

(　　) 5. 透過【推特】帳戶，隨時掌握最新米其林餐廳座位狀態

(　　) 6. 使用信用卡禮賓服務訂位

Match the Chinese-English Translations

a. 餐廳評價	f. 是 no 比較親切的說法	k. 就試一試吧！
b. 有位子的可能性	g. 上策 / 最安全可靠的辦法	l. 哪是不可能的！
c. 注冊 / 登錄	h. 電話忙線 / 佔線信號	m. 直接打電話到餐廳
d. 保證	i. 一直重撥	n. 禮賓服務『使用信用卡禮賓服務訂位』
e. 在餐廳用餐	j. 鈴聲	o. 不幸地 / 可惜

(　) 1. dine in
(　) 2. Nope!
(　) 3. restaurant review
(　) 4. availability
(　) 5. log in
(　) 6. guarantee
(　) 7. concierge service
(　) 8. unfortunately
(　) 9. That's out of the question!
(　) 10. Call the restaurant directly
(　) 11. best bet
(　) 12. busy signal
(　) 13. keep dialing
(　) 14. ringtone
(　) 15. Let's give it shot!

Listen and Pronounce

track 19

Listen to the audio first. Then, try pronouncing each one of the following.

1. Michelin restaurant	米其林餐廳
2. restaurant review	餐廳評價
3. One Star Michelin restaurant	米其林一星餐廳
4. Two Star Michelin restaurant	米其林二星餐廳
5. Three Star Michelin restaurant	米其林三星餐廳
6. The Michelin Plate	米其林餐盤餐廳
7. Michelin Bib Gourmand	米其林畢比登超值餐廳
8. American Express (AMEX) Platinum Card	美國 AMEX 運通白金卡
9. credit card concierge services	信用卡禮賓服務
10. Twitter account	推特帳號
11. OpenTable online booking -	OpenTable 網站訂位
12. Reservation Genie online booking -	Reservation Genie 網站訂位

Listen and fill in the blanks

track 20

Listen to the conversation and fill in the blanks.

1. Alain Ducasse at the Dorchester has a 4.7 star ______________ and Restaurant Gordon Ramsay has a 4.5 Star review.
2. One way to make a Michelin restaurant reservation is through the restaurant's ______________ .
3. Another way to make a Michelin restaurant reservation is to ______________ to a Twitter account to get updates on cancellations
4. The couple decided to call the restaurant ______________ .

 Photographs - How are Michelin stars defined?

Look at the pictures and match it with the answers given below:

(　) 1. Three Star Michelin Restaurants

(　) 2. One Star Michelin Restaurants

(　) 3. The Michelin Plate

(　) 4. Michelin Bib Gourmand

(　) 5. Two Star Michelin Restaurants

(a)

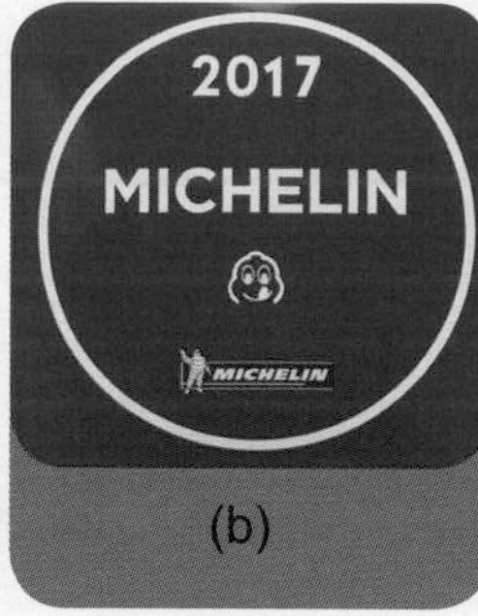

(b)

(c)

(d)

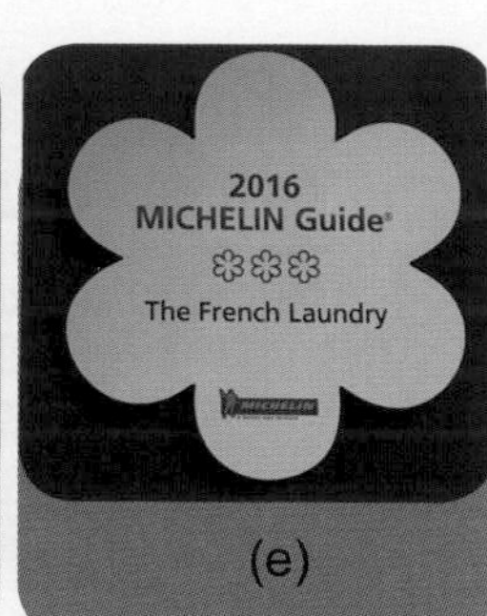

(e)

LONDON CITY SIGHTSEEING

Learning Objectives

What you will learn in this unit...

- Discover different ways to see a city.
- Things you could do when visiting a city.
- Things you could see when visiting a city.
- Different ways to sightsee a city.
- Some London sightseeing attractions.
- Some useful knowledge about city sightseeing.
- City sightseeing related keyword verbs, phrases and idioms.

Brainstorming

1. What does the way you do your city sightseeing say about you?

Walking tour
步行旅遊

You are an economical and practical person. You like to see the world and exercise. You love to take the world at your own pace – stop and smell the roses along the way.

Biking tour
觀光單車旅遊

You like to feel connected to the environment, at the same time making sure you not miss any part of the city. Smelling the air and hearing the sounds of a place makes you feel a part of the place.

Hop-on, hop-off bus
跳上跳下旅遊巴士

You like to "feel" like a tourist and don't want to miss the major attractions in the city. You also love to take as many photo and video shots as possible, making sure that you don't miss out all the interesting spots in the city.

Balloon ride
氣球之旅

You have had this in your bucket list for a long time. You like to feel high up in the air, as in your own personal life. You also often view the world from a different perspective. Taking beautiful 360 degree panoramic photo and video shots is also one of your hobbies.

Helicopter tour
直升機旅遊

You don't mind paying more for a lifetime experience you'll never forget. You are also the kind who wants a panoramic view of life and places in whatever you do and wherever you go.

2. What are some different ways of which you could see a city?
   Example: walking tour, etc.
3. What are some things you could do or see when visiting a city?
   Example: visiting the museum, going to the amusement park, etc.
4. What do you like to do when you go city sightseeing? Where can you find it in London?
   Example: Art & Museums - National Gallery in London, etc.
5. Ask your partner what is his/her favorite way of doing city sightseeing.
6. Ask your partner what may be some things that he/she must do when visiting a new country/city?

BASIC WORDS

brochure
旅遊小冊子

skyline
（尤指建築物在天空映襯下的）天際線

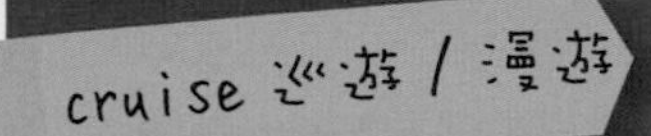

cruise 巡遊 / 漫遊

The London Eye
倫敦眼

The River Thames 泰晤士河

CityPass / CityCard
城市通行證 / 城市卡
(The London Pass 倫敦旅遊卡)

Tower of London
倫敦塔

selfie 自拍

A. bus driver 巴士司機
B. passenger / tourist 乘客 / 觀光客
C. open-top bus 露天觀光巴士
D. hop-on, hop-off bus 跳上跳下旅遊巴士
E. bus conductor 巴士售票員

board (a bus)
上（船、車或飛機）

House of Parliament
國會大廈

The Big Ben
大笨鐘

night tour 夜遊

Conversation Preview

Practice Phrases

Work with a partner to practice saying the phrases between a tourist and a bus conductor of a Hop-on, Hop-off bus.

Tourist	Bus Conductor
★ Hi! We'd like two 72-hour tickets, please.	★ Sure! Your total will be £86, please.
★ How long are the tickets valid for?	★ They are valid for 72 hours from the time of your first use.
★ Here you are. (Ken handed £86 in cash to the bus conductor).	★ Here are your tickets! ★ Just show your tickets to the bus conductor or driver whenever you board the bus.
★ Excuse me, where are the headphones and maps?	★ The headphones and maps are right in the front of the bus. ★ Enjoy your tour, folks!

track 21

Listening Practice

Listen to the conversation and choose the correct answer.

( ) 1. (a) A bus conductor asked for two 72-hour tickets and the total price is £86.
(b) A tourist asked for two 86-hour tickets and the total price is £72.

( ) 2. (a) The bus ticket can only be used once.
(b) The bus tickets can be used for 72 hours.

( ) 3. (a) The tourist has to show £86 in cash to the bus conductor or driver whenever he boards the bus.
(b) The tourist has to show his tickets to the bus conductor or driver whenever he boards the bus.

( ) 4. (a) The tourist can get some headphones and maps in the front of the bus.
(b) The tourist can get some headphones and maps from the bus conductor.

Test Yourself

Fill in the blanks with the correct answers given below.

a. attractions	d. sightseeing
b. public transport	e. tickets & options
c. open-top bus	f. brochures

1. Michelle collected some ________ from the airport yesterday.
2. The London Eye, Big Ben and Thames River are all interesting ________ .
3. There are many ways to do ________ in London including the balloon ride, helicopter tour, walking tour and hop-on, hop-off bus.
4. The CityPass includes ________ to main attractions, a pass for cable cars and ________ .
5. The ________ is perfect for photo shots and selfies!

Conversation

track 22

New Words & Phrases

track 23

1. A good night's rest (phrase)
   一夜的充分休息 / 一晚好睡
2. Woke up feeling completely refreshed
   (phrase) 醒來感到徹底恢復了精力
3. city sightseeing (n.) 城市觀光
4. attractions (n.) 旅遊景點
   同 attractions / places of interest
5. tour (n.) 旅遊 / 觀光 / 旅行
6. brochure (s) (n.) 小冊子
   同 pamphlet, booklet, leaflet
7. collect (ed) (adj.) 收集
8. I really don't know where to start! (phrase)
   我真的不知道從哪裡開始！
9. I know exactly how you feel! (phrase)
   我知道你的感受！
10. points of interests (n.) 景點
    同 attractions / places of interest
11. landmarks (n.) 地標
12. walking tour (n.) 徒步旅行
13. helicopter tour (n.) 直升機旅遊（觀光）
    同 chopper
14. limited time (adj.) 時間有限
    反 unlimited time
15. energy (n.) 活力 同 vigor
16. balloon ride (n.) 氣球之旅
17. I bet (phrase) 我敢打賭
18. view (n.) 景色
19. spectacular (adj.) 壯觀的
20. skyline (n.)
    尤指建築物在天空映襯下的天際線
21. get hold of yourself (idiom) 控制住自己
    同 calm down
22. You are right! (phrase) 你是對的！
    美國人常常會用 so 在你想不到的地方來加強語氣。例如：可以在 "You are right." 的 be 動詞 are 之後加上一個 so，就變成了 "You are so right." 語氣上的程度就不一樣。

Michelle and Ken had a good night's rest[1] and woke up feeling completely refreshed[2], ready to do some city sightseeing[3] in London.

Michelle: Honey, there are so many attractions[4] and tours[5] in the brochures[6] we collected[7] from the airport yesterday. I really don't know where to start! [8]

Ken: I know exactly how you feel! [9] There are so many points of interests[10] and landmarks[11], from walking tours[12] to helicopter tours[13]!

Michelle: But, honey...We have limited time[14].

Ken: Yes, you're right. The walking and biking tours take up too much time and energy[15]. What about the helicopter or balloon rides[16]? I bet[17] the view[18] is spectacular[19] and would give us a skyline[20] of the whole city!

Michelle: Honey, get hold of yourself[21]! Those tours are too expensive!

Ken: You are right! [22]

Michelle: Oh... look! There's also the London CityPass[23]. It includes tickets & options[24] to main attractions[25], a pass[26] for cable cars[27] and public transport[28].

Ken: I don't think taking the public transport will give us good photo shots[29].

Michelle: You are right. Here's another one! It's a hop-on, hop-off bus[30]. It says we can catch a glimpse of[31] the House of Parliament[32] and the Tower of London[33], set your watches[34] by the time on the Big Ben[35], and even take a leisurely[36] spin,[37] on the London Eye[38]!

Ken: Look, it also says that a three-day ticket includes a night tour[39], a walking tour and a cruise[40] by River Thames[41]!

Michelle: Plus, the open-top bus[42] is perfect for photos and selfies[43]!

Ken: Sounds like the hop-on, hop-off bus is our best choice!

New Words & Phrases

23. London CityPass (n.) 倫敦旅遊卡 / 倫敦通行證 / 城市通行證
    同 CityCard 城市卡
24. tickets & options (n.) 門票及選項
25. main attractions (n.) 主要旅遊景點
26. pass (n.) 乘車證
27. cable cars (n.) 纜車
28. public transport (n.) 公共交通
    反 private transport
29. photo shots (n.) 照片拍攝
30. hop-on, hop-off bus (n.) 跳上跳下旅遊巴士
    同 jump on and off bus
31. catch a glimpse of (idiom) 瞥見 / 瞥一眼
    同 catch sight of something or someone
32. House of Parliament (n.) 國會大廈
33. Tower of London (n.) 倫敦塔
34. set your watch (phrase) 按照 [大笨鐘] 的報時對錶
    同 adjust your watch
35. Big Ben (n.) 大笨鐘
36. leisurely (adj.) 悠閒
    同 easygoing 反 hurried
37. spin (n.)（汽車等的）疾馳 / 兜風
38. London Eye (n.) 倫敦眼
39. night tour (n.) 夜遊 反 day tour
40. cruise (v.t.) 巡航於 / 航遊於 / 緩慢巡行於
41. River Thames (n.) 泰晤士河
42. open-top bus (n.) 露天觀光巴士
43. selfie (s) (n.) 自拍

Michelle: Look, honey! There's a hop-on, hop-off bus parked right across the street[44]!

A bus conductor[45] was standing by the door of a hop-on, hop off bus.

Ken: [a] Hi! We'd like two 72-hour tickets[46], please.

Bus conductor: [b] Sure! Your total will be £86, please.

Ken: [c] How long are the tickets valid[47] for?

Bus conductor: [d] They are valid for 72 hours from the time of your first use.

Ken: [e] Here you are.

(Ken handed £86 in cash to the bus conductor).

Bus conductor: [f] Here are your tickets! [g] Just show your tickets to the bus conductor or driver whenever you board[48] the bus.

Michelle: Excuse me, where are the headphones and maps?

Bus conductor: [h] The headphones and maps are right in the front of the bus. [i] Enjoy your tour, folks[49]!

New Words & Phrases

44. right across the street (phrase) 街的正對面
45. bus conductor (n.) 巴士售票員
46. 72-hour ticket (n.) 七十二小時票券
47. valid (adj.) 有效 反 invalid
48. board (vt.) 上（船、車或飛機） 同 get on/get in 反 get off
49. folks (n.) (口頭用語) 親人，或表示 [各位] 及人們 同 people

Q & A

1. What did Ken say about the walking and biking tours?

 ____

2. What did Michelle say about the helicopter and balloon rides?

 ____

3. What does the CityPass include?

 ____

4. What attractions can they see and do if Ken and Michelle choose the hop-on, hop-off bus?

 ____

5. How much are the hop-on, hop-off bus tickets, and how long are they valid for?

 ____

Important Sentences

a. Hi! We'd like two 72-hour tickets, please.
嗨！我們要買兩張三天票。

b. Sure! Your total will be £86, please.
當然！總共是 86 英鎊。

c. How long are the tickets valid for?
請問票的有效期限是多久？

d. They are valid for 72 hours from the time of your first use.
票的有效期限是七十二小時，從你使用第一次開始計算起。

e. Here you are...
這裡是…[86 英鎊]。

f. Here are your tickets!
這是你的票！

g. Just show your tickets to the bus conductor or driver whenever you board the bus.
只要你一上車就給巴士售票員或司機看你的票就可以了。

h. The headphones and maps are right in the front of the bus.
耳機及地圖在巴士的右前方。

i. Enjoy your tour, folks!
各位，玩的開心點！

Conversation Review

Match the Chinese-English Translations

a. 城市觀光
b. 小冊子
c. 景點
d. 地標
e. 城市通行證
f. 時間有限
g. (尤指建築物在天空映襯下的)天際線
h. 地平線，以天空爲背景的輪廓
i. 門票及選項
j. 主要旅遊景點
k. 巴士售票員

( ) 1. brochure
( ) 2. points of interests
( ) 3. landmarks
( ) 4. limited time
( ) 5. skyline
( ) 6. tickets & options
( ) 7. main attractions
( ) 8. bus conductor
( ) 9. city sightseeing
( ) 10. CityPass

Choose the incorrect answer

( ) 1. Types of tours:
(a) walking tour (b) helicopter tour
(c) skyline (d) cruise

( ) 2. Types of tours:
(a) Thames River (b) night tour
(c) day tour (d) balloon ride

( ) 3. Types of tours:
(a) biking tour (b) hop-on, hop-off bus
(c) public transport (d) night tour

( ) 4. Types of tours:
(a) electric tour (b) historical tour
(c) photography tour (d) river cruise

( ) 5. Attractions:
(a) hop-on, hop-off bus (b) Big Ben
(c) London Eye (d) House of Parliament

track 24

Listen and Pronounce

Listen to the audio first. Then, try pronouncing each one of the following:

1. Balloon tour	氣球旅遊
2. Biking tour	單車旅遊
3. Cultural tour	文化旅遊
4. Food tour	美食旅遊
5. Helicopter tour	直升機旅遊
6. Historical tour	歷史古蹟旅遊
7. Hop-on, hop-off bus tour	跳上跳下旅遊巴士
8. Photography tour	攝影旅遊
9. Running tour	跑步旅遊
10. Speedboat tour	高速遊艇旅遊

track 25

Listen and fill in the blanks

Listen to the conversation and fill in the blanks.

1. The couple is looking at attractions and tours from the brochures they collected at the airport, and is planning to do some London city s ________.
2. There are many points of interests and landmarks, from walking tours to ________, but the couple has limited time.
3. Ken suggests the helicopter and balloon rides would give them a spectacular v ________ and s ________ of the London city!
4. Looks like the couple decided to catch the h ________ - ________, h ________- ________ bus where they can visit the House of Parliament, Tower of London, Big Ben, and London Eye!
5. The couple bought two 72-hour ________ for a total of £ ________.

Photographs-Types of tours

Match the photos to the answers given below:

a. Running tour
b. Balloon tour
c. Biking tour
d. Helicopter tour
e. Photography tour
f. River cruise

1.

2.

3.

4.

5.

6.

LONDON BROADWAY MUSICAL

Unit 06

Learning Objectives

What you will learn in this unit...

- What are some of the most popular Broadway musicals?
- What are some ways to purchase discounted Broadway tickets?
- What is the dress code to attend a Broadway musical?
- Websites you can purchase a Broadway ticket.
- Understanding Broadway theater seating arrangements.
- Understanding the different items on a Broadway theater ticket.
- Some useful knowledge about Broadway musicals.
- Broadway musical related keyword verbs, phrases and idioms.

Brainstorming

1. What are some of the most popular Broadway musicals?

The Lion King
獅子王

This story is of Simba, a young lion who is to succeed his father, Mufasa, as King of the Pride Lands. Simba's uncle, Scar murders Mufasa. Simba is then manipulated into thinking he was responsible and flees into exile. Upon maturation, Simba returns to end Scar's tyranny, and takes his place as the rightful King.

The Aladdin
阿拉丁

The story is of a poor young man who is granted three wishes by a genie in a lamp, of which he uses to woo a princess and to thwart the Sultan's evil, Grand Vizier.

The Phantom of the Opera
歌劇魅影

This is the story of the Phantom, who Lives in an underground cavern in the Paris Opera House. The Phantom tutors and composes operas for Christine, a gorgeous young soprano star-to-be. As Christine's star rises, and a handsome suitor from her past enters the picture, the Phantom grows mad, terrorizing everyone.

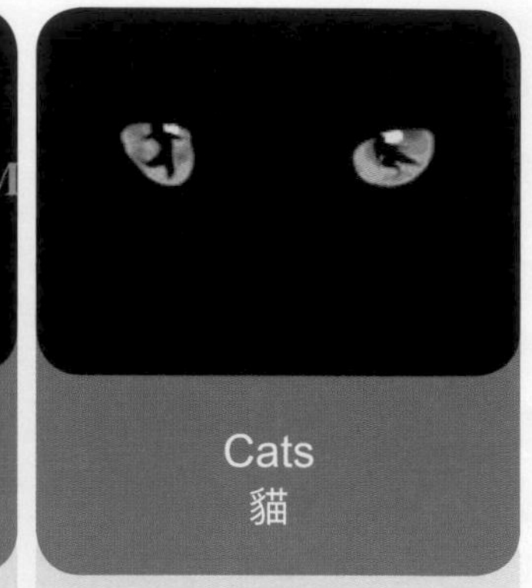

Cats
貓

This story is of Jellicle cats. Each cat's individual quest is to be selected as the lucky one who will ascend to "The Heaviside Layer."

2. What is the dress code to attend a Broadway musical?
3. If you could only pick one show on Broadway, which one would it be?
   Example: The Phantom of the Opera, etc.
4. What are some of the websites you can purchase a Broadway ticket?
   Example: Ticketmaster, etc.
5. What are some ways to get discounted Broadway tickets?
   Example: student rush tickets, etc.
6. Can you name the types of seating at a Broadway theater?
   Example: mezzanine, etc.

BASIC WORDS

Broadway Seating
百老匯座位區

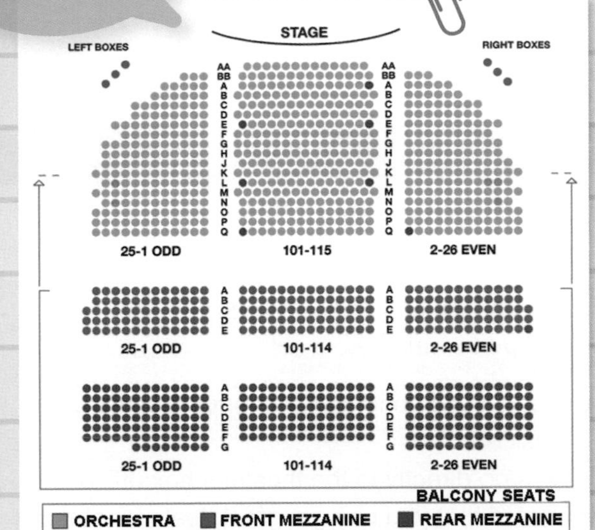

* Stage 舞臺
* Box seats (left boxes / right boxes) 包廂座位
* Orchestra seats 管弦樂隊區座位
* Front mezzanine seats (FMEZZ) 二樓前半部座位
* Rear mezzanine seats (RMEZZ) (2nd or 3rd oor) 二樓或三樓夾層樓座位
* Balcony seats (劇院的)樓廳座位

Broadway musical (play/show)
百老匯音樂劇(戲劇/秀)

Broadway theater
百老匯劇院

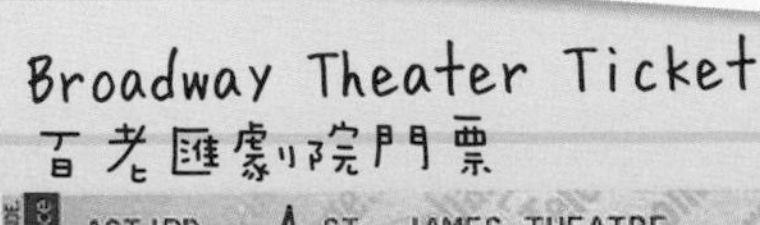

Broadway Theater Ticket
百老匯劇院門票

A. Name of theatre-ST. JAMES THEATER 劇院名稱－詹姆斯劇院
B. Street Address of Theatre-246 WEST 44TH STREET
劇院地址－西44街246號
C. Name of Broadway musical-THE PRODUCERS 百老匯音樂劇名稱－製片人
D. Time of Broadway musical-8:00 Pm, Saturday
百老匯音樂劇開演時間－晚上8點，禮拜六
E. Date of Broadway musical-February 3, 2007
百老匯音樂劇開演日期－2月3日，2007年
F. Price of ticket - $111.25 (includes $1.25 facility fee)
門票價格－111.25英鎊(包含1.25英鎊設施使用費)
G. How ticket was paid using cash (or creditcard)
門票付費方式－使用現金或信用卡
H. Telephone number of ticket agent-212-239-6200
門票上的聯絡電話－代理人－212-239-6200
I. Ticket agent-Telecharge.com 門票上的代理公司名稱－Telecharge.com
J. Seat Position-FMEZZC Front - MEZZanine Center
座位位置－二樓前半部中間
k. Seat：E106 座位號碼：E106

box office
售票處/票房
box office clerk 售票員工

Program
節目單

Conversation Preview

Practice Phrases

Work with a partner to practice saying the phrases below.

Partner A	Partner B
★ They are showing The Phantom of the Opera.	★ Yes, I'd love to watch a Broadway musical in London.
★ They are also showing Lion King, Aladdin and Cats.	★ They all sound like great choices! ★ I'd love to watch them all!
★ Yes, I agree. But, I'd really love to watch The Phantom of the Opera. ★ It is the longest running show in the history of Broadway.	★ Yes, it is also one of my favorite Broadway musicals. ★ Let's go directly to the theater's box office. ★ I heard that you can get great deals for standby tickets, General Rush tickets and Lottery tickets prior to its opening.
★ Wow! There's such a long queue!	★ Maybe, we should purchase our tickets online at Telecharge, Ticketmaster, PlayBill or TheaterMania.
★ Purchasing our tickets online help us save time.	★ But... isn't there are service charge added to the price of ticket?
★ Yes, there is. ★ And, because we are using a foreign credit card, exchange rates may apply as well.	★ It'd be more expensive this way.
★ Yes, it would. Why don't we just return early first thing in the morning?	★ Great idea!

Listening Practice

track 26

Listen to the audio. Listen to the conversation between the box office clerk at Broadway and customer, and then choose the correct answer.

( ) 1. (a) It seems most likely that they are going to watch the Lion King.
(b) It seems most likely that they are going to watch The Phantom of the Opera.

( ) 2. (a) They are going to purchase their tickets online.
(b) They are going to purchase their tickets at the theater's box office.

( ) 3. (a) They are thinking of purchasing their tickets online at Telecharge, Ticketmaster, PlayBill or TheaterMania because it is more expensive.
(b) They are going to purchase their tickets online at Telecharge, Ticketmaster, PlayBill or TheaterMania because it is cheaper.

( ) 4. (a) The customer asked for the orchestra seats in the third row right of the stage.
(b) The customer asked for the front center mezzanine seats.

Test Yourself

Mix & match the questions and answers below

a. mezzanine	d. program
b. £55	e. The Phantom of the Opera
c. General Rush	f. orchestra

1. Box office clerk: Hi, may I help you?
   Customer: Do you still have two __________ tickets for __________ ?
2. Box office clerk: Well, it's your lucky day! We have __________ seats in the third row right of the stage, front center __________ seats and balcony seats.
   Customer: We'd like two front center mezzanine seats, please.
3. Box office clerk: Would you also like a __________ ?
   Customer: Yes, please.
4. Box office clerk: The programs are £5 each. Your total is __________ , please.
   Customer: Here you are.

Conversation

track 27

New Words & Phrases

track 28

1. Broadway (n.) 百老匯
2. central London (n.) 倫敦市中心
3. Apollo Victoria Theater (n.)
   阿波羅維多利亞劇院
4. theater (n.) 劇院
   [英式拼音爲 theater, (re) 結尾；美式拼音則爲 theater, (er) 結尾]
5. The Phantom of the Opera (n.) 歌劇魅影
6. Broadway musical (n.) 百老匯音樂劇
   同 Broadway play 戲劇 /
   Broadway show 秀
7. Lion King (n.) 獅子王
8. Aladdin (n.) 阿拉丁
9. Cats (n.) 貓
10. longest running show in the history of Broadway (phrase)
    史上百老匯經久不衰的音樂劇
11. Let's go directly (phrase) 我們直接去吧，好嗎？ Let's go 是 Let us go 的簡寫。「起程 / 出發」或鼓勵「加油」。
12. box office (n.) 售票處
13. great deals (n.) 很不錯的買賣 /
    很划算的買賣
14. standby tickets (n.) 開演前的零散折扣票 /
    等候票
15. General Rush tickets (n.) 一般當天上演前的折扣票。（註：劇院留一定量的票在當天賣，且提供較折扣的優惠或售票模式。）
16. Lottery tickets (n.) 樂透票。
    分爲 (a) In-person Lotteries 現場個人抽籤樂透票 – 現場抽籤的情形爲開演前兩個半小時到戲院門口填寫個人資料，半小時後立即現場開票；(b) Online Ticket Lottery 網路線上抽籤票，及 (c) Mobile Ticket Lottery 手機 TodayTix APP 購票。

Michelle and Ken are walking along Broadway[1] in central London[2] when they came across Apollo Victoria Theater[3,4].

Michelle: Honey, look! They are showing The Phantom of the Opera[5].

Ken: Yes, I'd love to watch a Broadway musical[6] in London.

Michelle: Honey, they are also showing Lion King[7], Aladdin[8] and Cats[9].

Ken: Wow! They all sound like great choices!

Michelle: Yes, I agree. But, I'd really love to watch The Phantom of the Opera. It is the longest running show in the history of Broadway[10].

Ken: Yes, it is also one of my favorite Broadway musicals.

Michelle: Let's go directly[11] to the theater's box office[12]. I heard that you can get great deals[13] for standby tickets[14], General Rush tickets[15] and Lottery tickets[16] before its opening.

Michelle and Ken then walked towards[17] Apollo Victoria Theater's box office.

Ken: Wow! There's such a long queue[18]!

Michelle: Maybe, we should purchase[19] our tickets online at Telecharge[20], Ticketmaster[21], PlayBill[22] or TheaterMania[23].

Ken: Purchasing our tickets online help us save time.[24]

Michelle: But... isn't there are service charge[25] added to the price of ticket?

Ken: Yes, there is. And, because we are using a foreign[26] credit card[27], exchange rates[28] may apply[29] as well.

Michelle: It'd be more expensive this way.

Ken: Yes, it would. Why don't we just return early first thing in the morning[30]?

Michelle: Great idea!

New Words & Phrases

17. walked towards (prep.) 朝某人或某物的方向走去 .
18. queue (vi.) 排隊
19. purchase (a ticket) (v.) 買 (票)
    同 buy 反 sell
20. Telecharge (website) (n.) 百老匯購票網站
21. Ticketmaster (website) (n.) 百老匯購票網站
22. PlayBill (website) (n.) 百老匯購票網站
    同 brochure / flyer
23. TheaterMania (website) (n.)
    百老匯購票網站
24. save time (idiom) 節省時間
    反 waste time
25. service charge (n.) 服務費
26. foreign (adj.) 國外的 同 overseas
    反 local / national)
27. credit card (n.) 信用卡 同 charge
    反 cash
28. exchange rates (n.) 匯率
29. apply (vt.) 應用
30. first thing in the morning (phrase)
    明天頭一件要做的事

Early next morning, Michelle and Ken returned to Apollo Victoria Theater's box office. They were fifth in line[31] and waited for three hours...

Box office clerk[32]: Hi, may I help you?

Ken: [a] Do you still have two General Rush tickets for The Phantom of the Opera?

Box office clerk: [b] Well, it's your lucky day! [c] We have orchestra seats[33] in the third row right of the stage, front center mezzanine seats[34] and balcony seats[35].

Ken: [d] We'd like the front center mezzanine seats, please.

Box office clerk: Ok. Two front center mezzanine tickets. [e] Your total will be **£**50[36].

Ken: [f] Do you accept credit cards?

Box office clerk: [g] Sorry, sir. For General Rush tickets, we only accept cash. [h] Would you also like a program[37]?

Ken: Yes, please.

Box office clerk: [i] The programs are £5 each. [j] Your total will be £55.

Ken: [k] Here you are.

New Words & Phrases

31. fifth in line（idiom）排在第五順位
32. box office clerk (n.) 售票員工
33. orchestra seats (n.) 管弦樂隊區座位
34. front center mezzanine seats (n.) 二樓前半部中間的座位 反 rear (center) mezzanine seats 二樓或三樓後半部 [中間] 的座位)。百老匯票上坐位顯示的簡稱爲 Front = F, Center = C, Rear = R, Mezzanine =MEZZ / MEZ
35. balcony seats (n.)（劇院等的）樓廳座位
36. £ (n.) British Pound 英鎊
37. program (n.) 節目單 同 schedule

Q & A

1. Which theater in central London did Michelle and Ken come across?

____

2. Which show did Ken and Michelle decide to watch?

____

3. Which websites can Ken and Michelle also purchase their Broadway tickets from?

____

4. What kinds of seats did the box office clerk offer Ken?

____

5. How much was the total price of the tickets?

____

Important Sentences

a. Do you still have two General Rush tickets for The Phantom of the Opera?
請問你還有兩張歌劇魅影的一般 Rush 折扣票嗎？

b. Well, it's your lucky day!
嗯，這是你的幸運日！

c. We have orchestra seats in the third row right of the stage, front center mezzanine seats and balcony seats.
我們有管弦樂隊區座位靠舞台右邊的第三排座位、二樓前半部靠中間的座位及樓廳座位。

d. We'd like the front center mezzanine seats, please.
請給我們兩張二樓前半部靠中間的座位。

e. Your total will be £50.
總共是 50 英鎊。

f. Do you accept credit cards?
你們接受信用卡嗎？

g. Sorry, sir. For General Rush tickets, we only accept cash.
對不起，先生。一般當天上演前的折扣票，我們只接受現金。

h. Would you also like a program?
你要不要買一張節目單？

i. The programs are £5 each.
一張節目單是 5 英鎊。

j. Your total will be £55.
總共是 55 英鎊。

k. Here you are.
這裡是 ...[55 英鎊]。

Conversation Review

Match the Chinese-English Translations

a. 歌劇魅影	f. 樓廳座位	k. 阿拉丁
b. 百老匯音樂劇	g. 節目單	l. 售票處
c. 售票處	h. 英鎊	m. 開演前的零散折扣票 / 等候票
d. 獅子王	i. 劇院	n. 一般當天上演前的折扣票
e. 二樓前半部的座位	j. 樂透票	o. 管弦樂隊區座位

(　) 1. theater
(　) 2. The Phantom of the Opera
(　) 3. Broadway musical
(　) 4. Lion King
(　) 5. Aladdin
(　) 6. box office
(　) 7. standby tickets
(　) 8. General Rush tickets
(　) 9. Lottery tickets
(　) 10. box office
(　) 11. orchestra seats
(　) 12. front mezzanine seats
(　) 13. balcony seats
(　) 14. program
(　) 15. £

track 29

Listen and Pronounce

Listen to the audio first. Then, try pronouncing each one of the following Broadway musicals.

1. A Chorus Line	歌舞線上
2. Aladdin	阿拉丁
3. Blue Man	藍人秀
4. Cats	貓
5. Chicago	芝加哥
6. Kinky Boots	長靴妖
7. Le Petit Prince	小王子
8. Les Misérables	悲慘世界
9. Lion King	獅子王
10. Mamma Mia!	媽媽咪呀！
11. Miss Saigon	西貢小姐
12. The Book of Mormon	摩門經
13. The Phantom of the Opera	歌劇魅影
14. The Wizard of Oz	綠野仙蹤
15. Wicked	女巫

track 30

Listen and fill in the blanks

Listen to the conversation and fill in the blanks.

1. Sounds like they are going to watch a Broadway musical called ____________ .
2. The customer would like to buy two ____________ Rush tickets for the Phantom of the Opera.
3. The customer asked for the front center ____________ seats.
4. Looks like the customer is going to pay for his tickets using a ____________ .
5. The customer bought a ____________ for £5 each.

Photographs – Broadway Seating

a. Mezzanine seats (2nd or 3rd floor)
b. Orchestra seats
c. Balcony seats
d. Stage
e. Box seats (left boxes / right boxes)

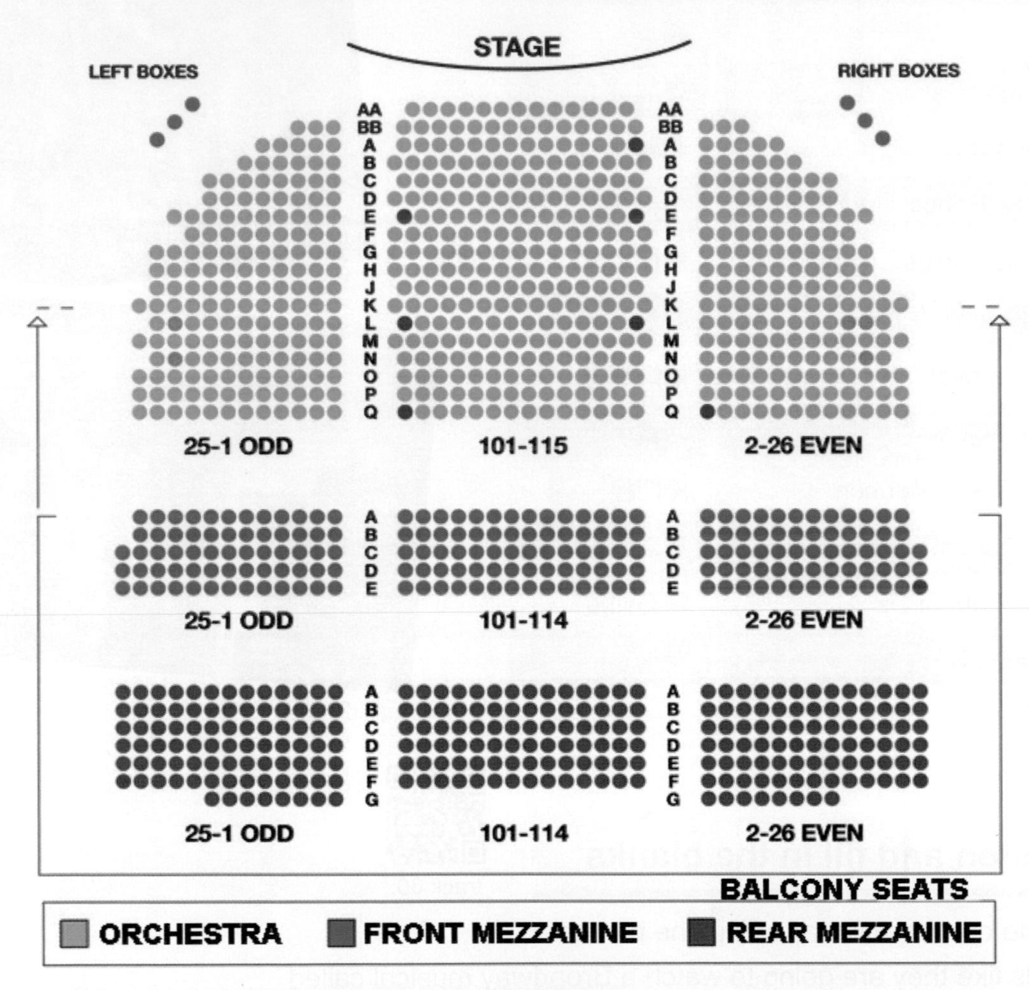

1. 舞臺：____________________
2. 包廂座位：____________________
3. 管弦樂隊區座位：____________________
4. 二樓或三樓夾層樓座位：____________________
5. 劇院的樓廳座位：____________________

Seven Wonders of the World

Unit 07

Learning Objectives

What you will learn in this unit...

- What are some of the Seven Wonders of the World?
- Why the number "7" was chosen for the "Seven Wonders of the World?
- Names of some of the world's most mysterious stone circles or standing stones, and where they are located?
- More information about Stonehenge in the United Kingdom, one of the Seven Wonders of the World.
- Some useful phrases to introduce the Seven Wonders of the World for a tour guide.
- Some useful questions to learn to ask a tour guide as a tourist.
- Some useful knowledge about many other Seven Wonders of the World.
- Seven Wonders of the World -related keyword verbs, phrases and idioms.

Brainstorming

1. What are some examples of the Seven Wonders of the World?

Porcelain Tower of Nanjing 大報恩寺琉璃塔

Location 地點 Nanjing, China
Size 大小 **Height**: 79 m, 9 stories, spiral staircase of 184 steps
Built: 15th century **Re-built**: 19th century
Type 類別 Pagoda

Catacombs of Kom El Shoqafa 亞歷山卓地下陵墓

Location 地點 Alexandria, Egypt
Size 大小 **Height**: 100 feet
Built: 2nd century
Type 類別 tomb / burial chamber

Colosseum 羅馬競技場

Location 地點 Rome, Italy
Size 大小 Holds between 50,000 and 80,000 spectators
Built: 70–80 AD
Type 類別 Amphitheatre

Great Wall of China 萬里長城

Location 地點 China **Size** 大小 21,196 km
Built by: Qin Shi Huang, the first Emperor of China
Built: 220-206BC
Type 類別 Fortification

Hagia Sophia 聖索菲亞大教堂

Location 地點 Istanbul, Turkey
Size 大小 **Length**: 82 meters, **Width**:73 meters, **Height**: 55 meters
Built: 532 - 537
Type 類別 Cathedral

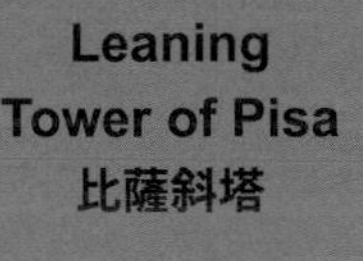

Leaning Tower of Pisa 比薩斜塔

Location 地點 Pisa, Italy
Size 大小 Height (max) 55.86m
Built:1372
Type 類別 : Cathedral

Stonehenge 巨石陣

Location 地點 Wiltshire, England
Size 大小 Each standing stone is around 4.1 metres high
Built: 3000 BC-2000 BC
Type 類別 : Monument

2. Do you know why the number "7" was chosen for the "Seven Wonders of the World?
3. Can you name some other Seven Wonders of the World?
   Example: Seven Wonders of the Ancient World
4. Can you name the Seven Wonders of the Ancient World?
   Example: Great Pyramid of Giza 吉薩金字塔
5. Can you name the Seven Natural Wonders of the World?
   Example: Grand Canyon 科羅拉多大峽谷
6. Can you name the Seven Man-made Wonders of the World?
   Example: Channel Tunnel 英法海底隧道
7. Can you name some of the world's most mysterious stone circles or standing stones, and find out where they are located?
   Example: Stonehenge, United Kingdom 巨石陣，英國

BASIC WORDS

Map of United kingdom (UK)
英國地圖

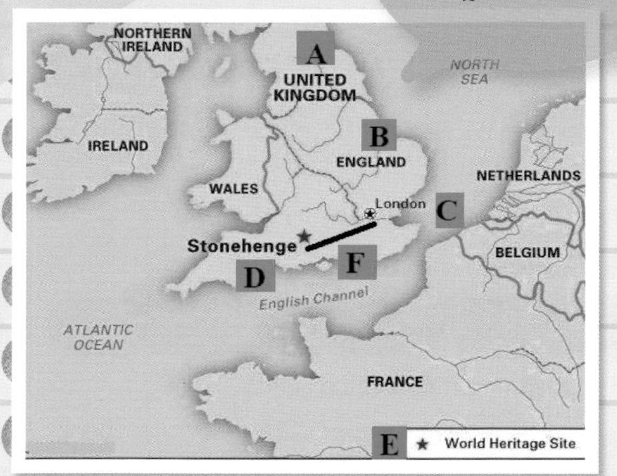

A. United kingdom (UK) 英國
B. England 英格蘭
C. London 倫敦
D. Stonehenge 巨石陣
E. UNESCO's World Heritage Site
聯合國教科文組織的世界遺產
F. Stonehenge is 90 miles from London 巨石陣離倫敦 90 英里

Approximate Size of Each Standing Stone
巨石陣每個立石大約大小
2.1 meters wide: 2.1 米寬
4 meters high : 4 米高
Weight: 25 tons 重量 : 25 噸

stone circle 石圈／環狀土

standing stones 立石

surfing the Internet using a cellphone
使用手機上網

I'm so thrilled!
我很興奮！

Conversation Preview

Phrasal Words

Below are some good phrases that a tourist can ask, and a tour guide may use to answer questions during a tour. Practice the phrases below with a partner.

Tourist	Tour Guide
★ Do you know that we actually visited one of the Seven Wonders of Europe on our London sightseeing tour? ★ The Tower of London is considered one of the Seven Wonders in Europe.	★ Are you kidding me? Which one?
★ Are there any more Seven Wonders of the World?	★ In fact, there are several – Seven Wonders of the Ancient World Seven Natural Wonders of the World New Seven Wonders of the World Seven Wonders of the Industrial World Seven Wonders of the Modern World New Seven Wonders Cities Seven Wonders of the Underwater World
★ I'd sure like to visit another Seven Wonder of the World while we are still in the UK.	★ Which one do you have in mind?
★ I heard that there's a Seven Wonder of the Ancient World in the UK.	★ Let's check it out.
★ What is the Stonehenge?	★ The Stonehenge is one the Seven Wonders of the Ancient World. ★ It is also considered as one of UNESCO's list of World Heritage.
★ What does it look like?	★ Here, look at this picture. ★ It looks like a stone circle. ★ There's a ring of 100 standing stones. ★ Each standing stone is around 4 meters high, 2.1 meters wide and weighs around 25 tons.
★ I wonder how long it took them to erect the stone circle?	★ The stone circle was constructed in a number of stages over hundreds of years. ★ It took around 1500 years to erect them.
★ What was the stone circle for?	★ The purpose of the stone circle is unknown, but possibly ritualistic. ★ Many modern scholars agree that Stonehenge was once a burial ground.

Surf the Internet Exercise

Use the following table to fill out the different Seven Wonders of the World. You may surf the Internet to find your answers:

Type of Seven Wonder of the World	List 7 each
Seven Wonders of the World 中古世界七大奇蹟	1. 2. 3. 4. 5. 6. 7.
Seven Natural Wonders of the World 世界七大自然奇觀	1. 2. 3. 4. 5. 6. 7.
Seven Wonders of the Industrial World 世界七大工程奇蹟	1. 2. 3. 4. 5. 6. 7.
New Seven Wonders Cities 世界七大奇蹟城市	1. 2. 3. 4. 5. 6. 7.

Listening Practice

track 31

Listen to the audio. Listen to the conversation and then choose the correct answer.

( ) 1. (a) London is considered a Seven Wonder of Europe.
(b) The Tower of London is considered a Seven Wonder of Europe.

( ) 2. (a) They wish to visit another Seven Wonder of the Ancient World in the UK.
(b) They wish to visit another Seven Wonder of the New World in the UK.

( ) 3. (a) Stonehenge looks like a stone ring and has 100 stones lying on the ground.
(b) Stonehenge looks like a stone circle and has a ring of 100 standing stones.

( ) 4. (a) The purpose of the stone circle at Stonehenge was probably a burial ground in the olden days.
(b) The purpose of the stone circle at Stonehenge is probably a burial ground for people of United Kingdom today.

Test Yourself

Fill in the blanks with the correct answers given below.

a. standing stones
b. ritualistic
c. constructed
d. Seven Wonder of the Ancient World
e. World Heritage Site

1. There's a________ called Stonehenge approximately 90 miles from London.
2. The Stonehenge is considered one of UNESCO's _________.
3. The Stonehenge looks like a stone circle and has a ring of 100 __________.
4. The stone circle was__________in a number of stages over hundreds of years.
5. The purpose of the stone circle is unknown, but possibly_______.

Conversation

track 32

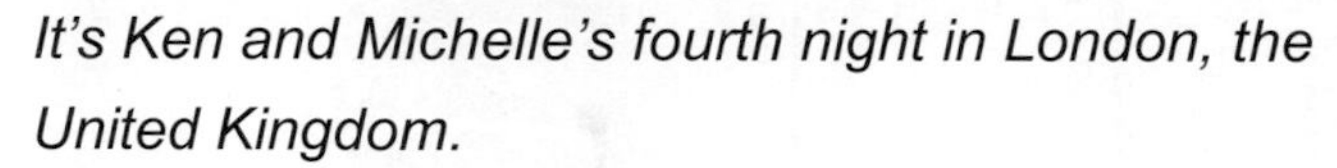

It's Ken and Michelle's fourth night in London, the United Kingdom.

Michelle: Do you know that we actually[1] visited one of the Seven Wonders of Europe[2] on our London sightseeing tour?

Ken: Are you kidding me? [3] Which one?

Michelle: The Tower of London[4] is considered one of the Seven Wonders in Europe.

Ken: I didn't know that?[5] Are there any more Seven Wonders of the World?

Michelle: In fact, there are several[6] – The Seven Wonders of the Ancient World[7], Seven Natural Wonders of the World[8], New Seven Wonders of the World[9], Seven Wonders of the Industrial World[10], Seven Wonders of the Modern World[11], New Seven Wonders Cities[12], and Seven Wonders of the Underwater World[13].

Ken: I'd sure like to visit another Seven Wonder of the World while we are still in the UK[14].

Michelle: Which one do you have in mind?

Ken: I heard that there's a Seven Wonder of the Ancient World in the UK.

Michelle: Let's check it out.[15]

Ken and Michelle started surfing the Internet[16] on their cellphones[17]...

New Words & Phrases

track 33

1. actually (adv.) 實際上／竟然
2. Seven Wonders of the Europe (n.) 歐洲七大奇蹟
3. Are you kidding me? (phrase) 你在跟我開玩笑吧？同 Are you joking?
4. Tower of London (n.) 倫敦塔（位於倫敦市中心的一座宮殿和城堡）
5. I didn't know that (expression) 我並不知道
6. several (pronoun) 幾個 同 some 反 few
7. Seven Wonders of the Ancient World (n.) (or Seven Wonders of the World) 古代世界七大奇蹟。常稱七大奇蹟，爲最早被提出的七大奇蹟觀念。
8. Seven Natural Wonders of the World (n.) 世界七大自然奇觀
9. New Seven Wonders of the World (n.) 世界新七大奇蹟
10. Seven Wonders of the Industrial World (n.) 世界七大工程奇蹟
11. Seven Wonders of the Modern World (n.) 現代世界的七大奇蹟
12. New Seven Wonders Cities (n.) 世界七大奇蹟城市
13. Seven Wonders of the Underwater World (n.) 世界七大水下世界奇蹟
14. UK (n.) 英國（簡稱：UK (U.K) 是 United Kingdom 的簡稱英國）同 England
15. Let's check it out! (phrase) 查查看！
16. surfing the Internet (phrase) 上網 同 surf the net
17. cellphone (n.) 手機 同 mobile phone / hand phone

New Words & Phrases

18. As a matter of fact (phrase) 事實上 / 實際上 同 actually
19. Stonehenge (n.) 巨石陣
20. approximately (adv.) 大約 同 close to / about 反 exactly
21. 90 miles (n.) 90 英里
22. London (n.) 倫敦
23. UNESCO (n.) 聯合國教科文組織 The United Nations Educational, Scientific and Cultural Organization
24. world heritage site (n.) 世界文化遺址 / 世界遺產地
25. Let me see! (phrase) 讓我想一下！
26. stone circle (n.) 石圈 / 環狀土
27. standing stones (n.) 立石
28. meter (n.) 米，公尺
29. high (height) (adj.) 高度
30. wide (width) (adj.) 寬度 反 long / length
31. weigh (weight) (vt.) 稱 ...... 的重量
32. ton (n.) 噸 / 公噸 [C]

Ken: Hmm...As a matter of fact[18], there's one called the Stonehenge[19]. It's approximately[20] 90 miles[21] from London[22].

Michelle: [a] What is the Stonehenge?

Ken: [b] The Stonehenge is one the Seven Wonders of the Ancient World. It is also considered as one of UNESCO's[23] world heritage site[24].

Michelle: Let me see! [25] Let me see! [c] What does it look like?

Ken: [d] Here, look at this picture. [e] It looks like a stone circle[26]. There's a ring of 100 standing stones[27]. Each standing stone is around 4 meters[28] high,[29] 2.1 meters wide[30] and weighs[31] around 25 tons[32].

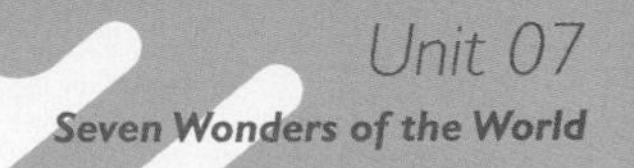

Michelle: [f] I wonder how long it took them to erect[33] the stone circle?

Ken: [g] It was constructed[34] in a number of stages[35] over hundreds of years. And, [h] it took around 1500 years to erect them.

Michelle: [i] What was the stone circle for?

Ken: [j] The purpose[36] of the stone circle is unknown[37], but possibly ritualistic[38]. Many modern scholars[39] agree that Stonehenge was once a burial ground[40].

Michelle: Honey, I'm so thrilled! [41] [k] What are we waiting for?

Ken: Ok! [l] Let's catch a train there right now!

Scan the QR Code for "Interactive Maps of the Stonehenge Landscape"
掃描 QR 碼
[巨石陣景觀的互動地圖]

http://www.english-heritage.org.uk/visit/places/stonehenge/history/stonehenge-landscape/#

Discover what the landscape around Stonehenge has looked like from before the monument itself was first built through to the present day. Move between the four maps to see the Stonehenge landscape at different periods, and open the image windows to find out more about each feature

探索巨石陣周圍的景觀，從紀念碑本身建成到現在的樣子。在四個地圖之間移動以查看不同時期的巨石陣景觀，並打開圖像窗口找出有關每個要素的信息

Q & A

1. What was the first Seven Wonder of Europe that Ken and Michelle visited?

______

2. List three different Seven Wonders of the World that Michelle mentioned.

______

3. How far is Stonehenge from London?

______

4. Describe how the Stonehenge looks like.

______

5. What was the stone circle for?

______

New Words & Phrases

33. erect (vt.) 建造 / 豎立 / 搭建
34. constructed (vt.) 建造 / 構成 同 erect
35. number of stages (phrase) 階段數
36. purpose (n.) 目的 同 objective)
37. unknown (adj.) 未知的
    同 anonymous 反 known
38. ritualistic (adj.) 儀式的 / 固守儀式的 / 慣例的
39. modern scholars (n.) 現代學者
    反 traditional scholars
40. burial ground (n.) 墓葬地 同 burial site)
41. I'm so thrilled! (phrase) 我很興奮！
    同 I'm so excited!

Important Sentences

a. What is the Stonehenge?
什麼是巨石陣？

b. The Stonehenge is one the Seven Wonders of the Ancient World.
巨石陣是古代世界的七大奇蹟之一。

c. What does it look like?
它看起來像什麼？

d. Here, look at this picture.
讓我們先來看看這張照片。

e. It looks like a stone circle.
它看起來像一個石圈。

f. I wonder how long it took them to erect the stone circle?
我想知道他們建立石圈需要多長時間？

g. It was constructed in a number of stages over hundreds of years.
千百年來，這個石陣歷經數代才終于建成。

h. It took around 1500 years to erect them.
他們需要大約 1500 年把它建立起來。

i. What was the stone circle for?
石圈的用途爲何？

j. The purpose of the stone circle is unknown, but possibly ritualistic.
堆疊石圓環的目的已無法稽考，但大抵與祭祀儀式有關。

k. What are we waiting for?
我們還在等什麼？

l. Let's catch a train there right now!
那我們現在就趕火車吧！

Conversation Review

Match the Chinese-English Translations

a. 世界七大自然奇觀	e. 石圈 / 環狀土	i. 世界七大工程奇蹟
b. 世界新七大奇蹟	f. 立石	j. 世界七大水下世界奇蹟
c. 世界七大奇蹟城市	g. 墓葬地	k. 使用手機上網
d. 古代世界七大奇蹟	h. 我很興奮	l. 現代世界的七大奇蹟

(　) 1. Seven Wonders of the Ancient World
(　) 2. Seven Natural Wonders of the World
(　) 3. New Seven Wonders of the World
(　) 4. Seven Wonders of the Industrial World
(　) 5. Seven Wonders of the Modern World
(　) 6. New Seven Wonders Cities
(　) 7. Seven Wonders of the Underwater World
(　) 8. surfing the Internet using a cellphone
(　) 9. stone circle
(　) 10. standing stones
(　) 11. burial ground
(　) 12. I'm so thrilled

track 34

 Listen and Pronounce

Listen to the audio first. Then, try pronouncing each one of the following Seven Wonders of the Ancient World and Seven Natural Wonders of the World.

New Seven Wonders of the World 世界新七大奇蹟

1. Christ the Redeemer	里約熱內盧基督像 (Brasil 巴西)
2. Great Wall of China	萬里長城 (China 中國)
3. Petra	佩特拉 (Jordan 約旦)
4. The Colosseum	羅馬競技場 (Italy 義大利)
5. Chichen Itza	契琴伊薩 (Mexico 墨西哥)
6. Machu Picchu	馬丘比丘 (Peru 秘魯)
7. Taj Mahal	泰姬瑪哈陵 (India 印度)

Seven Natural Wonders of the World 世界七大自然奇觀

1. Grand Canyon	科羅拉多大峽谷 (United States of America 美國)
2. Great Barrier Reef	大堡礁 (Australia 澳大利亞)
3. Guanabara Bay	里約熱內盧 瓜納巴拉灣 (Brazil 巴西) 高緯度（北極和南極）的天空中
4. Mount Everest	珠穆朗瑪峰（聖母峰）- 世界最高峰 (Nepal / China 尼泊爾 / 中國)
5. Victoria Falls	維多利亞瀑布 (Zimbabwe, South Africa 尚比亞、辛巴威共有)
6. Parícutin	帕里庫廷火山 (Mexico 墨西哥)
7. Aurora (Northern Lights)	極光 (北極光) Northern lights (aurora borealis) or Southern lights (aurora australis) is a natural light display in the Earth's sky, around the Arctic and Antarctic. 在高緯度（北極和南極）的天空中

track 35

Listen and fill in the blanks

Listen to the conversation and fill in the blanks.

1. Michelle and Ken visited one of the Seven ____________ of Europe on their London sighseeing tour called the ____________ of London.
2. There's a Seven Wonder of the Ancient World in the UK called the ____________ which is approximately 90 miles from London.
3. The Stonehenge is a Seven Wonder of the Ancient World and also considered one of ________'s world heritage site.
4. The Stonehenge looks like a ____________ .
5. The Stonehenge was ____________ a number of stages over hundreds of years.

Choose the incorrect answer

( ) 1. Size-related words of each Stonehenge standing stone:
(a) meter (b) erect (c) width (d) height

( ) 2. Words related to Stonehenge:
(a) Stonehenge
(b) UNESCO's World Heritage Site
(c) Seven Wonder of the Ancient World
(d) Tower of London

( ) 3. Some Seven Wonders of the World:
(a)Old Seven Wonders Cities
(b)Seven Wonders of the Ancient World
(c)Seven Natural Wonders of the World
(d)New Seven Wonders of the World

( ) 4. Some Seven Wonders of the World:
(a)Seven Wonders of the Stonehenge World
(b)Seven Wonders of the Modern World
(c)New Seven Wonders Cities
(d)Seven Wonders of the Underwater World

( ) 5. Cities in the United Kingdom:
(a) London (b) Stonehenge
(c) Manchester (d) stone circle

Photographs

1. Which sentence best describes the picture?

   (a) Some tourists are very thrilled to be at the Stonehenge.
   (b) Some tourists are performing a ritual at the Stonehenge.
   (c) Some tourists are surfing the Internet at the Stonehenge.
   (d) Some tourists are erecting some stones at the Stonehenge.

Your Answer: (   )

2. Which sentence best describes what the people are doing in the picture?

   (a) They are performing a ritual at the Stonehenge.
   (b) They are trying to erect some stones at the Stonehenge.
   (c) They are visiting the Stonehenge.
   (d) They are thrilled to be at the Stonehenge.

Your Answer: (   )

Scottish Whisk(e)y Tour

Unit 08

Learning Objectives

What you will learn in this unit...

- Which countries produce whisk(e)y?
- Whiskey or whisky?
- What are the different categories of Scotch whisk(e)y?
- What are some of the most popular whiskies in the world, and which country are they made from?
- What are some popular Scottish whisk(e)y brands?
- What are some different ways to drink your whisk(e)y?
- Whisk(e)y -related keyword verbs, phrases and idioms.

Brainstorming

1. What your choice in whisk(e)y really says about you?

Starward 斯達瓦威士忌	Jack Daniels 傑克丹尼爾斯威士忌	Chivas Regal 皇家起瓦士威士忌	Suntory 三得利威士忌	Canadian Club 加拿大俱樂部威士忌
Australia 澳洲	USA 美國	Scotland 蘇格蘭	Japan 日本	Canada 加拿大

You question everything, but your intuition. You also make use of what's around you, and don't take yourself too seriously.	You are a confident person and one who enjoys the finer aspects of life. You silently sip your drink and let your looks do the talking	You don't want to be disturbed when drinking your Scotch. You are also an introverted person and often like to be by yourself.	You are a mysterious person, and often like to sit at the end of the bar.	You like to play safe. But, when that whisk(e) y gets into your bloodstream, you start dancing and loosening up
Standish Yellow Tail Two Hands Wine	Jack Daniel Blanton High West	Laphroaig Highland Park Glendronach	Nikka Yamazaki Kikori	Crown Royal Forty Creek

2. Which countries produce whisk(e)y?
   Example: Scotland.
3. What are the different categories of Scotch Whisk(e)y?
   Example: Single Malt Scotch Whisk(e)y.
4. What are some of the most popular whiskies in the world, and which country are they made from?
   Example: Jack Daniels (America).
5. What are some popular Scottish whisk(e)y brands?
   Example: Johnnie Walker.
6. What are some ways to drink whisk(e)y?
   Example: on the rocks.
7. What are some popular whisk(e)y cocktails?
   Example: Highball.

BASIC WORDS

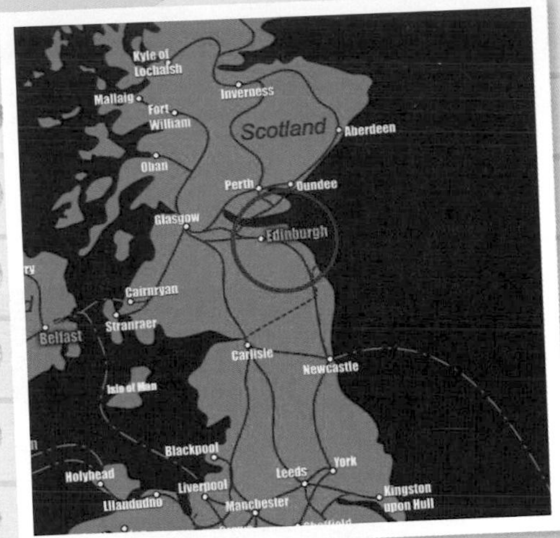

Scotland
蘇格蘭
Edinburgh
愛丁堡

whisk(e)y vault
威士忌保護櫃

whisk(e)y collection
威士忌收藏品

whisk(e)y sommelier
威士忌侍酒師

amber glow
琥珀色的輝光

single cask whisk(e)y
單桶威士忌

feeling tipsy
感覺有點微醉／感覺有點醉

whisk(e)y tasting
品嚐威士忌

How would you like your whisk(e)y?

neat 純飲

straight up / Up 去冰 (Martini straight up with olives)

on the rocks 加冰塊

single shot /
one shot of whisk(e)y
一杯單份威士忌 (1.5 盎司)
double shot / two shots of whisk(e)y 一杯雙份威士忌 (3 盎司)

neat, with water 加水
加入 1~2 滴水 (或多一點) 來喝

water back (chaser) 水伴
另外再上一杯水

Whisk(e)y Cocktails 威士忌調酒

Whisk(e)y Sour
威士忌酸酒

Whisk(e)y Cola
威士忌加可樂

Highball 高球

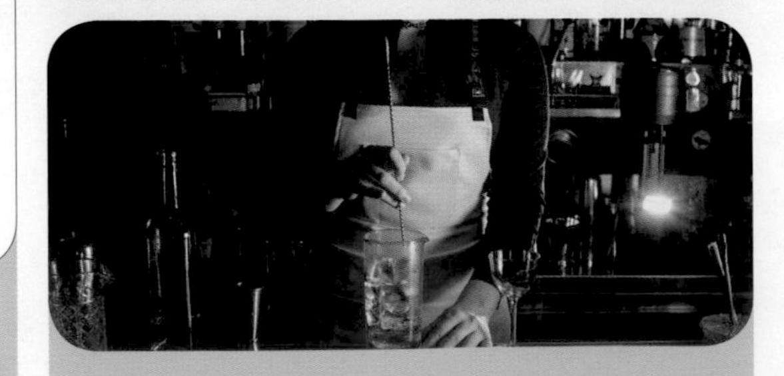

Mizuwari 水割

Conversation Preview

 Phrasal Words – Whiskey Tour

Practice the phrases between a tourist and a whisk(e) y sommelier.

Tourist	Whisk(e)y Sommelier
★ *A tourist is on a whiskey tour...*	★ Good afternoon, ladies and gentlemen. ★ We are in a whisk(e)y vault. ★ You are looking at the biggest whisk(e)y collection in the world.
★ How many bottles of whisk(e)y are here in this whisk(e)y vault?	★ We have about 4000 different bottles of whisk(e)y. ★ Our Scotch Whisk(e)y Experience is also known as one of the Seven Wonders of the Whisk(e)y World.
★ *{A tourist is in a whiskey vault listening to a whiskey sommelier}*	★ We have a collection of the finest and rarest single cask and single malts. ★ They have been carefully selected from The Scotch Malt Whisk(e)y Society.
★ When do we get a chance to taste a dram of whisk(e)y?	★ In fact, you will taste your dram of Scotch whisk(e)y right here in this whisk(e)y vault. ★ Here's our list of whiskies.
★ Where are your whiskies from?	★ Our whiskies arc from Scotland, Ireland, the United States, Canada and Japan.
★ How many whisk(e)y tastings do we get?	★ You get four whisk(e)y tastings per person.
★ Can you tell us what are some of your customer's favorites?	★ Some of our customers' favorites are the Royal Salute, Johnnie Walker, Chivas Regal, Dewar and Macallan.

track 36

Listening Practice

Listen to the audio. Listen to the conversation and then choose the correct answer.

( ) 1. (a) The tourist is looking at about 4000 whisk(e)y vaults.
(b) The tourist is looking at about 4000 bottles of whisk(e)y.

( ) 2. (a) The tourist gets four whisk(e)y tastings.
(b) The sommelier gets four whisk(e)y tastings.

( ) 3. (a) The customer would like a single shot Chivas Regal with ice.
(b) The customer would like a double shot Chivas Regal without ice.

( ) 4. (a) The customer is a neat person.
(b) The customer would like a double shot whiskey, neat.

Test Yourself

Fill in the blanks with the correct answers given below.

a. single cask	d. whiskey vault
b. On the rocks	e. Ireland
c. double shot	

1. Whiskey Sommelier: We are in a ________. You are looking at the biggest whiskey collection in the world.
2. Tourist: Where are your whiskies from?
   Whiskey Sommelier: Our whiskies are from Scotland, ________, the United States, Canada and Japan.
3. Whisk(e)y Sommelier: We have a collection of the finest and rarest ________ and single malts. They have been carefully selected from The Scotch Malt Whisk(e)y Society.
4. Whiskey Sommelier: What would you like, sir?
   Customer: I'd like a ________ Royal Salute, please.
5. Whiskey Sommelier: How would you like your whiskey?
   Customer: ________, please.

Conversation

track 37

Michelle and Ken are at the Royal Mile[1] in Edinburgh[2], Scotland[3]. They have signed up[4] for a whisk(e)y tasting experience[5] at the Scotch Whisk(e)y Experience[6].

Whisk(e)y Sommelier[7]: Good afternoon, ladies and gentlemen. [a] We are in a whisk(e)y vault[8]. You are looking at the biggest whisk(e)y collection[9] in the world

Ken: How many bottles of whisk(e)y are here in this whisk(e)y vault?

Whisk(e)y Sommelier: We have about 4000 different bottles of whisk(e)y. The Scotch

Whisk(e)y Experience is well-known as one of the Seven Wonders of the Whisk(e)y World[10].

New Words & Phrases

track 38

1. Royal Mile (n.) 皇家一哩路
2. Edinburgh (n.) 愛丁堡
3. Scotland (n.) 蘇格蘭
4. signed up (phrasal verb) 報名參加
5. whisk(e)y tasting experience (phrase) 威士忌品嚐體驗
6. Scotch Whisk(e)y Experience (n.) 蘇格蘭威士忌體驗館
7. whisk(e)y sommelier (n.) 威士忌侍酒師
8. whisk(e)y vault (n.) 威士忌保護櫃
9. whisk(e)y collection (n.) 威士忌收藏品
10. Seven Wonders of the Whisk(e)y World (n.) 世界七大威士忌奇蹟

Conversation

New Words & Phrases

11. amber glow (n.) 琥珀色的輝光
12. finest (n.) 最高級 反 low-grade
13. rarest (adj.) 最稀罕的 / 最珍貴的 反 common
14. single cask whisk(e)y (n.) 單桶威士忌 同 single barrel whisk(e)y) 直接從單一酒廠中，單一橡木桶中的酒裝瓶出廠的威士忌。這種酒在酒標上往往會標明桶號，以及這瓶是幾百瓶中的編號 XX 瓶。每一批的 Single Cask 都是最獨特的，就算是同一酒廠，出自不同桶內，酒的味道與香氣，往往大相逕庭。
15. single malt whisk(e)y (n.) 單一麥芽 / 單一純麥威士忌。指完全來自同一家蒸餾廠，運用大麥芽釀造、儲存於不同橡木桶中的酒，加水稀釋調配的威士忌，酒精濃度約 40%~50%。
16. The Scotch Malt Whisk(e)y Society (簡稱 SMWS) (n.) 蘇格蘭麥芽威士忌協會 SMWS 是以單一麥芽威士忌（Single Malt）為基礎建立的品牌，它們的特色是直接採用單一酒桶的單桶原酒（Single Cask），不稀釋、不冷過濾裝瓶，綠色酒瓶裏裝的就是 100% 原酒桶裏的酒，比市面上經過特殊處理的 Single Malt 更能呈現威士忌的原始風味及口感。
17. dram (a dram of whisk(e)y) (n.) 秤小重量時所用的法定衡量單位，大多被用來描述了一杯威士忌 同 whisk(e)y
18. Ireland (n.) 愛爾蘭
19. whisk(e)y tastings (n.) 品嚐威士忌

Michelle: Honey, look at the amber glow[11] from the 4000 bottles of whisk(e)y!

Ken: Yes, it's marvelous, isn't it?

Whisk(e)y Sommelier: [b]We have a collection of the finest[12] and rarest[13] single cask[14] and single malts[15]. They have been carefully selected from The Scotch Malt Whisk(e)y Society[16]

Michelle: When do we get a chance to taste a dram[17] of whisk(e)y?

Whisk(e)y Sommelier: In fact, you will taste your dram of Scotch whisk(e)y right here in this whisk(e)y vault. [c] Here's our list of whiskies.

Ken: Where are your whiskies from?

Whisk(e)y Sommelier: Our whiskies are from Scotland, Ireland,[18] the United States, Canada and Japan.

Michelle: How many whisk(e)y tastings[19] do we get?

Whisk(e)y Sommelier: [d] You get four free whisk(e)y tastings per person.

Ken: What are some of your customer's favorites?

Whisk(e)y Sommelier: [e] Some of our customers' favorites are the Royal Salute[20], Johnnie Walker[21], Chivas Regal[22], Dewar[23] and Macallan[24].

Michelle: [f] I'd like a single shot[25] of Chivas Regal, please.

Whisk(e)y Sommelier: [g] How would you like your whisk(e)y?

Michelle: [h] On the rocks,[26] please.

Whisk(e)y Sommelier: What about you, sir? What would you like?

Ken: [i] I'd like a double shot[27] of Royal Salute, please.

Whisk(e)y Sommelier: And, how would you like your whisk(e)y?

Ken: [j] Neat[28], please.

Ken and Michelle went on to try some other whisk(e)y cocktails[29].

Ken: I'd like to have Martini[30] straight up[31], please.

Michelle: And, I'll have a Whisk(e)y Sour[32], please.

Ken and Michelle were feeling tipsy[33] after a few shots of whisk(e)y, and decided to head back[34] to their hotel.

Q & A

1. Where are Michelle and Ken?

2. How many bottles of whiskey are there in the whiskey vault?

3. What are some customers' favorite whiskies?

4. What whiskey did Michelle order, and how did she want her whiskey?

5. What whiskey cocktail did Ken order?

New Words & Phrases

20. Royal Salute (Scotland) (n.)
皇家禮炮威士忌（蘇格蘭）
21. Johnnie Walker (Scotland) (n.)
尊尼獲加威士忌（蘇格蘭）
22. Chivas Regal (Scotland)(n.)
皇家起瓦士威士忌（蘇格蘭）
23. Dewar (Scotland)(n.) 帝王威士忌（蘇格蘭）
24. Macallan (Scotland) (n.) 麥卡倫威士忌（蘇格蘭）
25. single shot (of whisk(e)y) (n.)
一杯單份威士忌 (1.5 盎司)
同 one shot of whisk(e)y
26. on the rocks (as in whisk(e)y) (phrase)
加冰塊 同 with ice 反 straight up
27. double shot (of whisk(e)y) (n.)
一杯雙份威士忌（3 盎司）
同 two shots of whisk(e)y
28. neat (as in whisk(e)y) (n.)
純飲，直接從酒瓶中倒出（室溫酒）
同 whiskey from the bottle
29. whisk(e)y cocktails (n.) 威士忌調酒
Examples: Manhattan Cocktail, Whisk(e)y Sour, Irish Coffee, Jack & Coke, Highball, Whiskey Cola, Mizuwari.
30. Martini (n.) 馬丁尼
31. straight up (as in whisk(e)y) 去冰
在酒精飲料中加冰搖拌，再將冰濾除，倒入高腳雞尾酒杯中飲用 同 Up (Example: Martini Up / Martini Straight Up)
32. Whisk(e)y Sour (n.) 威士忌酸酒
（一種調酒形式，最原始的酸酒是由基酒、檸檬汁以及糖漿組成）
33. feeling tipsy (adj.) 感覺有點微醉 / 感覺有點醉 同 feeling a little drunk 反 sober
34. head back (to their hotel) (phrasal verb)
回頭走向旅館

Important Sentences

a. We are in a whisk(e)y vault.
我們正在威士忌保護櫃前。

b. We have a collection of the finest and rarest single cask and single malts.
我們收藏最高級及最稀有的單一橡木桶及單一麥芽。

c. Here's our list of whiskies.
這是我們威士忌的清單。

d. You get four free whisk(e)y tastings per person.
每個人可品嘗四杯免費威士忌。

e. Some of our customers' favorites are the Royal Salute, Johnnie Walker, Chivas Regal, Dewar and Macallan.
我們最受客戶歡迎有皇家禮炮威士忌、尊尼獲加威士忌、皇家起瓦士威士忌、帝王威士忌及麥卡倫威士忌。

f. I'd like a single shot of Chivas Regal, please.
請給我一杯單份皇家起瓦士威士忌。

g. How would you like your whisk(e)y?
你想怎麼喝你的威士忌？

h. On the rocks, please.
請給我加冰塊。

i. I'd like a double shot of Royal Salute, please.
請給我一杯雙份皇家禮炮威士忌。

j. Neat, please.
請給我純威士忌（不加冰）。

Conversation Review

Match the Chinese-English Translations

a. 一杯雙份威士忌	f. 加冰塊	k. 威士忌收藏品
b. 純飲直接從酒瓶中倒出(室溫酒)	g. 感覺有點微醉 / 感覺有點醉	l. 世界七大威士忌奇蹟
c. 去冰	h. 單桶威士忌	
d. 威士忌侍酒師	i. 單一麥芽 / 單一純麥 威士忌	
e. 威士忌品嚐體驗	j. 威士忌保護櫃	

( ) 1. whisk(e)y sommelier
( ) 2. whisk(e)y tasting experience
( ) 3. whisk(e)y vault
( ) 4. whisk(e)y collection
( ) 5. Seven Wonders of the Whisk(e)y World
( ) 6. single cask whiskey
( ) 7. single malt whiskey
( ) 8. on the rocks
( ) 9. double shot (of whiskey)
( ) 10. neat (as in whiskey)
( ) 11. straight up (as in whiskey)
( ) 12. feeling tipsy

track 39

Listen and Pronounce

Listen to the audio first. Then, try pronouncing each one of the following types of whisk(e)y.

1. Ballantine's (Scotland) 百齡壇（蘇格蘭）
2. Black Velvet (Canada) 黑色天鵝絨（加拿大）
3. Canadian Club (Canada) 加拿大俱樂部（加拿大）
4. Chivas Regal (Scotland) 皇家起瓦士（蘇格蘭）
5. Crown Royal (Canada) 皇家皇冠（加拿大）
6. Dewar's (Scotland) 帝王（蘇格蘭）
7. Jack Daniel's (USA) 傑克丹尼爾斯（美國）
8. Jameson (Ireland) 尊美醇 (愛爾蘭)
9. Jim Beam (USA) 金賓（美國）
10. Johnnie Walker (Scotland) 尊尼獲加（蘇格蘭）
11. Macallan (Scotland) 麥卡倫（蘇格蘭）
12. Glenfiddich (Scotland) 格蘭菲迪 (蘇格蘭)
13. Royal Salute (Scotland) 皇家禮炮（蘇格蘭）
14. Seagram's Seven Crown (Canada) 施格蘭七王冠（加拿大）
15. Suntory (Japan) 三得利（日本）

Choose the incorrect answer

( ) 1. Scottish whisk(e)y brands:
(a) Royal Salute (b) Walker
(c) Chivas Rega l(d) Dewar

( ) 2. Whiskey brands:
(a) Jameson (b) Jack Daniels
(c) Suntory (d) Canada

( ) 3. Ways to drink whisk(e)y:
(a) rocks (b) straight up
(c) neat (d) water back

( ) 4. Ways to drink whisk(e)y
(a) double shot (b) one shot
(c) straightly (d) neat, with water.

( ) 5. Whiskey cocktails:
(a) Whiskey Sour (b) Irish Coffee
(c) Jack & Coke (d) Lowball

track 40

Listen and fill in the blanks

Listen to the conversation and fill in the blanks.

1. A whisk(e)y ____________ is introducing the biggest whisk(e)y collection in the world.
2. The tourist will taste a ____________ of whisk(e)y in the whiskey vault.
3. The customer ordered a single shot of Johnnie Walker, ____________ .
4. The customer ordered a double shot of Macallan ____________ .

Photographs – How would you like your whisk(e)y?

Mix and match the photos with the answers given below

a. single shot / one shot of whisk(e)y
b. neat
c. straight up / Up (Martini straight up with olives)
d. on the rocks
e. neat, with water
f. water back (chaser)
g. double shot / two shots of whisk(e)y

1.
2.
3.
4A
4B
5.
6.

Luxury Shopping

Unit 09

Learning Objectives

What you will learn in this unit...

- Names of some luxury shopping items.
- Names of international designer brands.
- Some of the most popular international cosmetic brand names.
- Some of the most popular international designer watches.
- Some of the most popular international designer sunglasses.
- Some of the most popular international designer handbags.
- Some of the most popular international designer stereo brands.
- Luxury shopping related keyword verbs, phrases and idioms.

Brainstorming

1. What international designer brand you like says about you?

Coach 寇馳	Chanel 香奈兒	Gucci 古馳	Hermes 愛馬仕	Prada 普拉達
You are from the suburbs and fashionably stunted.	You are a classically polished and timeless woman.	You are loud, pretentious, and also lack sophistication.	You are wealthy and refined. You also have a major appreciation for art.	You appreciate good quality, and are not overly concerned about trends.

2. What are some luxury items you'd go shopping for when overseas?
   Example: cosmetics.
3. What are some of the most popular international cosmetic brand names?
   Example: Chanel.
4. What are some of the most popular international designer watches?
   Example: Cartier.
5. What are some of the most popular international designer sunglasses?
   Example: Ray-Ban.
6. What are some of the most popular international designer handbags?
   Example: Bottega Veneta.
7. What are some of the most popular international designer stereos?
   Example: BOSE.

BASIC WORDS

déjà vu
曾經看過 / 似曾相識

Swarovski flagship store (Vienna, Austria)
施華洛世奇旗艦店（維也納，奧地利）

designer handbags / luxury handbags
名牌包包

EU (European Union) 歐盟

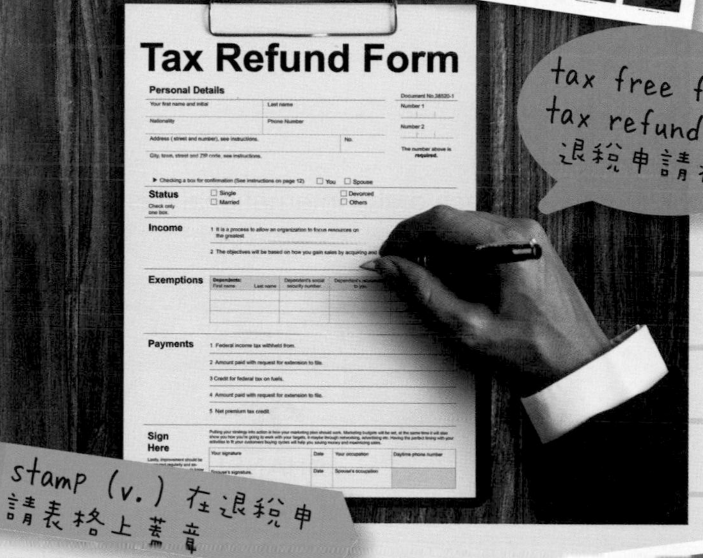

tax free form / tax refund form
退稅申請表格

stamp (v.) 在退稅申請表格上蓋章

Mozart chocolates
莫札特巧克力

invoice 發票 / 單據

stamp (n.) 蓋章

customs authorities 海關

Conversation Preview

Phrasal Words

Below are some good phrases between a salesperson and tourist. Practice the phrases below with a partner.

Salesperson	Tourist
★ Your total will be €2,065 after VAT.	★ What is the VAT rate?
★ The VAT rate is 20%, ma'am/sir.	★ Can I get a tax refund?
★ Are you an EU-resident?	★ No, I'm from Taiwan.
★ In this case, you are entitled to a tax refund.	★ Oh, that's wonderful!
★ I'll fill up a tax free form for you.	★ Thank you.
★ Please fill out your name and permanent address right here.	(Action) ★ Michelle writes down her name and home address on the tax free form.
★ Here you are. ★ Remember to show your purchased goods, invoice and passport to customs authorities.	★ Ok. Thank you. ★ I'll take note of that. Thanks.

Surf the Internet Exercise

Draw the logos on the right column in the table below for each of the international designer brand names below. You may surf the Internet to find your answers.

International Designer Brands Names	Draw the logo
Example: Chanel	CHANEL
1. Calvin Klein	
2. Fendi	
3. Louis Vuitton	
4. Dolce & Gabbana	
5. Christian Dior	

track 41

Listening Practice

Listen to the audio. Listen to the conversation and then choose the correct answer.

( ) 1. (a) Chanel, Louis Vuitton and Hermes are Parisian brands.
(b) Chanel, Louis Vuitton and Hermes are British brands.

( ) 2. (a) She will buy a Prada handbag.
(b) She will buy a Bottega Veneta handbag.
(c) She will buy a Givency handbag.
(d) She will buy a Versace handbag.

( ) 3. (a) The total price of the Bottega Veneta shoulder bag is €3,065 after 20% VAT.
(b) The total price of the Bottega Veneta shoulder bag is €3,065 before 20% VAT.

( ) 4. (a) Michelle cannot get a tax refund because she is an EU-resident.
(b) Michelle can get a tax refund because she is not an EU-resident.

Test Yourself

Fill in the blanks with the correct answers given below.

a. international designer brands	d. Value Added Taxes (VAT)
b. flagship stores	e. tax refund
c. purchased goods	f. invoice

1. There are many high-end ________ at the shopping mile in Vienna, Austria.
2. Vienna's famous shopping mile has many ________ including Prada, Bottega Veneta, Givency, Versace, Salvatore Ferragamo and Tod's.
3. Michelle's total for her Bottega Veneta handbag is €3,035 after ________ .
4. If you are not an EU-resident, then you are entitled to a ________ in Vienna, Austria.
5. A tourist has to show his/her ________ , ________ and passport to customs authorities.

Conversation

track 42

New Words & Phrases

track 43

1. Vienna (n.) 維也納（奧地利首都）
2. Austria (n.) 奧地利
3. shopping mile (n.) 購物英里
4. déjà vu (n.) 意指「曾經看過」，中文又譯（「似曾相識」），是人類在現實環境中（相對於夢境），突然感到自己「曾於某處親歷某畫面或者經歷一些事情」的感覺。依據人們多數憶述，是先於夢境中見過某景象，但並不以爲意，是眞正到了景象該處時，便會對陌生的環境突然浮現出「似曾相識」的感覺
   同 a strange feeling of having already experienced the present situation
5. I feel the same way too (phrase)
   我也有同感
6. grown (adj.) 生長
7. middle ages (n.) 中世紀 (西元 476 至 1453 年的歐洲歷史時期)
8. historic (adj.) 歷史 同 memorable
9. ambience (adj.) 氛圍 同 atmosphere
10. high-end (adj.) (產品）高價位的，高檔的，上層的 反 low-end
11. flagship stores (n.) 旗艦店
12. international designer brands (n.)
    國際設計師的標籤 反 local designer brands
13. British brands (n.) 英國品牌
14. Aquascutum (n.) 雅格獅丹 (英國品牌)
15. Burberry (n.) 巴寶利
    （或稱博柏利，英國品牌）
16. Parisian (adj.) 巴黎的 / 巴黎人的 / 和巴黎有關的
17. Chanel (n.) 香奈兒（法國品牌）
    香奈兒在 1910 年創辦的頂級法國女性知名時裝店。
18. Louis Vuitton (LV) (n.) 路易威登（法國品牌）
19. Hermès (n.) 愛馬仕（法國品牌）

Ken and Michelle have arrived in Vienna[1], Austria[2].

Michelle: Honey, we are actually walking along the famous shopping mile[3] in Vienna, Austria. [a] I feel a sense of déjà vu[4].

Ken: I feel the same way too[5]. Did you know that wine was grown[6] right here in the middle ages[7]?

Michelle: No wonder I feel a historic[8] ambience[9]!

Ken: Look at those high-end[10] flagship stores[11] of international designer brands[12].

Michelle: Yes, I see British brands[13] – Aquascutum[14] and Burberry[15]!

Ken: There are Parisian[16] brands too– Chanel[17], Louis Vuitton[18] and Hermes[19] !

Michelle: There are international designer brands for all mankind[20] – Prada[21], Bottega Veneta[22], Givency[23], Versace[24], Salvatore Ferragamo[25], Tod's[26].

Ken: Alright, I get the message[27].

Michelle: Love you to bits! [28]

Ken: You'd better! Honey, you have to make up your mind[29] what you want. We have a limited[30] budget[31] and time[32].

Michelle: Alright. Alright...I'll settle for[33] a Bottega Veneta designer handbag.

Ken and Michelle stopped by a Bottega Veneta store and purchased[34] a shoulder bag[35].

Salesperson: [b] Your total will be €2,065 after VAT[36].

Michelle: [c] What is the VAT rate?

Salesperson: [d] The VAT rate is 20%, ma'am.

Michelle: [e] Is it possible to get a tax refund[37]?

Salesperson: [f] Are you an EU-resident[38]?

Michelle: [g] No, I'm from Taiwan.

Salesperson: [h] In this case, you are entitled to[39] a tax refund.

Michelle: Oh, that's wonderful!

New Words & Phrases

20. mankind (n.) 人類 同 humankind
21. Prada (n.) 普拉達 (義大利品牌)
22. Bottega Veneta (n.) 葆蝶家
(義大利品牌）是一個義大利奢侈品及高級時裝品牌，以行銷全球的皮具產品及男女時裝知名。品牌於 1966 年在位於義大利東北部威尼托區的維琴。
23. Givency (n.) 紀梵希（法國品牌）
由時裝設計師于貝爾・德・紀梵希（Hubert de Givenchy）於 1952 年成立，主營高級服裝訂製、成衣、鞋履、皮革製品及飾品。
24. Versace (n.) 範思哲（義大利品牌）
25. Salvatore Ferragamo (n.) 薩瓦托・菲拉格慕 (義大利品牌）
26. Tod's (n.) 陶德斯（義大利品牌）
27. Alright, I get the message (phrase)
好吧！我知道了
28. Love you to bits (phrase) 愛你的全部 / 每一部分 同 love you to pieces
29. make up your mind (idiom) 下定決心
同 decide
30. limited (adj.) 有限的 反 unlimited
31. budget (n.) 預算
32. limited budget and time (phrase)
有限的預算和時間
33. I'll settle for... (phrasal verb)
我只好勉強接受 同 I'll decide to have ...
34. purchase (vt.) 購買 同 buy 反 sell
35. shoulder bag (n.) 肩背包
36. VAT（Value Added Tax）(n.) 增值稅。
增值稅是指對納稅人生產經營活動的增值額徵收的一種間接稅。
37. tax refund (n.) 退稅
38. EU-resident (European Union resident) (n.)
歐盟居民 反 non-EU resident
39. entitled to (v.) 使有資格 / 使有權
(entitle 的過去式和過去分詞)

New Words & Phrases

40. tax free form (n.) 退稅申請表格
    同 tax refund form
41. home address (n.) 永久地址 / 戶籍地址 / 通訊地址 同 permanent address
42. purchased goods (n.) 購買的商品
43. invoice (n.) 發票 / 單據 同 bill
44. customs authorities (n.) 海關
    同 customs officer
45. stamp (v. / n.) 在該文件 (退稅申請表格) 上蓋章 / 蓋章
46. I'll take note of that (phrase) 我會記下來的
47. limited edition (n.) 限量版
48. Swarovski (n.) 施華洛世奇（Daniel Swarovski）於 1895 年創立，現更從生產精確切割水晶首飾石的製造商，發展成全球首屈一指的水晶設計。
49. crystal (n.) 水晶
50. decoration (n.) 裝飾品
51. Mozart chocolates (n.) 莫札特巧克力，Mozartkugel 莫札特球，是大家去奧地利必買伴手禮，是一種包裝紙上印有莫札特肖像。

Salesperson:[i] I'll fill up a tax free form[40] for you.

Michelle: Thank you.

Salesperson:[j] Please fill out your name and home address[41] right here.

Michelle writes down her name and home address on the tax free form.

Salesperson:[k] Remember to show your purchased goods[42], invoice[43] and passport to customs authorities[44]. Also, remember to have your tax free form stamped[45] by customs authorities.

Michelle: I'll take note of that[46]. Thank you!

Michelle and Ken then made two last shopping stops. They bought a limited edition[47] Swarovski[48] crystal[49] decoration[50] and five boxes of Mozart chocolates[51].

Q & A

1. What are some British brands that Michelle mentioned she saw along the shopping mile in Vienna, Austria?

   ____

2. What does it mean by "déjà vu"?

   ____

3. Why does Ken say that Michelle has to make up her mind of what she wants?

   ____

4. What international designer brand and item did Michelle decide to get?

   ____

5. How much is the VAT for the Bottega Veneta handbag?

   ____

Important Sentences

a. I feel a sense of déjà vu.
我突然感到自己夢境中見過這景象。

b Your total will be €2,065 after VAT.
增值稅後，妳的總金額將爲 2,065 歐元。

c. What is the VAT rate?
增值稅稅率是多少？

d. The VAT rate is 20%, ma'am.
女士，增值稅稅率爲 20%。

e. Is it possible to get a tax refund?
是否有可能獲得退稅？

f. Are you an EU-resident?
妳是歐盟居民嗎？

g. No, I'm from Taiwan.
不，我是從台灣來的。

h. In this case, you are entitled to a tax refund.
在這種情況下，妳有資格權獲得退稅。

i. I'll fill up a tax free form for you.
我會爲你填寫一張退稅申請表格。

j. Please fill out your name and home address right here.
請在這裡填寫妳的姓名和居住國永久地址。

k. Remember to show your purchased goods, invoice and passport to customs authorities.
請記得出示妳購買的商品，發票及護照給海關。

Conversation Review

Matching Pictures & Words

Match the pictures with the correct answers given below:

a. tax free form
b. credit card
c. export validation stamp
d. passport
e. invoice
f. purchased good (Bottega Venega shoulder handbag)

1.

2.

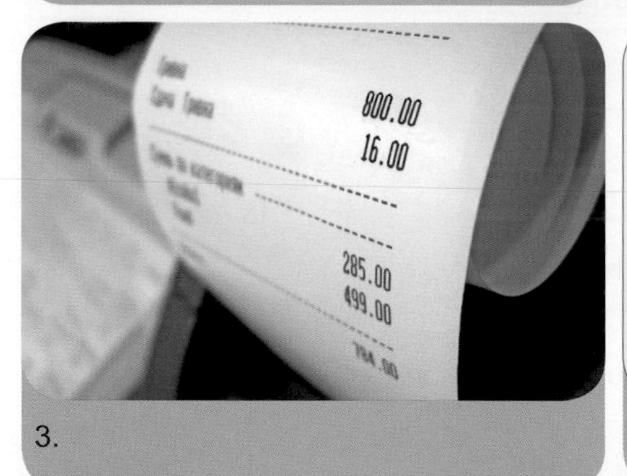

3.

4.

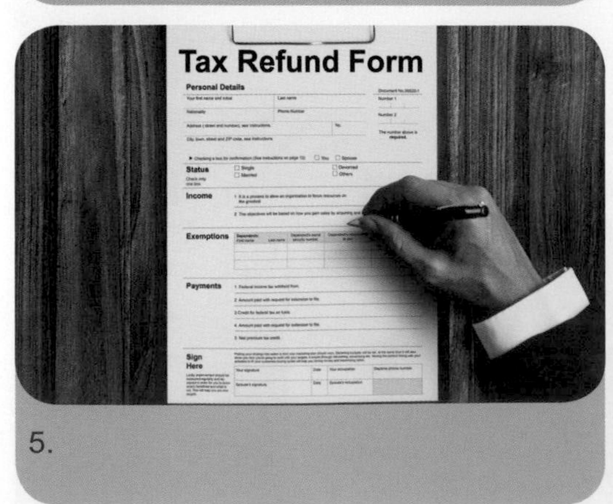

5.

6.

Fill Up a Tax Free Form

Instructions:

1. Fill out the below tax free form using your personal information.
2. You may use the given information above for items 6 and 10.
3. For item 10, "validate" the tax free form by cutting out and pasting the customs stamp.

TAX FREE FORM

1. Last Name: ____________
2. First Name: ____________ Mr/Mrs/Miss/Ms/Other (circle one)
3. Home / Permanent Address
   ____
4. City ______________________________
5. Country ____________________
6. Passport No. ____________________
7. Email ______________________________
8. Credit card number ______________________________

   | | | | | | | | | | | | | | | | | | | |

9. Shopper Signature
   ____
10. Export Validation Stamp (Stamp by Customs Authorities)

track 44

Listen and Pronounce

Listen to the audio first. Then, try pronouncing each one of the following international designer brands below.

1. Aquascutum	雅格獅丹
2. Balenciaga	巴黎世家
3. Bally	百麗
4. Chanel	香奈兒
5. Coach	寇馳
6. Dior (CD / Christian Dior)	迪奧
7. DKNY	唐納卡倫
8. Ermenegildo Zegna	傑尼亞
9. Fendi	芬迪
10. Gucci	古馳（古琦）
11. Hermes	愛馬仕
12 . Louis Vuitton	LV 路易．威登
13 . Moschino	莫斯奇諾
14 . Prada	普拉達
15 . Valentino	瓦倫蒂諾

track 45

Listen and fill in the blanks

Listen to the conversation and fill in the blanks.

1. The couple are walking along the famous __________ in Vienna, Austria.
2. The couple sees many high-end flagship stores international __________ brands such as Aquascutum, Burberry, Chanel, Louis Vuitton and Hermes.
3. The total price for the shoulder bag is €2,065 after __________ , and the VAT rate is __________ .
4. The tourist is entitled to a __________ because she is from Taiwan, and not an EU-resident.
5. The tourist has to show her purchased goods, __________ and passport to customs authorities.

Match the Chinese-English Translations

a. 似曾相識	e. 有限的預算	i. 巴黎的 / 巴黎人的 / 和巴黎有關的
b. 施華洛世奇水晶裝飾品	f. 名牌包包	j. 奧地利
c. 旗艦店	g. 限量版	
d. 購物英里	h. 國際設計師的標籤	

(　　) 1. Austria
(　　) 2. shopping mile
(　　) 3. déjà vu
(　　) 4. flagship stores
(　　) 5. international designer brands
(　　) 6. Parisian
(　　) 7. limited budget
(　　) 8. designer handbag
(　　) 9. limited edition
(　　) 10. Swarovski crystal decoration

Choose the incorrect answer

(　　) 1. International Designer Brand Names:
(a) Chanel　(b) Louis Vuitton　(c) Prada　(d) Parisian

(　　) 2. International Designer Brand Names:
(a) Burberry　(b) Tod's　(c) Flagship　(d) Bottega Veneta

(　　) 3. Items related to a tourist tax refund in Europe:
(a) Brand name　(b) 20% VAT rate　(c) Value Added Tax　(d) tax free form

(　　) 4. Items to fill out on a tax free form:
(a) name　(b) home address　(c) hotel address　(d) passport number

(　　) 5. Things to show to the customs authorities for your tax refund:
(a) purchased good(s)　(b) invoice　(c) luggage　(d) passport

Photographs

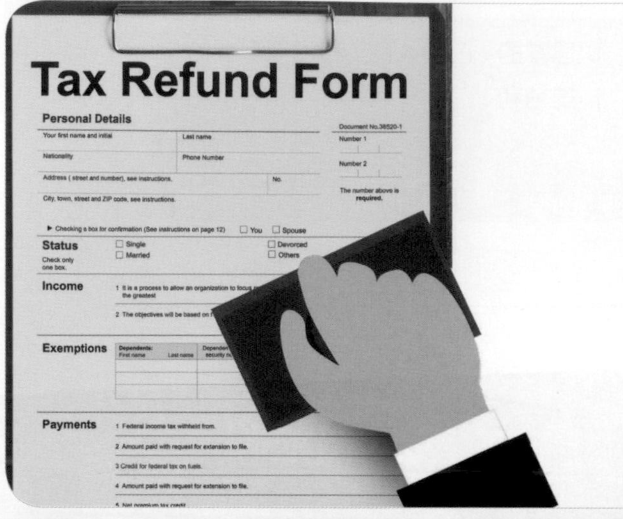

1. Which of the following statements best describes the picture?
   (a) A salesperson is stamping on an invoice.
   (b) A customs authority is stamping on an invoice.
   (c) A salesperson is stamping on a tax free form.
   (d) A customs authority is stamping on a tax free form.

   Your Answer: (   )

© Helen Page / Travelsignposts.com

2. Which of the following statements best describes the picture?
   (a) Tourists are queueing up at the airport immigration.
   (b) Tourists are showing their tax free form and purchased goods to customs authorities.
   (c) Tourists are checking in their bags at the airport.
   (d) Tourists are queueing up for their VAT refunds.

   Your Answer: (   )

French Vineyard Tour

Unit 10

Learning Objectives

What you will learn in this unit...

- What does AOC (Appellation d`Origine Controlee) mean?
- Can you name some major wine regions with AOC designations in Provence?
- Types of wine that can be made from grapes, and what are some popular wines in each category?
- Names of some major wine regions in France.
- Names of the two different types of rosé wines.
- Types of grapes used to make dry rosé wines.
- Types of grapes used to make sweet rosé wines.
- Some common rosé wine shades (colors), from light to dark
- What are three methods to make rosé wine?
- Learn what important verbs, phrases and vocabulary related to rosé wine and French wine.

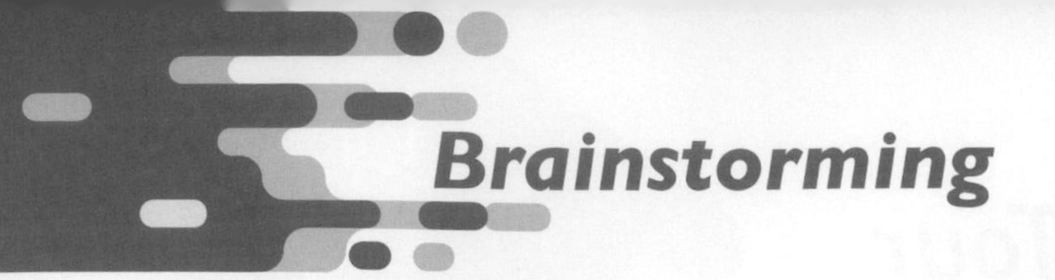

Brainstorming

1. What does the type of rosé wine you like say about you?

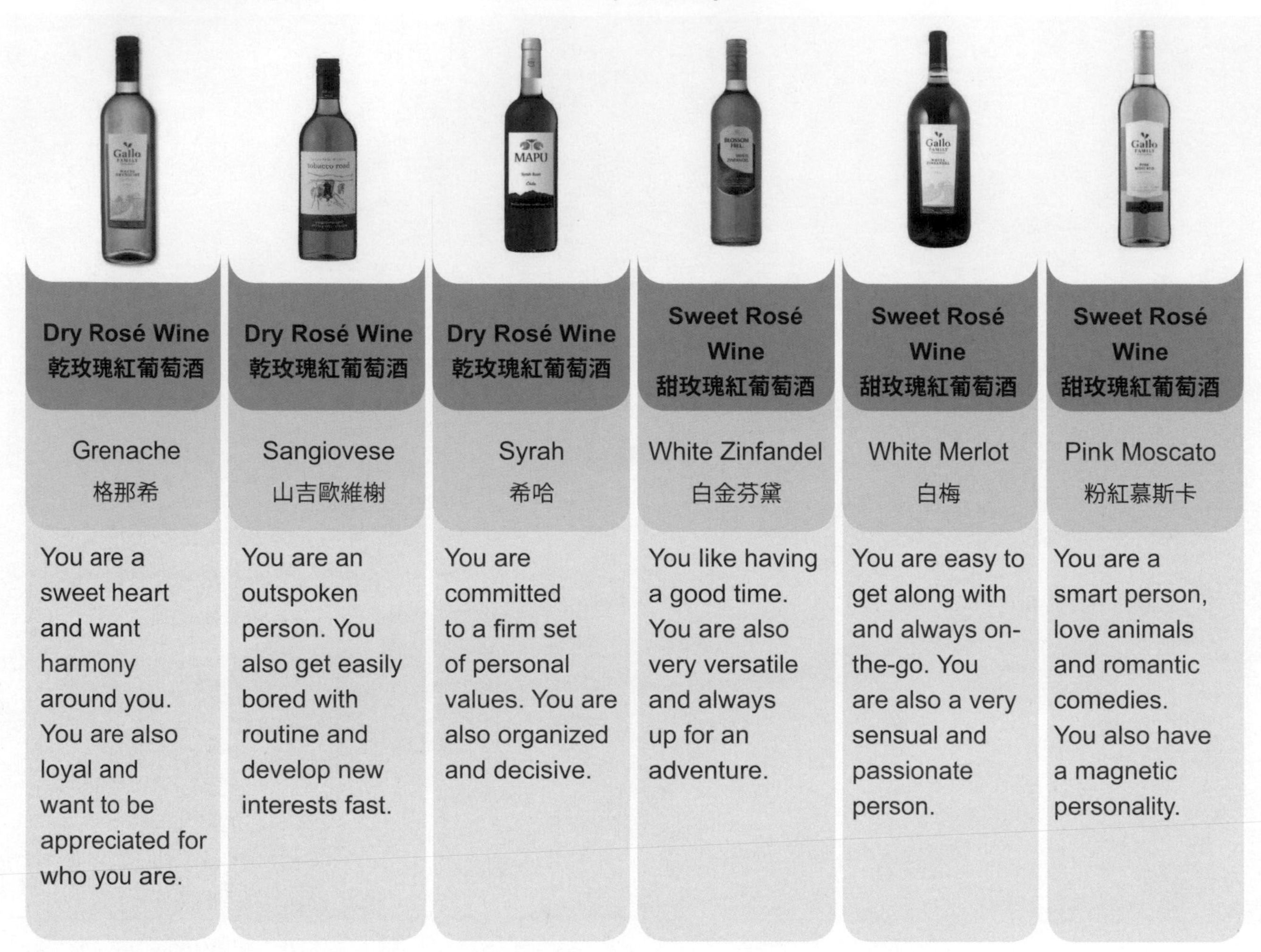

Dry Rosé Wine 乾玫瑰紅葡萄酒	Dry Rosé Wine 乾玫瑰紅葡萄酒	Dry Rosé Wine 乾玫瑰紅葡萄酒	Sweet Rosé Wine 甜玫瑰紅葡萄酒	Sweet Rosé Wine 甜玫瑰紅葡萄酒	Sweet Rosé Wine 甜玫瑰紅葡萄酒
Grenache 格那希	Sangiovese 山吉歐維榭	Syrah 希哈	White Zinfandel 白金芬黛	White Merlot 白梅	Pink Moscato 粉紅慕斯卡
You are a sweet heart and want harmony around you. You are also loyal and want to be appreciated for who you are.	You are an outspoken person. You also get easily bored with routine and develop new interests fast.	You are committed to a firm set of personal values. You are also organized and decisive.	You like having a good time. You are also very versatile and always up for an adventure.	You are easy to get along with and always on-the-go. You are also a very sensual and passionate person.	You are a smart person, love animals and romantic comedies. You also have a magnetic personality.

2. What does AOC (Appellation d`Origine Controlee) mean?
3. Can you name some major wine regions with AOC designations in Provence?
   Example: Côtes de Provence
4. Do you know what types of wine can be made from grapes, and what are some popular wines in each category?
   Example: red wine – Syrah; white wine – Chardonnay Sauvignon.
5. Can you name some major wine regions in France?
   Example: Champagne.

BASIC WORDS

Major French Wine Regions
主要法國葡萄酒產區

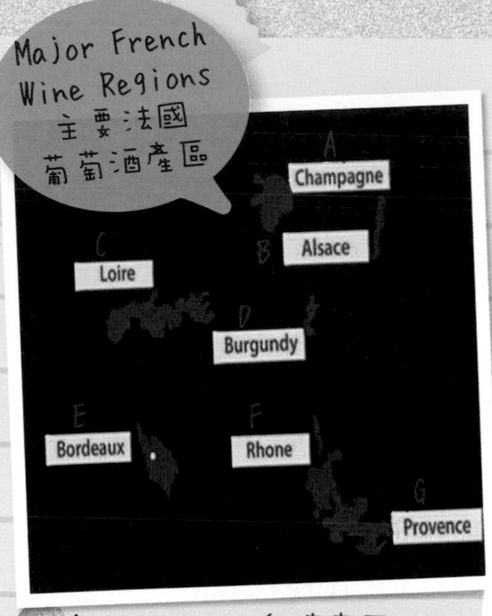

A. vintner 釀酒師／葡萄酒商
B. vineyard 葡萄園
C. vineyard tour 葡萄園之旅

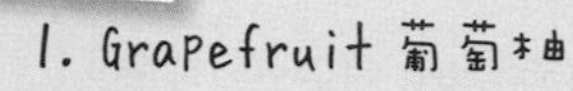

A. Champagne 香檳產區
B. Alsace 阿爾薩斯產區
C. Loire Valley 羅亞爾河谷產區
D. Burgundy (Bourgogne) 勃根地
E. Bordeaux 波爾多產區
F. Rhone Valley 羅納河谷產區
G. Provence 普羅旺斯產區

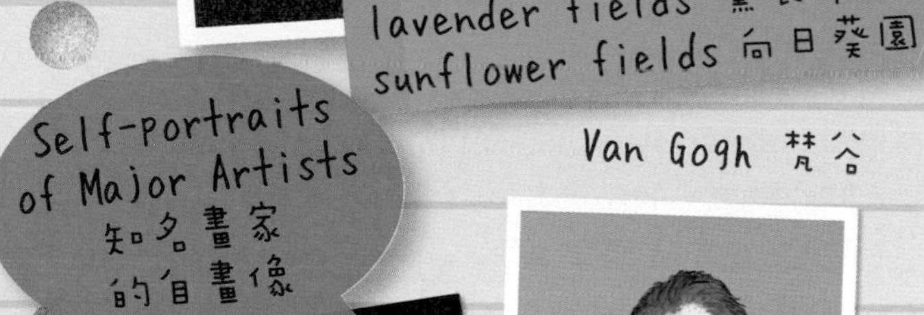

lavender fields 薰衣草園
sunflower fields 向日葵園

Different Shades of Rose Wine from Light to Dark
玫瑰紅葡萄酒顏色從淺到深的粉紅酒風味描述

1. Grapefruit 葡萄柚
2. Strawberry 草莓
3. Tart Cherry 酸櫻桃
4. Sweet Cherry 甜櫻桃
5. Raspberry 覆盆子
6. Wild Strawberry 野草莓
7. Blood Orange 血橙
8. Raspberry Sauce 覆盆子醬
9. Red Bell Pepper 紅甜椒
10. Black Currant 黑醋栗
11. Blackberry 黑莓
12. Berry Jam 貝瑞果醬

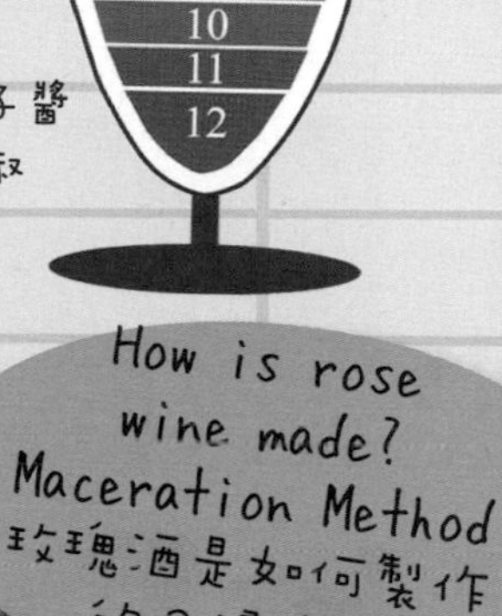

Self-portraits of Major Artists
知名畫家的自畫像

Matisse
馬蒂斯

Van Gogh 梵谷

Picasso
畢卡索

Renoir
雷諾瓦

How is rose wine made? Maceration Method
玫瑰酒是如何製作的？浸皮法

A. Harvest red grapes 收成紅葡萄
B. Crush red grapes 壓碎紅葡萄
C. Maceration Method 浸皮法（製作紅酒時，通常整個釀造期都會浸漬果皮，玫瑰紅則會在酒色過深之前將果皮從果汁剔除）
D. Fementation 發酵
E. Bottling 裝瓶

Conversation Preview

Phrasal Words

Below are some phrases between a tourist and a vintner. Practice the phrases below with a partner.

Tourist 觀光客	Vintner 釀酒師 / 葡萄酒商
★ How many wine regions are there in France?	★ There are seven major wine regions in France – Champagne, Alsace, Loire Valley, Burgundy, Bordeaux, Rhone Valley and Provence. ★ Côtes de Provence AOC is the largest appellation of the Provence wine region in south-eastern France.
★ What types of grapes are grown here?	★ Provence grows a lot of red grapes – the Grenache, Syrah, Mourvèdre, Cinsaut, Carignan, Tibouren and Cabernet Sauvignon.
★ I heard that Provence produces a lot of rosé wines.	★ That's true. Today, Provence is known predominantly for rosé wine and produces 34% of all rosé wines made in the world.
★ How is rosé wine made?	★ There are three methods to make rosé wine – the maceration method, blending method and saignée method. ★ Our rosé wine is made using the maceration method. ★ First, we crush red grapes. Then, the juice is left in contact with the skin from a few hours to a few days. Afterward, the entire batch of juice is finished into rosé wine.
★ Why is it that rosé wine has different shades?	★ Well, the longer the juice from red grapes spends in contact with the skins, the darker the color. ★ There are more than ten shades of rosé wine, from grapefruit, blood orange to berry jam.
★ What types of rosé wines are there?	★ There are two types of rosé wines – dry rosé wine and sweet rosé wine.
★ What are some of your most popular dry rosé wines?	★ Some of our most popular dry rosé wines are the Grenache, Sangiovese, Syrah, Mourvèdre, Carignan, Cinsault and Pinot Noir.
★ Can you also recommend some popular sweet rosé wines?	★ Some of our popular sweet rose wines are the White Zinfandel, White Merlot and Pink Moscato.

Listening Practice

track 46

Listen to the audio. Listen to the conversation between a tourist and a vintner during a vineyard tour in France. Then choose the correct answer.

( ) 1. (a) There are seven major wine regions in France including Champagne and Provence.
(b) There are two major wine regions in France including Champagne and Provence.

( ) 2. (a) Provence grows a lot of red grapes including the Grenache, Syrah, Mourvèdre, Cinsaut, Carignan, Tibouren and Cabernet Sauvignon.
(b) Provence grows a lot of white grapes including the Grenache, Syrah, Mourvèdre, Cinsaut, Carignan, Tibouren and Cabernet Sauvignon.

( ) 3. (a) The maceration method and 'saignée' method are two ways to make rose wines.
(b) The maceration method and blending method are two ways to make rosé wines.

( ) 4. (a) Rosé wine has different shades because the longer the juice the red grapes spends in contact with the skins, the lighter the color.
(b) Rosé wine has different shades because the longer the juice from red grapes spends in contact with the skins, the darker the color.

( ) 5. (a) There are two types of rosé wines : dry rosé wine and sweet rosé wine.
(b) There are two types of rosé wines : dry rosé wine and non-sweet rosé wine.

Test Yourself

Fill in the blanks with the correct answers given below.

a. dry rosé wine	d. Alsace
b. Sangiovese	e. maceration
c. Cinsault	f. contact

Michelle and Ken are taking a vineyard tour in Côtes de Provence, France.

1. Michelle: How many wine regions are there in France?
   Vintner: There are seven major wine regions in France – Champagne, ______ , Loire Valley, Burgundy, Bordeaux, Rhone Valley and Provence.
2. Ken: How is rosé wine made?
   Vintner: There are three methods to make rosé wine – the ______ method, blending method and saignée method.
3. Michelle: Why is that rosé wine has different shades?
   Vintner: Well, the longer the juice from red grapes spends in ______ with the skins, the darker the color.
4. Ken: What types of rosé wines are there?
   Vintner: There are two types of rosé wines – ______ and sweet rosé wine.
5. Michelle: What are some of your most popular dry rosé wines?
   Vintner: Some of our most popular dry rosé wines are the Grenache, ______ , Syrah, Mourvèdre, Carignan, ______ and Pinot Noir.

Conversation

track 47

Michelle and Ken are on a vineyard tour in Côtes de Provence[1], France[2].

Vintner[3]: On your right, you see lavender fields[4]. And, on your left are the sunflower fields[5]. Because Provence has a spectacular view[6], it has attracted[7] many great artists such as Van Gogh[8], Picasso[9], Matisse[10] and Renoir[11].

Michelle: [a] How many wine regions[12] are there in France?

Vintner: [b] There are seven major wine regions in France – Champagne[13], Alsace[14], Loire Valley[15], Burgundy[16], Bordeaux[17], Rhone Valley[18] and Provence[19]. Côtes de Provence AOC[20] is the largest appellation[21] of the Provence wine region in south-eastern France.

Ken: [c] What types of grapes are grown here?

New Words & Phrases

track 48

1 Côtes de Provence (n.) 普羅旺斯丘（是法國最主要的 AOC 法定產區，以生產清淡爽口的粉紅酒爲主）
2. France (n.) 法國
3. vintner (n.) 釀酒師 / 葡萄酒商 同 winemaker / wine merchant
4. lavender fields (n.) 薰衣草園
5. sunflower fields (n.) 向日葵園
6. spectacular view (phrase) 壯觀的景色
7. attract (v.) 吸引 同 draw 反 repel
8. Van Gogh (n.) 梵谷（文森・威廉・梵谷 [Van Gogh, Vincent, 1853-1890] 是荷蘭畫家，畫風屬於後期印象派）
9. Picasso (n.) 畢卡索（巴勃羅・伊斯・畢加索 [Pablo Ruiz Picasso,1881-1973] 是西班牙著名的藝術雕塑家、版畫家、陶藝家、舞台設計師及作家）
10. Matisse (n.) 馬蒂斯（亨利・馬蒂斯 [Henri Matisse, 1869-1954] 是法國畫家，野獸派的創始人及主要代表人物）
11. Renoir (n.) 雷諾瓦（雷諾瓦・彼得・菲斯特 [Pierre-Auguste Renoir, 1841-1919] 是法國印象派畫家、雕刻家）
12. wine region (n.) 葡萄酒地區
13. Champagne (n.) 香檳區
14. Alsace (n.) 阿爾薩斯
15. Loire Valley (n.) 羅亞爾河谷
16. Burgundy (n.) 勃根地 同 Bourgogne
17. Bordeaux (n.) 波爾多
18. Rhone Valley(n.) 羅納河谷
19. Provence (n.) 普羅旺斯（是法國南端的省份濱臨地中海。在炎熱多陽光的普羅旺斯有80%的葡萄酒都是清淡可口的玫瑰红葡萄酒）
20. AOC (n.) [Appellation d`Origine Controlee] 在薄酒萊地區生產的葡萄酒，分別屬於十二個法定產區（Appellation d'Origine Contrôlée, AOC）。AOC《Appellation ＋加上地名或酒莊名＋ contrôlée》這就是代表法國“國寶級”或“國產級”的產酒中，最高品質保證的名酒
21.Appellation (n.) (1) 指定 (法文)，(2) 名稱 / 名號 / 稱謂 （英文），(3) 在洋酒界中的意思是審核標準控制一級某城堡酒莊榮譽頂級佳釀。〈contrôlée〉法文在中文裏的意思是控制。同 designation

Conversation

New Words & Phrases

22. Grenache (n.) 格那希
23. Syrah (n.) 希哈
24. Mourvèdre (n.) 慕維得爾
25. Cinsault (n.) 仙梭 同 Cinsaut
26. Carignan (n.) 卡利濃
27. Tibouren (n.) 提布宏
28. Cabernet Sauvignon (n.) 卡本內蘇維翁
29. rosé wine (n.) 玫瑰紅葡萄酒 / 粉紅酒
(原料是紅葡萄，經過直接壓榨法或出血法使果汁含有少量色素，然後與白酒作法相同)
30. predominantly (adv.) 佔絕大多數地
同 mainly 反 secondary
31. maceration method (n.) 浸皮法
(製作紅酒時，通常整個釀造期都會浸漬果皮，玫瑰紅則會在酒色過深之前將果皮從果汁剔除，是最常見的方法之一)
32. blending method (n.) 混合法
33. saignée method (n.) 放血法
同 bled method
34. in contact with (phrase) 與 ... 接觸
35. entire (adj.) 全部的
同 whole 反 partial
36. batch (n.) 一批 同 lot 反 one
37. different shades (phrase) 顏色深淺不同
同 different hues / colors
38. grapefruit (shade) (n) 葡萄柚顏色
39. blood orange (shade) (n.) 血橙顏色
40. berry jam (shade) (n.) 貝瑞果醬顏色

Vintner: [d] Provence grows a lot of red grapes – the Grenache[22], Syrah[23], Mourvèdre[24], Cinsaut[25], Carignan[26], Tibouren[27] and Cabernet Sauvignon[28].

Michelle: I heard that Provence produces a lot of rosé wine[29].

Vintner: That's true. Today, Provence is known predominantly[30] for rosé wine and produces 34% of all rosé wines made in the world.

Ken: [e] How is rosé wine made?

Vintner: There are three methods to make rosé wine – the maceration method[31], blending method[32] and saignée method[33]. Our rosé wine is made using the maceration method. First, we crush red grapes. Then, the juice is left in contact with[34] the skin from a few hours to a few days. Afterward, the entire[35] batch[36] of juice is finished into rosé wine.

Michelle: [f] Why does rosé wine have different shades[37]?

Vintner: Well, the longer the juice from red grapes spends in contact with the skins, the darker the color. There are more than ten shades of rosé wine, from grapefruit,[38] blood orange[39] to berry jam[40].

Ken: [g] What types of rosé wines are there?

Vintner: There are two types of rosé wines – dry rosé wine[41] and sweet rosé wine[42].

Michelle: [h] What are some of your most popular dry rosé wines?

Vintner: Some of our most popular dry rosé wines are the Grenache, Sangiovese[43], Syrah, Mourvèdre, Carignan, Cinsault and Pinot Noir[44]

Ken: [i] Can you also recommend some popular sweet rosé wines?

Vintner: Some of our popular sweet rose wines are the White Zinfandel,[45] White Merlot[46] and Pink Moscato[47].

Michelle: Honey, I'm really looking forward to our wine tasting session[48].

Ken: I'd love that too!

Q & A

1. What great artists did Provence attract?

   ____

2. What types of red grapes are grown in Provence?

   ____

3. Describe the maceration method used to make rosé wine.

   ____

4. Can you name three different shades of rosé wine?

   ____

5. What dry rosé wines did the vintner recommend?

   ____

New Words & Phrases

41. dry rosé wine (n.) 乾玫瑰紅葡萄酒
    反 sweet rosé wine
42. sweet rosé wine (n.) 甜玫瑰紅葡萄酒
43. Sangiovese (n.) 山吉歐維榭
44. Pinot Noir (n.) 黑皮諾
45. White Zinfandel (n.) 白金芬黛
46. White Merlot (n.) 白梅洛
47. Pink Moscato (n.) 粉紅慕斯卡
48. wine tasting session (n.) 品葡萄酒會

Important Sentences

a. How many wine regions are there in France?
法國有多少個葡萄酒產區？

b. There are seven major wine regions in France – Champagne, Alsace, Loire Valley, Burgundy, Bordeaux, Rhone Valley and Provence.
法國有七個主要的葡萄酒產區包含香檳區、阿爾薩斯、羅亞爾河谷、勃根地、波爾多、羅納河谷及普羅旺斯。

c. What types of grapes are grown here?
在這裡種植那些葡萄種類？

d. Provence grows a lot of red grapes – the Grenache, Syrah, Mourvèdre, Cinsaut, Carignan, Tibouren and Cabernet Sauvignon.
普羅旺斯種植了許多紅葡萄包含格那希、希哈、慕維得爾、仙梭、卡利濃、提布宏及卡本內蘇維翁。

e. How is rosé wine made?
玫瑰紅葡萄酒是如何製成的？

f. Why does rosé wine have different shades?
為什麼玫瑰紅葡萄酒顏色深淺會不同呢？

g. What types of rosé wine are there?
有幾種玫瑰紅葡萄酒呢？

h. What are some of your most popular dry rosé wines?
您最受歡迎的乾玫瑰紅葡萄酒有哪些？

i. Can you also recommend some popular sweet rosé wines?
您還可以推薦一些受歡迎的甜玫瑰紅葡萄酒嗎？

Match the Chinese-English Translations

a. 浸皮法	e. 薰衣草園	i. 顏色深淺不同
b. 混合法	f. 向日葵園	j. 釀酒師 / 葡萄酒商
c. 放血法	g. 葡萄酒地區	k. 普羅旺斯
d. 玫瑰紅葡萄酒	h. 乾玫瑰紅葡萄酒	l. 甜玫瑰紅葡萄酒

( ) 1. vintner
( ) 2. lavender fields
( ) 3. sunflower fields
( ) 4. wine region
( ) 5. Provence
( ) 6. rosé wine
( ) 7. maceration method
( ) 8. blending method
( ) 9. saignée method
( ) 10. different shades
( ) 11. dry rosé wine
( ) 12. sweet rosé wine

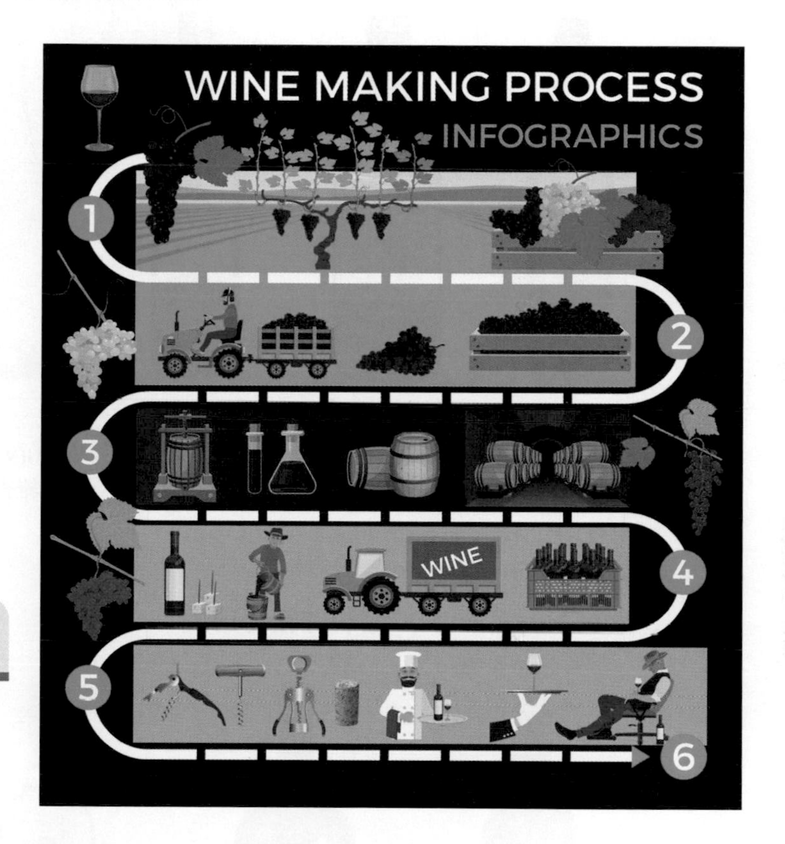

Choose the incorrect answer

( ) 1. Major French wine regions:
(a) Champagne (b) Alsace
(c) Rome Valley (d) Burgundy

( ) 2. Methods to make rosé wines:
(a) vintner method (b) maceration method
(c) blending method (d) saignée method

( ) 3. Different shades of rosé wine:
(a) grapefruit (b) tart cherry
(c) jam (d) wild strawberry

( ) 4. Types of dry rosé wines:
(a) Grenache (b) Sangiovese
(c) Syrah (d) Pink Moscato

( ) 5. Types of sweet rosé wines:
(a) White Zinfandel (b) White Merlot
(c) Pinot Noir (d) Pink Moscato

Listen and Pronounce

track 49

Listen to the audio first. Then, try pronouncing each one of the following dry rosé wines and sweet rosé wines.

Dry Rosé Wines 乾玫瑰紅葡萄酒

Grenache
格那希

Sangiovese
山吉歐維樹

Syrah
希哈

Mourvèdre
慕維得爾

Carignan
卡利濃

Cinsault / Cinsaut
仙梭

Pinot Noir
黑皮諾

Sweet Rosé Wines 甜玫瑰紅葡萄酒

White Zinfandel
白金芬黛

White Merlot
白梅洛

Pink Moscato
粉紅慕斯卡

track 50

Listen and fill in the blanks

Listen to the conversation and fill in the blanks.

1. Michelle and Ken see __________fields and __________fields on their way to a vineyard tour in Côtes de Provence, France.
2. There are seven major__________ in France including Champagne, Alsace, Loire Valley, Burgundy, Bordeaux, Rhone Valley and Provence.
3. Provence produces a lot of __________ , and produces up to 34% of all of all rosé wines made in the world.
4. There are three methods to make rose wine – the__________ method, blending method and saignée method.
5. Two types of rose wines are the__________ rosé wine and__________ rosé wine.

Photographs - How is rosé wine made? Maceration Method

Fill in the blanks with the correct answers given below:

1. Crush red grapes
2. Bottling
3. Maceration method
4. Fermentation
5. Harvest red grapes

A. ___________ B. ___________ C. ___________ D. ___________ E. ___________

Wine Tasting Tour

Learning Objectives

What you will learn in this unit...

- Learn how to serve wine.
- Learn how to order wine.
- Learn about the major wine-producing countries in the world.
- Learn the different types of red wines.
- Learn the different types of white wines.
- Learn about the wine tasting process.
- The 6 S's of wine tasting:
  See – Swirl – Sniff – Sip – Savor – Spit.
- What's on a wine label?
- Learn what important verbs, phrases and vocabulary related to wine tasting and wine tasting tours.

Brainstorming

1. What does the type of wine you drink say about you?

Red Wine 紅葡萄酒	Red Wine 紅葡萄酒	Red Wine 紅葡萄酒	White Wine 白葡萄酒	White Wine 白葡萄酒	White Wine 白葡萄酒
Pinot Noir 黑比諾	Cabernet Sauvignon 卡本內蘇維翁	Merlot 梅洛	Chardonnay 夏多內	Pinot Grigio 灰皮諾	Sauvignon Blanc 白蘇維翁
You are fresh, elegant and graceful. You are also unique and you like things your way.	You are super fancy, intelligent and worldly. You can be occasionally a bit pretentious.	You are easy to get along with and you are always a delightful partner.	You work hard and play hard. You are also fun and have lots of friends.	You are the type of person people love and hate.	You are smart and sexy. You are always in control of every aspect of your life.

2. Can you name some major wine-producing countries?
   Example: France, Spain, Chile, etc.
3. What kinds of red wines do you know of or drink?
   Example: Cabernet Sauvignon
4. What kinds of white wines do you know of or drink?
   Example: Chardonnay
5. Ask your partner what is his/her favorite type of wine.

What's on a wine label?
葡萄酒標籤

BASIC WORDS

A.Brand name / Producer name 葡萄酒品牌名稱 / 酒廠名稱	Chateau Les Valentines
B.Appellations (of origin) AOC [Appellation d`Origine Controlee] 指原產地法定區域管制餐酒，是法國葡萄酒的最高級別 -- 酒廠等級	Côtes de Provence
C.Vintage 葡萄採收年份 (The year of which the grapes were harvested)	2011
D.Country of production 生產國	France
E.Wine type (type of grape) 葡萄品種	red wine

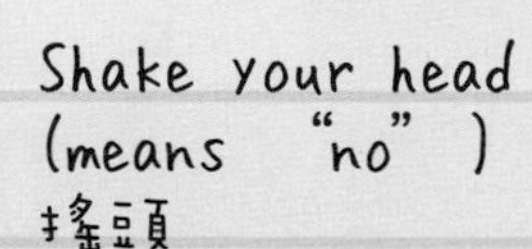

Shake your head
(means "no")
搖頭

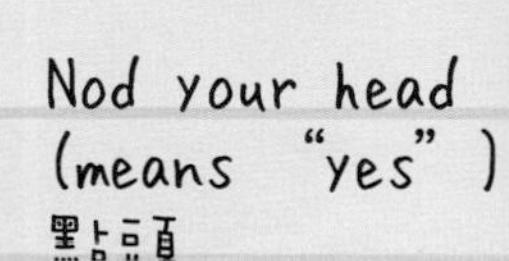

Nod your head
(means "yes")
點頭

A. Sommelier 侍酒師
B. Open a bottle of wine with a wine opener / corkscrew
使用開瓶器開一瓶葡萄酒

sniff the cork 聞軟木塞

Pour wine into a wine glass
倒葡萄酒到酒杯裡

Wine Tasting Process

The 6 S's of Wine Tasting: See – Swirl – Sniff – Sip – Savor - Spit

See / look at (the color of wine)
觀察葡萄酒顏色

Swirl (the wine glass)
輕搖酒杯 / 醒酒

Sniff (the wine) / inhale deeply / whiff
聞酒 (將鼻子伸入杯中深呼吸)

Sip (the wine)
啜飲葡萄酒

Savor (the wine)
細細品嚐
(讓舌頭和臉頰所有細胞去感受酒的風味及酒的濃郁程度)

A. Spit wine
吐葡萄酒到葡萄酒吐桶
B. wine tasting spittoon
葡萄酒吐桶

Conversation Preview

 Phrasal Words

Below are some phrases between a sommelier and a tourist. Practice the phrases below with a partner.

Tourist 觀光客	Sommelier 侍酒師
★ *After their vineyard tour in Côtes De Provence, Ken and Michelle went for a wine tasting session.* ★ Honey, I'm really looking forward to our wine tasting session.	★ Good evening. Here's our wine menu. ★ Let me know if there's anything you like on the menu. ★ You are allowed four free wine tastings per person.
★ How much is it for extra tastings?	★ You can add on 3 extra tastings for €5 per person.
★ What red wines would you recommend?	★ Some of our favorites are the Cabernet Sauvignon, Malbec, Merlot, Pinot Noir and Shiraz.
★ I prefer white wine. ★ Can you recommend some white wines?	★ Some of our favorites are the Chardonnay, Moscato, Pinot Grigio, Riesling and Sauvignon Blanc.
★ I'll have a glass (bottle) of Chardonnay. ★ I'll have a glass of Moscato. ★ I'll have a glass of Pinot Grigio. ★ I'll have a glass of Riesling. ★ I'll have a glass of Sauvignon Blanc.	★ Ok. Coming right up! ★ Sure. What about you, sir/ma'am?
★ I'll have a glass of Malbec. ★ I'll have a glass of Cabernet Sauvignon. ★ I'll have a glass of Merlot. ★ I'll have a glass of Pinot Noir. ★ I'll have a glass of Shiraz.	★ I'll open a whole new bottle of Malbec for you, sir. ★ Sir, this is a bottle of French Malbec and its vintage is 2010.

Listening Practice

track 51

Listen to the audio. Listen to the conversation between a tourist and a sommelier during a wine tasting session. Then choose the correct answer.

( ) 1. (a) The tourist gets four free wine tastings.
(b) The tourist gets three free wine tastings.

( ) 2. (a) The tourist ordered a glass of Moscato.
(b) The tourist ordered a glass of Sauvignon Blanc.

( ) 3. (a) The tourist ordered a glass of Cabernet Sauvnignon.
(b) The sommelier recommended two red wines – Cabernet Sauvignon and Malbec.

( ) 4. (a) The tourist ordered a glass of Merlot.
(b) The tourist ordered a glass of Malbec.

( ) 5. (a) The tourist ordered a glass of Sauvignon Blanc.
(b) The tourist ordered a glass of Chardonnay.

Test Yourself

Fill in the blanks with the correct answers given below.

a. Chardonnay	d. Malbec
b. wine tastings	e. vintage
c. extra tastings	

1. Sommelier: Good evening. Here's our wine menu. Let me know if there's anything you like on the menu. You are allowed four free__________per person.
2. Michelle: How much is it for__________?
   Sommelier: You can add on 3 extra tastings for €5 per person, ma'am.
   Michelle: Sounds wonderful.
3. Ken: What red wines would you recommend?
   Sommelier: Some of our favorites are the Cabernet Sauvignon,__________ , Merlot, Pinot Noir and Shiraz.
4. Michelle: I prefer white wine. Can you recommend some white wines?
   Sommelier: Some of our favorites are the __________ , Moscato, Pinot Grigio, Riesling and Sauvignon Blanc.
5. *The sommelier first poured Michelle a glass of Chardonnay. He then turned to Ken.*
   Sommelier: Sir, this is a bottle of French Malbec and its __________ is 2010.

Conversation

track 52

After their vineyard tour in Côtes De Provence, Ken and Michelle went for a wine tasting session[1].

Sommelier[2]: Good evening. Here's our wine menu[3].

Michelle: How many free wine tastings are we allowed?

Sommelier: You are allowed four free wine tastings per person.

Michelle: [a] How much is it for extra tastings[4]?

Sommelier: You can add on 3 extra tastings for €5 per person, ma'am.

Michelle: Sounds wonderful.

Ken: [b] What red wines would you recommend?

Sommelier: [c] Some of our favorites are the Cabernet Sauvignon[5], Malbec[6], Merlot[7], Pinot Noir[8] and Shiraz[9].

Michelle: I prefer white wine. Can you recommend some white wines?

Sommelier: [d] Some of our favorites are the Chardonnay[10], Moscato[11], Pinot Grigio[12], Riesling[13] and Sauvignon Blanc[14].

New Words & Phrases

track 53

1. wine tasting session (n.) 品葡萄酒會
2. sommelier (n.) 侍酒師 同 wine waiter
3. wine menu (n.) 葡萄酒單 同 wine list
4. extra tastings (n.) 額外品酒
5. Cabernet Sauvignon (n.) 卡本內蘇維翁葡萄酒
6. Malbec (n.) 馬爾貝克葡萄酒
7. Merlot (n.) 梅洛葡萄酒
8. Pinot Noir (n.) 黑皮諾葡萄酒
9. Shiraz (n.) 西拉葡萄酒
10. Chardonnay (n.) 夏多內葡萄酒
11. Moscato (n.) 白莫斯卡托葡萄酒
12. Pinot Grigio (n.) 灰皮諾葡萄酒
13. Riesling (n.) 麗絲玲葡萄酒
14. Sauvignon Blanc (n.) 白蘇維翁葡萄酒

New Words & Phrases

15. French Merlot (n.) 法國馬爾貝克葡萄酒
16. vintage (adj.) 葡萄收成年分
17. wine opener (n.) 開瓶器
    同 bottle opener / corkscrew
18. cork (n.) 軟木塞
    （Notes: sniff the cork for cork taint 聞軟木塞涵義在於檢視軟木污染 (cork taint)。是一個廣義的術語，指的是一種不良狀況，主要指的是在一瓶葡萄酒中發現一系列不良氣味或味道，特別是在裝瓶、老化和開放後才能檢測到的腐敗）
19. inspection (n.) 視察 同 view
20. nod your head (phrasal verb) 點頭
    同 yes 反 shake your head / no
21. pour (v.) 倒 反 drip

A few moments later...

Sommelier: Ma'am, what would you like?

Michelle: [e] I'll have a glass of Chardonnay.

Sommelier: What about you, sir?

Ken: [f] I'll have a glass of Malbec, please.

Sommelier: [g] I'll open a whole new bottle of Malbec for you, sir.

Ken: That sounds great!

The sommelier first poured Michelle a glass of Chardonnay. He then turned to Ken.

Sommelier: [h] Sir, this is a bottle of French Malbec[15] and its vintage[16] is 2010.

The sommelier opened the bottle of Merlot with a wine opener[17]. He then placed the cork[18] in front of Ken for inspection[19]. Ken inspected the cork and then sniffed the cork. Ken then nodded his head[20]. The sommelier then poured[21] some wine into Ken's wine glass.

Sommelier: Ma'am, would you also like to try a glass of Merlot?

Michelle: Yes, please!

The sommelier poured Ken and Michelle each a glass of wine. They then picked up their wine glasses, and looked at[22] the color of their wines. A few moments later, they swirled[23] their wine glasses a few times. Then, they stuck their noses into their wine glasses[24], and sniffed[25] it before taking a sip[26]. Ken and Michelle then savored[27] the wine to pick up the different wine textures[28]. Ken and Michelle took a few more sips before spitting[29] their wine into a wine tasting spittoon[30].

Ken and Michelle paid for extra tastings and tasted a few other wines.

New Words & Phrases

22. look at (the color of wine) (phrasal verb) 觀察 同 see
23. swirl (the wine glass) (v.) 輕搖酒杯 / 固定方向順時針或逆時針搖晃杯子 同 swoosh
24. stuck their noses into the wine glass (phrase) 將鼻子伸入酒杯中 反 unstuck
25. sniff (wine) (v.) 深吸一口氣 同 whiff / inhale
26. sip (wine) (v.) 啜飲葡萄酒 反 gulp
27. savor (wine) (v.) 細細品嚐 （讓舌頭和臉頰內所有細胞去感受酒的風味及酒的濃郁程度）
28. wine texture (n.) 口感 （當我們談論葡萄酒的質地時，我們基本上描述了口感或觸感）
29. spit (wine) (v.) 吐葡萄酒
30. wine tasting spittoon (n.) 葡萄酒吐桶 同 wine tasting dump bucket / wine tasting spit bucket

Q & A

1. How many free wine tastings do Ken and Michelle each get?

____

2. What red wines did the sommelier recommend?

____

3. What wine did Michelle order?

____

4. Describe the bottle of wine that the sommelier opened for Ken.

____

5. Describe the six steps of the wine tasting processes (The 6 S's of Wine Tasting)

Step 1: ______________________________

Step 2: ______________________________

Step 3: ______________________________

Step 4: ______________________________

Step 5: ______________________________

Step 6: ______________________________

Important Sentences

a. How much is it for extra tastings?
請問如果額外品酒要加多少費用？

b. What red wines would you recommend?
你可以建議些紅酒嗎？

c. Some of our favorites are the Cabernet Sauvignon, Malbec, Merlot, Pinot Noir and Shiraz.
我們最受客戶歡迎的有卡本內蘇維翁、馬爾貝克、梅洛、黑比諾及西拉。

d. Some of our favorites are the Chardonnay, Moscato, Pinot Grigio, Riesling and Sauvignon Blanc.
我們最受客戶歡迎有霞多麗、白莫斯卡托、灰皮諾、麗絲玲及白蘇維翁。

e. I'll have a glass of Chardonnay.
請給我一杯霞多麗葡萄酒。

f. I'll have a glass of Malbec, please.
請給我一杯馬爾貝克葡萄酒。

g. I'll open a whole new bottle of Malbec for you, sir.
先生，我會開一瓶全新的馬爾貝克葡萄酒給您。

h. Sir, this is a bottle of French Malbec and its vintage is 2010.
先生，這是一瓶法國梅洛葡萄酒，葡萄收成年份是 2010 年。

Conversation Review

Match the Chinese-English Translations

a. 白莫斯卡托葡萄酒	e. 視察	i. 點頭
b. 馬爾貝克葡萄酒	f. 侍酒師	j. 倒
c. 黑比諾葡萄酒	g. 卡本內蘇維濃葡萄酒	k. 灰皮諾葡萄酒
d. 葡萄收成年份	h. 口感	l. 白蘇維翁葡萄酒

(　) 1. sommelier
(　) 2. Cabernet Sauvignon
(　) 3. Malbec
(　) 4. Pinot Noir
(　) 5. Moscato
(　) 6. Pinot Grigio
(　) 7. Sauvignon Blanc
(　) 8. vintage
(　) 9. inspection
(　) 10. nod your head
(　) 11. pour
(　) 12. wine texture

Wine Tasting Process (The 6 S's of Wine Tasting)

Place the following wine tasting process answers in the correct order: 1 ~ 6

(　) 1. Savor wine to pick up different textures of wine.
(　) 2. Swirl the wine glass a few times.
(　) 3. Sniff the wine.
(　) 4. Spit wine into a wine tasting spittoon.
(　) 5. See (look at) the color of wine.
(　) 6. Sip the wine.

Listen and Pronounce

track 54

Listen to the audio first. Then, try pronouncing each one of the following.

Red Wines 红葡萄酒

Barbera
巴貝拉葡萄酒

Cabernet Sauvignon
赤霞珠葡萄酒
(卡本內蘇維翁)

Grenache
歌海納葡萄酒

Malbec
馬爾貝克葡萄酒

Merlot
梅洛葡萄酒

Nebbiolo
內比羅奧

Pinot Noir
黑皮諾

Sangiovese
桑嬌維塞（基安蒂）

Shiraz
西拉

Zinfandel
仙粉黛

White Wines 白葡萄酒

Chardonnay
夏多內

Gewürztraminer
格烏茲塔明那

Moscato
蜜思嘉 /
白莫斯卡托

Pinot Grigio
灰皮諾

Riesling
麗絲玲

Sauvignon Blanc
白蘇維翁

Semillon
賽美蓉

Listen and fill in the blanks

track 55

Listen to the conversation and fill in the blanks.

1. The customer is allowed four free ____________ per person.
2. The sommelier recommended some red wines such as the ___________ , Malbec, Merlot, Pinot Noir and Shiraz.
3. The customer ordered a glass of _____________ .
4. The customer ordered a glass of _____________ .
5. The sommelier opened a bottle of French Malbec and its _______________ is 2010.

Choose the incorrect answer

( ) 1. What's on a wine label?
(a) brand name
(b) vintage
(c) wine type
(d) wine tasting spittoon

( ) 2. What's on a wine label?
(a) AOC
(b) country of production
(c) sniff
(d) appellation

( ) 3. Wine tasting process:
(a) wine opener
(b) swirl
(c) see
(d) savor

( ) 4. Wine tasting process:
(a) sip
(b) spit
(c) sniff
(d) cork

( ) 5. Things you need to taste wine:
(a) wine tasting spittoon
(b) a bottle of wine
(c) wine glass
(d) screwdriver

Photographs

1. What is the man doing?
   (a) He is sniffing wine from a wine tasting spittoon.
   (b) He is spitting wine into a wine tasting spittoon.
   (c) He is savoring wine from a wine tasting spittoon.
   (d) He is swirling wine into a wine tasting spittoon.

Your answer: (　　)

2. What is the woman doing?
   (a) She is spitting wine into a wine glass.
   (b) She is sniffing wine from a wine glass.
   (c) She is sipping wine from a wine glass.
   (d) She is swirling a wine glass.

Your answer: (　　)

Italian Coffee Bar

Learning Objectives

What you will learn in this unit...

- Names of different types of coffee.
- The Italian coffee menu.
- Names of different types of coffee beans.
- Some of the most popular coffee beans producing countries.
- Italian coffee drinking culture.
- How to order Italian coffee.
- Coffee related keyword verbs, phrases and idioms.

Brainstorming

1. What your coffee says about you?

Espresso / Caffé (義大利文) 濃縮咖啡

You are friendly and adaptive. You actually like the taste of coffee, a rare and admirable trait.

Doppio / Corsivo / Double Espresso 雙份濃縮咖啡

You are practical and hardworking. You like knowing that one shot just doesn't do it for you anymore.

Cappuccino 卡布奇諾

You are warm-hearted, but oblivious at times. Your friends have to remind you to wipe the foam off your lip.

Corretto 烈酒咖啡 / 卡瑞托咖啡

You try very hard to relax, but find it difficult. You also like the kick of caffèine, but also wished you were more laid back at the same time.

Latte Macchiato 拿鐵瑪奇朵

You are reflective, but often indecisive. In a world of unknowns, you like the safe pick.

2. Can you name some types of coffee?
   Example: Americano.
3. What is your favorite café?
   Example: Starbucks.
4. What are some coffee producing countries, and what are some types of coffee beans that they produce?
   Example: Indonesia produces Java coffee beans.
5. What is your favorite coffee?
6. Ask your partner what his/her favorite coffee is?

BASIC WORDS

Italian Coffee 義大利咖啡

A. Doppio 多皮奧（雙份濃縮咖啡）(Corsivo / Double Espresso)
B. Ristretto（或稱 Caff Corto）芮斯崔朵／蕊絲翠朵／芮斯崔朵（咖啡比濃縮咖啡更濃，用相同的咖啡但用較少量的水）
C. Corretto 卡瑞托咖啡／烈酒咖啡 {濃縮咖啡加上些許烈酒，如 Grappa（義大利白蘭地），干邑酒 Cognac，Sambuca（義大利甘草酒）或其他烈酒}
D. Macchiato 瑪奇朵
E. Latte Macchiato 拿鐵瑪奇朵
F. Americano 美式咖啡

Top 10 Cities in Italy 義大利十大城市 (Chinese-English-Italian 中英義文)

1. 羅馬 Rome
2. 威尼斯 Venice
3. 佛羅倫斯 Florence
4. 米蘭 Milan
5. 拿坡里 Naples
6. 維洛那 Verona
7. 杜林 Turin
8. 波隆納 Bologna
9. 卡塔尼亞 Catania
10. 熱那亞 Genoa

sparkling water 氣泡水

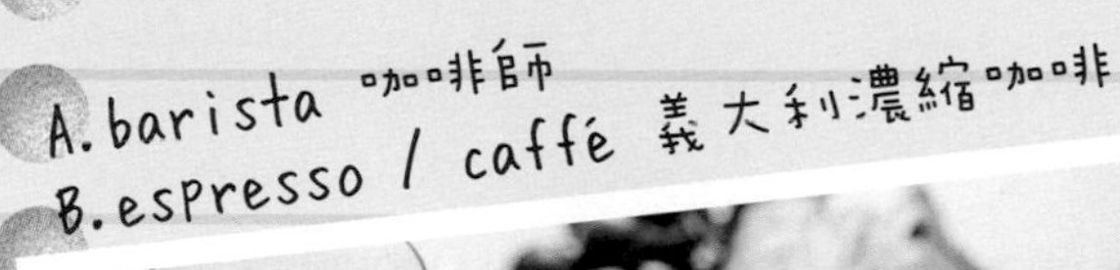

A. barista 咖啡師
B. espresso / caffé 義大利濃縮咖啡

A. coffee bar 咖啡吧
B. stood by the coffee bar 站在咖啡吧檯旁

A. change 零錢／找頭
B. receipt 收據／發票

Conversation Preview

Practice Phrases – Customer Service

Work with a partner to practice saying the phrases between a cashier and a customer below.

Cashier	Customer
★ What can I get for you today?	★ One Doppio, please. ★ I'd like a Corretto, please.
★ Any desserts for you?	★ I'll have a pistachio gelato, please. ★ I'll have a tiramisu, please.
★ That'll be €16.50, please. ★ Here's your change and receipt.	★ Here's €20.
★ Here you are. ★ One Doppio, one Corretto, two glasses of sparkling water, one tiramisu and one pistachio gelato.	★ Thank you.

Work with a partner to practice saying the phrases below.

Michelle	Ken
★ {It's after lunch time} I am craving for a cup of Cappuccino.	★ Honey, haven't you heard that the Italians only drink Cappuccino, Caffè Latte, Latte Macchiato, or any type coffee with milk as a breakfast beverage?
★ Did you know that coffee comes only in one size in Italy?	★ No, I didn't!
★ I'd love to try one of those quick, pick-me-up coffee bars.	★ Me too!
★ Honey, I think we are supposed to pay for our coffee to the cashier first.	★ Ok, let's join the queue!
★ I'd love something with strong caffeine.	★ What about Espresso, Ristretto, Doppio or Corretto?
★ I'd love to try something special.	★ What about Caffè Schiumato, Caffè Marocchino, Caffè Viennese, Corretto , Caffè al Ginseng or Caffè D'orzo?
★ It's almost our turn! ★ Have you made up your mind?	★ Yes, I have.
★ I heard that the Romans cleanse their palates with water before drinking coffee.	★ Ok. Just as they saying goes, "When in Rome, do as the Romans do."
★ Honey, let's drink our coffee in no more than three gulps!	★ Ok! On the count of three. One, two, three!

Listening Practice

track 56

Listen to the audio. Listen to the conversation and then choose the correct answer.

( ) 1. (a) The customer would like a tiramisu coffee and a Doppio for dessert.
(b) The customer would like a Doppio coffee and a tiramisu for dessert.

( ) 2. (a) The customer would like to have a pistachio gelato coffee and a Corretto for dessert.
(b) The customer would like to have a Corretto coffee and a pistachio gelato for dessert.

( ) 3. (a) The total price of the customer's order is €16.50.
(b) The total price of the customer's order is €20.

( ) 4. (a) The Italians drink water to cleanse their palates before drinking coffee.
(b) The Italians drink coffee to cleanse their palates before drinking water.

Test Yourself

Fill in the blanks with the correct answers:

a. caffè latte	e. cappuccino
b. pick-me-up	f. tiramisu
c. pistachio gelato	g. latte macchiato
d. sparkling water	h. one size

1. The Romans drink as__________ , __________ , __________ or any type of coffee with milk as a breakfast beverage.
2. The Italy, coffee only comes in______________ .
3. Look! There's a______________ coffee bar just around the corner.
4. The barista gave Ken a glass of ____________ to cleanse his palate before drinking his coffee.
5. Cashier: Would you like to have any desserts?
Customer: Yes, can I have a ___________ and one ____________ , please.

Conversation

track 57

New Words & Phrases

track 58

1. Rome (n.) 羅馬
2. Italy (n.) 義大利〔歐洲〕
3. pasta (n.) 廣稱的麵類 spaghetti，爲麵類中義大利麵的一種
4. exhausted (adj.) 極其疲憊的 / 精疲力竭的 同 extremely tired 反 energetic
5. craving (v.) 渴望 / 熱望
6. cappuccino (n.) 卡布奇諾
7. Caffè Latte (n.) 拿鐵咖啡 / 牛奶咖啡
8. Latte Macchiato (n.) 拿鐵瑪奇朵
9. breakfast beverage(s) (pl. n.) 早餐飲品
10. etiquette (n.) 禮儀 同 rules
11. one size (coffee) (adj.) 只有一種大小咖啡（義大利）
12. pick-me-up (coffee) (n.) 提神咖啡 同 energizer
13. coffee bar (n.) 咖啡吧（義大利）。有點類似「酒吧」的形式，只是販賣的東西變成了咖啡，多數爲有吧檯，前方有高腳椅的那種店。同 café / coffee shop

Michelle and Ken are in Rome[1], Italy[2]. They just had pasta[3] for lunch and are feeling rather exhausted[4] from walking around the city...

Michelle: Honey, I am craving[5] for a cup of Cappuccino[6].

Ken: Honey, haven't you heard that the Italians only drink Cappuccino, Caffè Latte[7], Latte Macchiato[8], or any type coffee with milk as breakfast beverages[9]?

Michelle: Oh, yes! I did read about it. The Italians have a coffee-drinking etiquette[10].

Ken: And, did you know that coffee comes only in one size[11] in Italy?

Michelle: Oh, really? I'd love to try one of those quick, pick-me-up[12] coffee bars[13].

Just then, they saw a coffee bar just around the corner[14]! They walked into the café.

Ken: Honey, I think we are supposed to pay for our coffee to the cashier[15] first.

Michelle: Let's take a look at the menu first.

Ken: I'd love something with strong caffèine[16].

Michelle: What about the Espresso[17], Ristretto[18], Doppio[19] or Corretto[20]?

Ken: They all look very enticing[21] to me.

Michelle: I'd love to try something special[22].

Ken: What about Caffè Schiumato[23], Caffè Marocchino[24], Caffè Viennese[25], Caffè Lungo[26], Caffè al Ginseng[27] or Caffè D'orzo[28]?

Ken: It's almost our turn![29] Have you made up your mind?[30]

Michelle: Yes, I have!

Cashier:[a] What can I get for you today?

Ken:[b] One Doppio, please.

Cashier:[c] Any desserts for you, sir?

Ken:[d] I'll have a tiramisu[31], please.

New Words & Phrases

14. just around the corner (idiom) 在街角附近 / 就在附近 同 nearby 反 far
15. cashier (n.)（商店、銀行、餐館等的）收銀員
16. caffèine (n.) 咖啡因
    反 decaf / decaffèinated
17. Espresso (n.) 義大利濃縮咖啡。
    在義大利，如果你想點濃縮義式咖啡 (Espresso)，只要點咖啡 (Caffé) 或是正常咖啡 (Caffé Normale) 就可以了。在義大利 Caffé 代表一般的咖啡，完全不添加任何東西的 espresso。同 Caffé（義大利）
18. Ristretto (n.) 芮斯崔朵 / 蕊絲翠朵（咖啡比濃縮咖啡更濃）
19. Doppio (n.) 多皮奧。雙份濃縮咖啡。
    同 Corsivo / Double Espresso
20. Corretto (n.) 卡瑞托咖啡 / 烈酒咖啡字面上的意思，其實是"正確的咖啡"。濃縮咖啡加上些許烈酒，如 Grappa（義大利白蘭地），干邑酒 Cognac，Sambuca（義大利甘草酒），或其他烈酒。
21. enticing (adj.) 有吸引力的
    同 attractive 反 unattractive
22. special (adj.) 特殊的 / 特別的
    同 unique 反 common
23. Caffè Schiumato (n.) 奶泡咖啡
24. Caffè Marocchino (n.) 摩洛哥式咖啡
25. Caffè Viennese (n.) 維也納咖啡
26. Caffè Lungo (n.) 長咖啡
27. Caffè al Ginseng (n.) 人參咖啡
28. Caffè D'orzo (n.) 大麥咖啡
29. It's almost our turn! (phrase) 快輪到我們了！
30. Have you made up your mind? (phrase) 你已經決定了嗎？同 decided 反 hesitant
31. tiramisu (n.) 提拉米蘇

Conversation

New Words & Phrases

32. pistachio gelato (n.) 開心果義式冰淇淋
33. gelato (n.) 義式冰淇淋
    兩種 gelato：gelato：內含乳製成份，常見像巧克力、榛果、咖啡 ... 等
    sorbet：以水爲底，一般以水果口味爲主，吃起來較爲清爽
34. change (n.) 零錢 / 找頭
35. receipt (n.) 收據 / 發票
36. stood by the coffee bar (phrasal verb) 站在咖啡吧檯旁
37. customers (n.) 顧客
38. barista (n.) 咖啡師
39. sparkling water (n.) 氣泡水
    同 mineral water 礦泉水
40. cleanse their palates with sparkling water before drinking coffee (phrase) 喝氣泡水把顎漱乾淨再喝咖啡
41. "When in Rome, do as the Romans do" (saying) 在羅馬的時候，要學習羅馬人，意思是「入境隨俗」When you are visiting another place, you should follow the customs of the people in that place.
42. gulps (n.) 咕嚕咕嚕地喝了下去
    同 swallow quickly 反 sip / drink slowly
43. On the count of three. One, two, three! (phrase) 我數到三，一、二、三！(命令某人執行某些動作)

Cashier: Ok. What can I get for you?

(Turning to Michelle)

Michelle: [e] I'd like a Corretto, please.

Cashier: Any desserts for you?

Michelle: [f] I'll have a pistachio gelato[32,33], please.

Cashier: [g] That'll be €16.50, please.

Ken: [h] Here's €20.

Cashier: [i] Here's your change[34] and receipt[35].

They stood by the coffee bar[36] with some other customers[37], and handed their receipt to the barista[38]. A few minutes later, the barista came by with their orders.

Barista: [j] Here you are. [k] One Doppio, one Corretto, two glasses of sparkling water[39], one tiramisu and one pistachio gelato.

Ken: I heard that the Romans cleanse their palates with sparkling water before drinking coffee[40].

Michelle: Ok. Just as they saying goes, "When in Rome, do as the Romans do.[41]"

Ken: Honey, let's drink our coffee in no more than three gulps[42]!

Michelle: Ok. On the count of three. One, two, three! [43]

Q & A

1. What size does Italian coffee come in?

____

2. What kinds of coffee did Michelle suggest to Ken?

____

3. What kind of coffee and dessert did Michelle order?

____

4. How much did Ken pay for their coffee and desserts?

____

5. What do the Romans do before drinking their coffee?

____

Important Sentences

a. What can I get for you today?
請問你今天想點什麼呢？

b. One Doppio, please.
請給我一杯雙份濃縮咖啡。

c. Any desserts for you, sir?
先生，要不要來個蛋糕甜點呢？

d. I'll have a tiramisu, please.
請給我一份提拉米蘇。

e. I'd like a Corretto, please.
請給我一杯烈酒咖啡 / 卡瑞托咖啡。

f. I'll have a pistachio gelato, please.
請給我一份開心果雞蛋奶泡義式冰淇淋。

g. That'll be €16.50, please.
總共是 €16.50。

h. Here's €20.
這是 €20。

i. Here's your change and receipt.
這是你的零錢及發票。

j. Here you are.
給你，都在這了

k. One Doppio, one Corretto, two glasses of sparkling water, one tiramisu and one pistachio gelato.
一份雙份濃縮咖啡、卡瑞托咖啡、兩杯氣泡水、提拉米蘇及一份開心果雞蛋奶泡義式冰淇淋。

Conversation Review

What can I get for you today?

Refer to the menu on page 167, and fill in the blanks below for the following:

(a) how many cups of coffee,

(b) type of Italian coffee, and

(c) calculate the total price of the coffee.

Example:

Customer: I'd like ______two______ ______Americano______, please.
(a) how many cups (b) type of coffee

Cashier: That'll be ______€1.80______, please.
(c) calculate total price

1. Customer: I'd like ____________ ____________, please.
(a) how many cups (b) type of coffee
Cashier: That'll be ____________, please.
(c) calculate total price

2. Customer: I'd like ____________ ____________, please.
(a) how many cups (b) type of coffee
Cashier: That'll be ____________, please.
(c) calculate total price

3. Customer: I'd like ____________ ____________, please.
(a) how many cups (b) type of coffee
Cashier: That'll be ____________, please.
(c) calculate total price

4. Customer: I'd like ____________ ____________, please.
(a) how many cups (b) type of coffee
Cashier: That'll be ____________, please.
(c) calculate total price

5. Customer: I'd like ____________ ____________, please.
(a) how many cups (b) type of coffee
Cashier: That'll be ____________, please.
(c) calculate total price

Mix and Match the Chinese-English translations

a. 雙份濃縮咖啡
b. 烈酒咖啡 / 卡瑞托咖啡
c. 早餐飲品
d. 禮儀
e. 咖啡吧
f. 義式冰淇淋
g. 咖啡師
h. 氣泡水
i. 入境隨俗
j. 咕嚕咕嚕地喝了下去

( ) 1. breakfast beverage
( ) 2. coffee bars
( ) 3. etiquette
( ) 4. Doppio
( ) 5. Corretto
( ) 6. When in Rome, do as the Romans do
( ) 7. gelato
( ) 8. barista
( ) 9. sparkling water
( ) 10. gulps

Choose the incorrect answer

( ) 1. Types of Italian food:
(a) pasta, (b) tiramisu, (c) gelato, (d) barista.

( ) 2. Types of Italian espresso:
(a) Corretto, (b) Espresso, (c) Ristretto, (d) Doppio,

( ) 3. Types of Italian breakfast beverages (with milk):
(a) Cappuccino, (b) Caffè Latte, (c) Doppio, (d) Latte Macchiato.

( ) 4. People at a coffee bar:
(a) cashier, (b) Rome, (c) barista, (d) customers.

( ) 5. Similar words to coffee shop:
(a) bar, (b) café, (c) coffee bar, (d) coffee house.

Listen and fill in the blanks

track 59

Listen to the conversation and fill in the blanks.

1. Michelle is craving for a cup of ____________ .
2. The Italians only drink Cappuccino, Caffè Latte, Latte Macchiato, or any type coffee with milk as _____________ .
3. The couple want to try one of those quick, ___________ - _________ - _________ coffee bars.
4. Michelle suggested some strong caffeine coffee to Ken such as the ________ , Ristretto, Doppio and Corretto.
5. Michelle and Ken ordered one __________ , one Corretto, two glasses of sparkling water, one tiramisu and one pistachio gelato.

Listen and Pronounce

track 60

Hot Coffee 熱咖啡系列

Americano 美式咖啡	€0.90
Espresso (Caffé) 濃縮咖啡	€1.00
Caffè al Ginsen 人蔘咖啡	€2.50
Caffè D'orzo 大麥咖啡	€1.40
Caffè Decafèinato 無咖啡因咖啡	€1.20
Caffè Hag 低咖啡因咖啡	€1.20
Caffè Latte 拿鐵咖啡 / 牛奶咖啡	€2.00
Caffè Lungo 長咖啡	€1.50
Caffè Marocchino 摩洛哥式咖啡	€1.50
Caffè Schiumato 奶泡咖啡	€1.75
Caffè Shakerato 雪克冰咖啡	€1.75
Caffè Viennese 維也納咖啡	€1.90
Cappuccino 卡布奇諾	€1.50
Chia Tea Latte 印度茶拿鐵	€1.30
Corretto 烈酒咖啡 / 卡瑞托咖啡	€2.00
Crema DiCaffè Fredda 咖啡奶昔	€2.50
Doppio (Corsivo / Double Espresso) 雙份濃縮咖啡	€1.20
Granita Di Caffè Con Panna 咖啡冰沙	€2.50
Latte Macchiato 拿鐵瑪奇朵	€1.50

Iced Coffee 冰咖啡系列

Espresso Freddo 濃縮冰咖啡	€1.90
Latte Freddo 拿鐵冰咖啡	€1.90
Cappuccino Freddo 卡布奇諾冰咖啡	€1.90
Americano Freddo 美式冰咖啡	€1.90
Caramel Macchiato Freddo 焦糖瑪奇朵冰咖啡	€1.90

Photographs

1. Which of the following sentences best describes the picture?

   (a) A barista is placing a cup of espresso onto a saucer.
   (b) A barista is making a cup of espresso for a customer.
   (c) A barista is serving the customer some sparkling water.
   (d) A barista is taking an order from a customer.

Your Answer: (　)

2. Which of the following sentences best describes the picture?

   (a) A man is drinking a cup of sparkling water to cleanse his palate.
   (b) A man is making a cup of espresso.
   (c) A man is eating a pistachio gelato.
   (d) A man is about to drink up his espresso in a gulp.

Your Answer: (　)

The Picasso Museum

Unit 13

Learning Objectives

What you will learn in this unit...

- Different types of museums.
- Names of famous artists of all times.
- Names of some of the most beautiful, famous and expensive paintings of all times.
- Names of some of the most famous works by Pablo Picasso.
- Some basic information about the Picasso Museum in Malaga, Spain.
- Some background information about Pablo Picasso.
- How to purchase and/or sell admission tickets and audio guides at a museum?

Brainstorming

- Museum related keyword verbs, phrases and idioms..

National Air and Space Museum(USA)
史密森尼學會旗下的航空與航太科學博物館【美國】

The National Air and Space Museum is the second most visited museum in the world, and the most visited museum in the United States. Almost all space and aircraft on display are originals or the original backup craft.

Louvre (France)
羅浮宮藝術博物館【巴黎】

The Louvre is the world's largest art museum and a historic monument. Approximately 38,000 objects from prehistory to the 21st century are exhibited.

British Museum (United Kingdom)
大英博物館【英國】

The British Museum is dedicated to human history, art and culture. It houses up to 8 million collections, originating from all continents.

Vatican Museums (Vatican City)
梵諦岡博物館【義大利】

The Vatican Museums are Christian and art museums. They display works from the immense collection amassed by Popes throughout the centuries.

The State Hermitage Museum (Russia)
冬宮博物館【俄羅斯】

The State Hermitage Museum is a museum of art and culture. It comprises over three million items including the largest collection of paintings in the world.

1. What are some of the most visited museums in the world?
2. What are some different types of museums?
   Example: art museum, etc.
3. Can you name some famous artists of all time?
   Example: Pablo Picasso, etc.
4. Can you name some of the most beautiful, famous and expensive paintings of all time?
   Example: Mona Lisa by Leonardo da Vinci.
5. Can you name the some of the most famous works of Pablo Picasso?
   Example: Three Musicians (1921), etc.

BASIC WORDS

MAP OF SPAIN
西班牙地圖

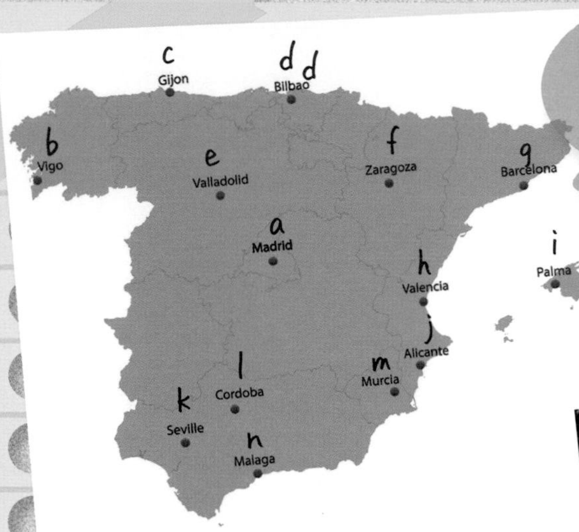

a. Madrid 馬德里【首都】
b. Vigo 維戈
c. Gijon 希洪
d. Bilbao 畢爾包
e. Valladolid 巴利亞多利德
f. Zaragoza 薩拉戈薩
g. Barcelona 巴塞隆那
h. Valencia 瓦倫西亞
i. Palma 帕爾馬島
j. Alicante 阿利坎特
k. Seville 塞維亞
l. Cordoba 哥多華
m. Murcia 穆爾西亞
n. Malaga 西班牙南部地中海沿岸的馬拉加，Malaga 是歐洲盛名的度假勝地

collections 收藏
artworks 藝術品 / 美術品

a. ticket window/ticket counter/ticket office 售票窗口
b. ticket attendant 票務員

Guinness World Records
吉尼斯世界紀錄

audio guide 語音導覽機

architecture
建築

tile 瓷磚
souvenir 紀念品

Conversation Preview

Practice Phrases

Work with a partner to practice saying the phrases below.

Partner A	Partner B
★ Honey, hurry up! ★ The location of Picasso Museum is quite hidden. Plus, we may have to queue for hours for the tickets.	★ Alight! Alight! ★ I'm coming! Picasso fan!
★ Honey...We are in Malaga, Spain. The birthplace of Picasso!	★ But, doesn't the museum only mainly cover the early years of Picasso's artistic life – the Blue Period from 1901 to 1904?
★ Yes. But, it houses one of the most extensive collections of Picasso's artworks – 4,251 to be exact! And, I'd really love to see some of his best paintings like The Frugal Repast (1904), The Old Guitarist (1903-1904), The Blindman's Meal (1903), The Portrait of Celestina (1903) and The Portrait of Soler (1903).	★ Ok, I'm impressed already!
★ I'm feeling a little tired. Let's call it the day!	★ I'm a little tired too... ★ I have to say that I just loved every part of the museum... from its Catalan architecture to all of Picasso's artworks!
★ I think that not only is Picasso a genius, but also, the most prolific artists of all time. ★ And, did you know that he also appears in the Guinness World Records?	★ Impressive! ★ Let's go get a tile with Picasso's painting on it as a souvenir!

Listening Practice

track 61

Listen to the audio, and then choose the correct answer.

( ) 1. (a) The Picasso museum has one of the most extensive collections of Picasso's artworks from the Rose Period from 1901 to 1904.
(b) The Picasso museum has one of the most extensive collections of Picasso's artworks from the Blue Period from 1901 to 1904.

( ) 2. (a) The tourist would like to purchase two permanent & temporary admission tickets.
(b) The tourist would like to purchase two temporary collection admission tickets.

( ) 3. (a) The ticket price for the permanent & temporary collections is €15.
(b) The ticket price for the permanent & temporary collections is €7.

( ) 4. (a) The tourist asked for two admission tickets for the permanent & temporary collections, and two Chinese audio guides.
(b) The tourist asked for two admission tickets for the temporary collections, and two Chinese audio guides.

Test Yourself

Fill in the blanks with the correct answers:

a. Artistic life
b. Collections
c. Permanent
d. Ticket attendant
e. Audio guide

1. The Picasso museum houses one of the most extensive __________ of Picasso's artworks – 4251 to be exact!
2. The Picasso museum mainly covers the early years of Picasso's __________. The Blue Period from 1901 to 1904.
3. Ken is at the Picasso museum ticket window:
A: I'd like two admission tickets, please?
B: Would you like tickets for the __________ & temporary collections, or just the temporary collection?
A: Definitely the permanent and temporary collections tickets!
4. B: Sure. Would you also like an __________?
A: Yes, please.
B: What language would you prefer?
A: Chinese, please.
B: Sure, your total will be €30 for the admission tickets, and €10 for the audio guides.
5. Ken bought the admission tickets at the Picasso museum from a __________.

Conversation

track 62

New Words & Phrases

track 63

1. Picasso museum (n.) 畢卡索博物館
2. Hurry up! (adj.) 趕快！/ 快！反 slow down
3. location (n.) 位置 / 地點 同 place / position
4. hidden (adj.) 隱藏的 / 神秘的
   同 covered 反 exposed
5. Picasso fan (n.) 畢卡索粉絲
6. Malaga (in Spain) (n.) 馬拉加
   西班牙南部地中海沿岸的馬拉加，Malaga 是歐洲盛名的度假勝地
7. Spain (n.) 西班牙
8. birthplace (n.) 出生地 同 homeland / native country
9. mainly (adv.) 大體上 / 主要地 同 mostly
10. cover (s) (vt.) 涵蓋
11. early years (n.) 早年 反 later years
12. artistic life (n.) 藝術生活
13. The Blue Period (from 1901 to 1904) (n.)
    憂鬱時期。畢卡索因在西班牙孤單的旅行受他的朋友卡洛斯・卡薩吉馬斯的自殺影響，使得藍色時期（1901 年－ 1904 年）期間的畫作常顯現出陰鬱的感覺。此時期的畫作以藍與藍綠的色調爲主，極少使用溫暖的顏色。
    反 The Rose Period - lasted from 1904 to 1906) 玫瑰時期是指畢卡索在 1904 年至 1906 年主要使用暖色調的橙色和粉色作畫的時期，與其之前的藍色時期形成了鮮明的對比。在畢卡索於 1904 年遇到了費爾南德之後他一直非常開心，這被認爲是它改變了他的畫風的一個重要原因。

Michelle is very excited this morning as they are going to visit the Picasso Museum[1].

Michelle: Honey, hurry up[2]! The location[3] of Picasso Museum is quite hidden[4]. Plus, we may have to queue for hours for the tickets.

Ken: Alright! Alright! I'm coming! Picasso fan[5]!

Michelle: Honey...We are in Malaga[6], Spain[7]. The birthplace[8] of Picasso!

Ken: But, doesn't the museum mainly[9] covers[10] the early years[11] of Picasso's artistic life[12] – the Blue Period[13] from 1901 to 1904?

Michelle: Yes. But, it houses[14] one of the most extensive[15] collections[16] of Picasso's artworks[17]– 4,251 to be exact[18]! And, I'd really love to see some of his best paintings like The Frugal Repast (1904)[19], The Old Guitarist (1903-1904)[20], The Blindman's Meal (1903)[21], The Portrait of Celestina (1903)[22] and The Portrait of Soler (1903)[23].

Ken: Ok, I'm impressed already!

After a forty-five minute walk, Michelle and Ken arrived at the museum entrance[24].

Michelle: We are lucky that the queue is not as long as we expected[25].

After a ninety-minute queue, [a] it was finally their turn at the ticket window[26]...

Ken: [b] We'd like two admission tickets, please.

Ticket attendant[27]: [c] Would you like tickets for the permanent & temporary collections,[28,29] or just the temporary collection?

Ken: [d] What are the ticket prices?

Ticket attendant: [e] It's €12[30] for the permanent & temporary collections, and €6 for the temporary collection.

Michelle: [f] Definitely[31] the permanent & temporary collections tickets!

Ticket attendant: [g] Would you like any audio guides[32]?

Ken: Yes, please.

Ticket attendant: [h] How many audio guides and in what language would you like?

Ken: [i] We'd like two Chinese audio guides, please.

Ticket attendant: [j] Ok, your total will be €24 for the admission tickets[33] and €14 for the audio guides. [k] Your total comes up to €38.

New Words & Phrases

14. houses (vt.) 供給 ... 房子 [用] 收藏
    同 hold / keep
15. extensive (adj.) 廣闊的 / 廣大的 / 廣博的
    同 broad / wide 反 limited
16. collections (n.) 收藏 同 accumulations
17. artworks (n.) 藝術品 / 美術品
18. to be exact (adj.) 精確地說〔插入語〕
19. The Frugal Repast (1904) (n.) 畢卡索藍色時期知名的蝕刻作品《儉樸的一餐》
20. The Old Guitarist (1903-1904) (n.)
    老吉他手（1903 年 ~190 年）
21. The Blindman's Meal (1903) (n.) 畢卡索的藍色時期常使用「失明」這個題材，像是《盲人的晚餐》(1903 年)
22. The Portrait of Celestina (1903) (n.) 《賽樂絲汀娜的肖像畫》（1903 年）畢卡索的藍色時期的作品
23. The Portrait of Soler (1903) (n.) 畢卡索的藍色時期的作品《索賴爾的肖像》(1903 年)
24. museum entrance (n.) 博物館入口
    反 museum exit
25. expected (v.) 預料 / 要求 / 認爲（某事）會發生 反 unexpected
26. ticket window (n.) 售票窗口
    同 ticket counter / ticket office
27. ticket attendant (n.) 票務員
28. permanent collection (n.) 永久收藏
    反 temporary collection
29. temporary collection (n.) 檔期收藏
30. €12 (n.) 12 Euro dollars 12 歐元
31. definitely (adv.) 一定地 / 肯定地
    同 absolutely 反 doubtfully
32. audio guides (n.) 語音導覽機
33. admission tickets (n.) 入場票

Ken: Here you are. (Ken handed the ticket attendant his credit card)

After spending three hours at the Picasso museum...

Michelle: I'm feeling a little tired. Let's call it the day! [34]

Ken: I'm a little tired too... I have to say that I just loved every part of the museum - from its Catalan[35] architecture[36] to all of Picasso's artworks!

Michelle: I think that not only is Picasso a genius[37], but also, the most prolific artist[38] of all time[39]. And, did you know that he also appears[40] in the Guinness World Records[41]?

Ken: Impressive! Let's go get a tile[42] with Picasso's painting on it as a souvenir[43]!

New Words & Phrases

34. Let's call it the day! (idiom)
今天就到此爲止吧！老外所謂的一天，就是整天的工作或任何活動告一段落。玩了或工作了一整天，累了～我不想再做任何事了。
35. Catalan (in Spain) (n.) (西班牙) 加泰蘭
36. architecture (n.) 建築
37. genius (n.) 天才 同 prodigy 反 amateur
38. prolific artist (n.) 多產藝術家
同 productive artist
39. of all time (idiom) 有史以來
40. appear (v.) 出現 同 be published
41. Guinness World Records (n.)
吉尼斯世界紀錄
42. tile (n.) 瓷磚
43. souvenir (n.) 紀念品

Q & A

1. Where was the birthplace of Picasso?

____

2. Name five of the best paintings that the Picasso museum houses.
(i) ____________________
(ii) ____________________
(iii) ____________________
(iv) ____________________
(v) ____________________

3. What are the ticket prices for the permanent & temporary collections, and temporary collection, respectively?

____

4. What did Ken and Michelle buy from the ticket attendant?

____

5. What did Ken love about the Picasso museum?

____

Important Sentences

a. It was finally their turn at the ticket window.
終於輪到他們到售票窗口了。

b. We'd like two admission tickets, please.
請給我們兩張入場票。

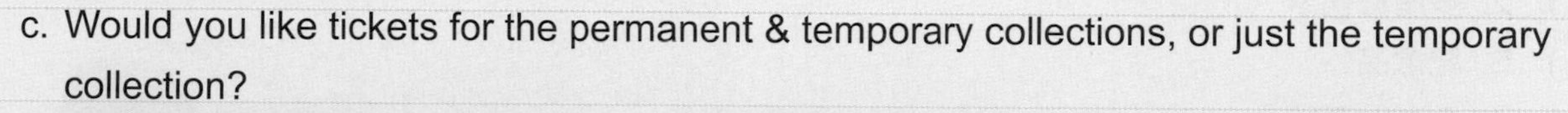

c. Would you like tickets for the permanent & temporary collections, or just the temporary collection?
您要含永久收藏和檔期收藏的門票或只是檔期收藏門票呢？

d. What are the ticket prices?
請問門票價格是多少？

e. It's €12 for the permanent & temporary collections, and €6 for the temporary collection.
永久收藏和檔期收藏的門票是十二歐元，檔期收藏門票是六歐元。

f. Definitely the permanent & temporary collections tickets!
當然是永久收藏和檔期收藏的門票！

g. Would you like any audio guides?
你需要語音導覽機嗎？

h. How many audio guides and in what language would you like?
你要幾個語音導覽機及什麼語文呢？

i. We'd like two Chinese audio guides, please.
我們要兩套中文語音導覽機。

j. Ok, your total will be €24 for the admission tickets and €14 for the audio guides.
好的，門票共是二十四歐元及導覽機共是十四歐元。

k. Your total comes up to €38.
總共是三十八歐元。

l. Here you are.
這裡是 ...[38 歐元]。

Conversation Review

Match the English-Chinese translations

a. Picasso museum	e. ticket window	i. audio guides
b. artistic life	f. ticket attendant	j. admission tickets
c. collections	g. permanent collection	k. prolific artist
d. museum entrance	h. temporary collection	l. souvenir

(　) 1. 票務員
(　) 2. 多產藝術家
(　) 3. 紀念品
(　) 4. 永久收藏
(　) 5. 檔期收藏
(　) 6. 語音導覽機
(　) 7. 入場票
(　) 8. 畢卡索博物館
(　) 9. 藝術生活
(　) 10. 收藏
(　) 11. 博物館入口
(　) 12. 售票窗口

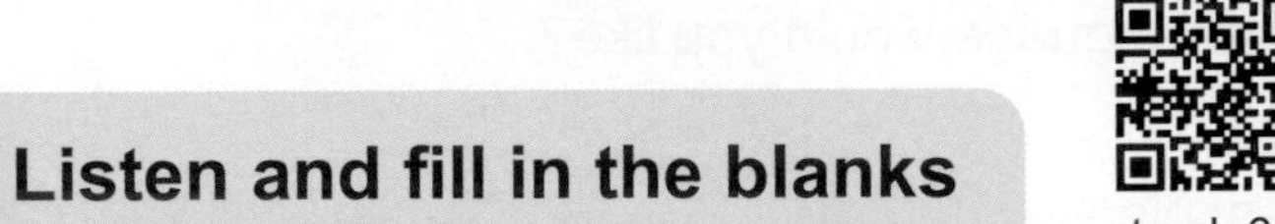

Listen and fill in the blanks

track 64

Listen to the conversation and fill in the blanks.

1. The Picasso museum mainly covers the early years of Picasso's ____________ during the Blue Period from 1901 to 1904.
2. The Picasso museum houses one of the most extensive ___________ of Picasso's artworks.
3. The tourist asked for two admission tickets for the permanent and __________ collections.
4. The tourist asked for two Chinese __________ __________.
5. The couple loved every part of the museum, from its Catalan architecture to all of Picasso's ___________.

Listen and Pronounce

track 65

Listen to the audio first. Then, try pronouncing each one of the following museums:

1. National Museum of China	中國國家博物館 (Beijing 北京)
2. National Air and Space Museum	國家航空航太博物館 (Washington, D.C. 華盛頓特區)
3. Louvre	羅浮宮 (Paris 巴黎)
4. Metropolitan Museum of Art	大都會藝術博物館 (New York City 紐約市)
5. British Museum	英國博物館 (London 倫敦)
6. National Palace Museum	故宮博物院 (Taipei 台北)
7. Vatican Museums	梵蒂岡博物館 (Vatican City 梵蒂岡城市)
8. National Gallery of Victoria	維多利亞國家美術館 (Melbourne 墨爾本)
9. National Museum of Natural Science	國家自然科學博物館 (Tokyo 東京)
10. Van Gogh Museum	梵谷博物館 (Amsterdam 阿姆斯特丹)

Choose the incorrect answer

( ) 1. Types of museum admission tickets:
(a) temporary collection (b) permanent collection
(c) temporary and permanent collection (d) Blue collection

( ) 2. Items you need to visit a museum:
(a) audio guides (b) admission tickets
(c) ticket attendant (d) money

( ) 3. Famous Picasso paintings:
(a) The Frugal Repast (b) The New Guitarist
(c) The Blindman's Meal (d) The Old Guitarist

( ) 4. Facts about Picasso:
(a) born in Italy (b) most prolific artist of all time
(c) appears in the Guinness World Records
(d) born in Spain

Photographs

Look at the pictures and match it with the answers given below:

1. Which one of the following __________ sentences best describes the picture?
   (a) There are some ticket attendants queueing to buy admission tickets.
   (b) There are some ticket attendants looking at Picasso's artworks.
   (c) There are some tourists queueing to buy admission tickets.
   (d) There are some tourists queueing to buy souvenirs.

Your Answer: ( )

2. Which one of the following __________ sentences best describes the picture?
   (a) A woman is looking at some Picasso paintings.
   (b) A woman is listening to audio guides.
   (c) A woman is buying admission tickets.
   (d) A woman is looking at some postcard souvenirs.

Your Answer: ( )

Unit 14

Northern Light Tour

Learning Objectives

What you will learn in this unit...

- What are the best places to see Northern lights (Aurora Borealis), and why?
- What are the top ten countries you can see the Northern Lights (Aurora Borealis)?
- What are some countries where you see the Southern Lights (Aurora Australis)?
- Do you know what is an aurora?
- Some differences between the Northern Lights (Aurora Borealis) and Southern Lights (Aurora Australis).
- Names of some Scandinavian countries.
- What are some things to do on a Scandinavian winter tour?
- Northern Light tour related keywords, verbs, phrases and idioms.
- Scandinavian tour related keyword verbs, phrases and idioms.

Brainstorming

1. Where in the world do you think are the best places to see Northern lights (Aurora Borealis), and why?

Iceland 冰島	**Finland** 芬蘭	**Sweden** 瑞典	**Canada** 加拿大	**Norway** 挪威
Iceland is the only location where you can spot the Borealis from almost anywhere in the country as long as you are outside Reykjavik.	The Northern Lights appear more than 200 nights a year in Finland, which is practically every winter evening.	Sweden is scientifically proven to be an ideal viewing spot due to its unique microclimate and already perfect dark winter nights.	The town of Yellowknife & the town of Whitehorse within Yukon Territory in Canada are some of the best places for seeing the Northern lights.	You can't go much higher than Svalbard. Generally, the higher the latitude, the better your chances of seeing the Northern Lights in Norway.

2. What are the top ten countries you can see the Northern Lights (Aurora Borealis)?
   Example: Iceland.
3. What are some countries where you see the Southern Lights (Aurora Australis)?
   Example: Australia.
4. Do you know what is an aurora?
5. Can you point out some differences between Northern Lights (Aurora Borealis) and Southern Lights (Aurora Australis)?
6. Name some Scandinavian countries.
   Example: Sweden.
7. What are some things to do on a Scandinavian winter tour?
   Example: See the Northern Lights.

A. Northern Lights / aurora borealis 北極光
B. Ice Hotel 冰酒店
BASIC WORDS
A
A. ice suite 冰套房
B. reindeer hides 馴鹿皮
C. ice bed 冰雕飾的床
snowmobile ride
騎摩托雪橇
glacier 冰川
ice cave 冰洞
ice fishing
冰上釣魚
A. musher 趕狗拉雪橇的人
B. sled 雪橇
C. Husky 哈士奇犬
D. wilderness / backwoods 荒野
A. ice bar 冰酒吧
B. vodka ice glass
伏特加冰酒杯
ICEBAR
STOCKHOLM
23
Give the Huskies a good belly rub!
好好摸一摸哈士奇犬的肚子

Conversation Preview

Practice Phrases

Work with a partner to practice saying the phrases below between a receptionist and a hotel guest at an Ice Hotel in Sweden.

Receptionist	Hotel Guest
★ Welcome to Ice Hotel. We are the biggest hotel made of ice in the world.	★ That sounds amazing! ★ Where do you get all that ice to build everything?
★ All the snow and ice is from the nearby Torne River.	★ It's no wonder Ice Hotel is listed as one of the Seven Wonders of Sweden. ★ Is everything really made from snow and ice?
★ Yes, sir. The reception area, restaurant, ice bar, chapel, and even the vodka glasses are ice sculptures.	★ That sounds amazing!
★ Let me ask our bellboy to show you to your ice suite.	★ That'll be great!

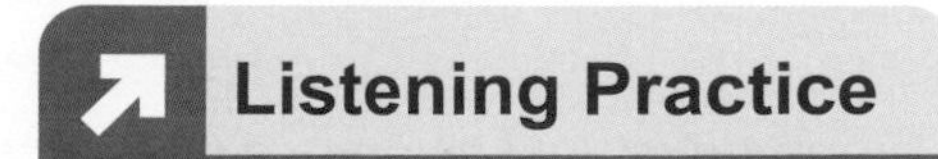

Listening Practice

track 66

Listen to the audio, and then choose the correct answer.

( ) 1. (a) The Ice Hotel is made of snow and ice from the nearby Torne River.
(b) The Ice Hotel is made of snow and ice from the Arctic Circle.

( ) 2. (a) The theme of each ice suite is from Kiruna, Germany, the United Kingdom and the United States.
(b) Each ice suite is hand-carved by artists from Kiruna, Germany, the United Kingdom and the United States.

( ) 3. (a) Each ice suite has the same design and has an ice bed covered with reindeer hides to keep hotel guests warm.
(b) Each ice suite has a different design and has an ice bed covered with reindeer hides to keep hotel guests warm.

( ) 4. (a) The Northern Lights dances across the sky in Jukkasjärvi, Sweden.
(b) The Northern Lights breathes across the sky in Jukkasjärvi, Sweden.

Test Yourself

Fill in the blanks with the correct answers:

a. Northern Lights	c. ice bar	f. hand-carved
b. breathtaking	d. vodka ice glasses	g. reindeer hides
	e. belly rub	

1. Receptionist: Welcome to Ice Hotel. We are the biggest hotel made of ice in the world.
   Hotel Guest: Is everything really made from snow and ice?
   Receptionist: Yes, sir. The reception area, restaurant,________ , chapel, and even the______ are ice sculptures.
2. Bellboy: Welcome to your ice suite. Each ice suite has a different theme, and is______by artists.
3. Hotel Guest: Is the bed over here also made of ice?
   Bellboy: Yes, it is. Your ice bed is covered with________and you will be sleeping in a thermal sleeping bag to keep you warm.
4. A: Honey! Wake up! The Northern Lights are about to appear!
   B: Wow! That's amazing! Looks like the________ is flaring up!
   A: Look how it's dancing across the sky – twisting and rolling away.
   B: Look, honey! It's fading away now.
   A: This is absolutely__________!
5. *Ken and Michelle watched the Northern Lights until they fell asleep. The next morning, they went on a Husky sledding tour.*
   Musher: Welcome to Kiruna Tours. Today, you will be mushers.
   But, before we start, let's give the Huskies a good_________ !

Conversation

track 67

New Words & Phrases

track 68

1. Jukkasjärvi (n.) 瑞典尤卡斯耶爾維（離北極圈 200 公里以內一個瑞典小鎮）
2. village (n.) 小鎮 / 村莊 同 small town 反 city
3. Sweden (n.) 瑞典
4. Arctic Circle (n.) 北極圈 同 north polar
5. Ice Hotel (n.) 冰酒店（位於瑞典北部的尤卡斯耶爾維（Jukkasjärvi）。館內設有冰雕客房，由採自托爾訥河（Torne River）的冰塊鑿建而成）。
6. Torne River (n.) 托爾訥河
7. Seven Wonders of Sweden (n.) 瑞典七大奇蹟
8. ice bar (n.) 冰酒吧
9. chapel (n.) （基督教）小教堂 同 church
10. vodka ice glass (n.) 伏特加冰酒杯
11. ice sculpture (n.) 冰雕
12. bellboy (n.) 旅館的服務生 / 旅館里爲客人搬運行李到房間裏的服務生 同 bellhop / bellman
13. ice suite (n.) 冰套房
14. theme (n.) 主題
15. hand-carved 手工雕刻 同 handmade
16. Kiruna (n.) 基律納市
17. unique (adj.) 獨一無二的 同 different 反 general
18. reindeer hides (n.) 馴鹿皮
19. thermal sleeping bag (n.) 保暖睡袋
20. sauna (n.) 三溫暖
21. hot spring (n.) 溫泉
22. outdoors (n.) 戶外的 / 露天的 反 indoors

Ken and Michelle have arrived in Jukkasjärvi[1], a village[2] in Sweden[3] just 200 km north of the Arctic Circle[4].

Receptionist: [a] Welcome to Ice Hotel[5]. We are the biggest hotel made of ice in the world.

Ken: That sounds amazing! Where do you get all that ice to build everything?

Receptionist: All the snow and ice is from the nearby Torne River[6].

Michelle: It's no wonder Ice Hotel is listed as one of the Seven Wonders of Sweden[7].

Ken: Is everything really made from snow and ice?

Receptionist: Yes, sir. [b] The reception area, restaurant, ice bar[8], chapel[9], and even the vodka ice glasses[10] are ice sculptures[11]. Let me ask our bellboy[12] to show you to your ice suite[13].

Michelle: That'll be great!

The bellboy brought Ken and Michelle to their ice suite.

Bellboy: Welcome to your ice suite. Each ice suite has a different theme[14], and is hand-carved[15] by artists.

Ken: Where are the artists from?

Bellboy: [c] The artists are from Kiruna[16], Germany, the United Kingdom and the United States.

Michelle: Is the design of each suite different?

Bellboy: Yes, it is. [d] Each ice suite is unique[17] and has never been created before.

Ken: Is the bed over here also made of ice?

Bellboy: Yes, it is. Your ice bed is covered with reindeer hides[18] and you will be sleeping in a thermal sleeping bag[19] to keep you warm.

Michelle: I don't see a bathroom in our ice suite.

Bellboy: We have no bathroom in your ice suite. But, we do have a sauna[20] and hot spring[21] outdoors[22]. Is there anything else I can help you with?

Michelle: Everything's great!

It was well after midnight. Ken and Michelle laid down on their ice beds. Just as they were about to fall asleep, the Aurora alarm"[23] beeped[24].

[Beep! Beep! Beep!]

Michelle: Honey! Wake up! The Northern Lights[25] are about to appear!

Ken then opened his eyes and looked up at the glass ceiling[26] from his bed.

Ken: Wow! That's amazing! Looks like the Aurora[27] is flaring up[28]!

Michelle: Look how it's dancing across the sky – twisting[29] and rolling away.

Ken: Look, honey! It's fading away[30] now.

Michelle: I see green and yellow lights!

Ken: It's turning green and red now.

Michelle: [e] This is absolutely breathtaking[31]!

Ken and Michelle watched the Northern Lights until they fell asleep. The next morning, they went on a Husky[32] sledding tour[33].

Musher[34]: Welcome to Kiruna Tours. Today, you will be mushers.

Ken: How far a distance will we be covering today?

Musher: [f] We will cover about 30 km, and travel over frozen lakes[35] and through forests.

Michelle: That sounds really exciting!

Musher: But, before we start, let's give the Huskies a good belly rub[36]!

Ken and Michelle received further instructions about sledding. When they hopped onto their sleds[37], the Huskies were already jumping, barking and rolling in the snow.

Musher: [g] All set? Let's head out into the wilderness[38]!

After their Husky dog sledding tour, Ken and Michelle signed up[39] for snowmobile ride[40], whale-watching[41], ice fishing[42]. They also explored a glacier[43] and entered an ice cave[44]!

New Words & Phrases

23. Aurora alarm (n.) 極光警示 / 歐若拉警示（當極光出現時，提醒你）
24. beep (n.) 嗶嗶聲
25. Northern Lights (n.) 北極光
    同 Polar Lights / Aurora Borealis
    反 Southern Lights / Aurora Australis
26. glass ceiling (n.) 玻璃天花板
27. Aurora (n.) 極光
28. flaring up (n.) 爆發
29. twisting (v.) 轉動 / 旋轉
30. fading away (phrasal verb) 逐漸消失
31. breathtaking (adj.) 使人透不過氣來的
32. Husky (plural Huskies) (n.) 哈士奇犬
33. sledding tour (n.) 雪橇之旅
34. musher (n.) 趕狗拉雪橇的人
35. frozen lake (n.) 冰凍的湖泊
36. belly rub (n.) 摸摸肚子
37. sled (s) (n.) 雪橇 同 sledge
38. wilderness (n.) 荒野
    同 nature / backwoods 反 city
39. sign up (phrasal verb) 報名參加（某項有組織的活動）
40. snowmobile ride (n.) 騎摩托雪橇
41. whale-watching (n.) 賞鯨魚
42. ice fishing (n.) 冰上釣魚
43. glacier (n.) 冰川
44. ice cave (n.) 冰洞

Q & A

1. Where in Sweden are Ken and Michelle?

2. Which parts of Ice Hotel is made from ice sculptures?

3. Describe the ice bed in the ice suite.

4. What colors of the Aurora did Ken and Michelle see?

5. What did the musher ask Michelle and Ken to do before receiving further instructions about Husky dog sledding?

Important Sentences

a. Welcome to Ice Hotel. We are the biggest hotel made of ice in the world.
歡迎來到冰酒店。 我們是世界上最大的冰酒店。

b. The reception area, restaurant, ice bar, chapel, and even the vodka ice glasses are ice sculptures.
接待區、餐廳、冰吧、小教堂，甚至伏特加酒杯都是冰雕的。

c. The artists are from Kiruna, Germany, the United Kingdom and the United States.
這些藝術家來自基律納市、德國、英國和美國。

d. Each ice suite is unique and has never been created before.
每間冰套房都是獨一無二的，以前從未創建過。

e. This is absolutely breathtaking!
這景色美得太令人無法呼吸！

f. We will cover about 30 km, and travel over frozen lakes and through forests.
我們將旅行約 30 公里，並通過冰凍的湖泊和森林。

g. All set? Let's head out into the wilderness!
都準備好了嗎？讓我們出發往荒野吧！

Match the Chinese-English

a. 馴鹿皮	f. 冰套房	l. 使人透不過氣來的
b. 保暖睡袋	g. 北極圈	m. 極光
c. 溫泉	h. 冰酒吧	n. 玻璃天花板
d. 小鎮 / 村莊	i. （基督教）小教堂	o. 爆發
e. 旅館的服務生 / 旅館裏爲客人搬運行李到房間裏的服務生	j. 伏特加冰酒杯	
	k. 冰雕	

( ) 1. village
( ) 2. Arctic Circle
( ) 3. ice bar
( ) 4. chapel
( ) 5. vodka ice glass
( ) 6. ice sculpture
( ) 7. bellboy
( ) 8. ice suite
( ) 9. reindeer hides
( ) 10. thermal sleeping bag
( ) 11. hot spring
( ) 12. Aurora
( ) 13. glass ceiling
( ) 14. flaring up
( ) 15. breathtaking

Conversation Review

track 69

Listen and fill in the blanks

Listen to the conversation and fill in the blanks.

1. Everything in Ice Hotel is made from snow and ice including the_____________ , chapel and vodka___________.
2. Each ice suite has a different theme and is ___________ - __________by artists.
3. There is no bathroom in the ice suite. But, the Ice Hotel has a sauna and ___________ outdoors.
4. Ken and Michelle are watching the _____________ and find it absolutely breathtaking.
5. Michelle signed up for a Husky_______________tour.

track 70

Listen and Pronounce

Below are some things a tourist can do on a Scandinavian winter tour. Listen to the audio first. Then, try pronouncing each of the following:

1. See the Northern Lights (Aurora Borealis)	賞北極光
2. Husky dog sledding	哈士奇狗拉雪橇
3. Ride on a snowmobile	駕駛雪橇
4. Stay at an Ice Hotel	住在冰酒店
5. Go ice fishing	冰上釣魚
6. Whale-watching	賞鯨魚
7. Explore glaciers	探索冰川
8. Explore an ice cave	探索冰洞
9. Go to an ice bar	去冰酒吧
10. See ice sculptures	賞冰雕
11. Explore the wilderness	探索荒野
12. Soak in a hot spring	泡溫泉

Choose the incorrect answer

( ) 1. Things made of sculptured ice in an Ice Hotel:
(a) ice bar, (b) reception,
(c) chapel, (d) bellboy.

( ) 2. Types of tours:
(a) Husky dog sledding tour, (b) snowmobile ride,
(c) musher, (d) whale-watching.

( ) 3. Things you would see in the winter in Sweden:
(a) frozen lakes, (b) glass ceiling,
(c) glacier, (d) ice cave.

( ) 4. Things on a Husky dog sled:
(a) musher, (b) Husky,
(c) sled, (d) snowmobile.

( ) 5. Words related to Aurora:
(a) Northern Lights, (b) Aurora Borealis,
(c) Southern, (d) Aurora Australis.

Photographs

1. Which of the following sentences best describes the picture?

   (a)The man is ice fishing.
   (b)The man is riding on a Husky dog sled.
   (c)The man is riding over a frozen lake.
   (d)The man is riding on a snowmobile.

Your answer: (   )

2. Which of the following sentences best describes the picture?

   (a) A man is watching the Northern Lights.
   (b) A man is standing in an ice cave.
   (c) A man is looking at a hot spring.
   (d) A man is looking at the wilderness.

Your answer: (   )

SELF-SERVICE CHECK-IN KIOSK

Unit 15

Learning Objectives

What you will learn in this unit...

- Learn about the different ways to check-in your flight.
- Learn more about airport self-service check-in kiosks.
- Learn how to check-in at a self-service check-in kiosk.
- Learn about the procedures involved in self-service check-in kiosks.
- Learn some ways of which your flight booking information can be retrieved at the self-service check-in kiosk.
- Learn about international airports that have self-service check-in kiosks.
- Self-service check-in kiosks related keyword verbs, phrases and idioms.

Brainstorming

1. What does the way you check-in at the airport say about you?

Self-service Check-in Kiosk
自助報到登機

You are a fast-learner and definitely don't like to waste time waiting in line at the airport. You are also always up to date on technological changes.

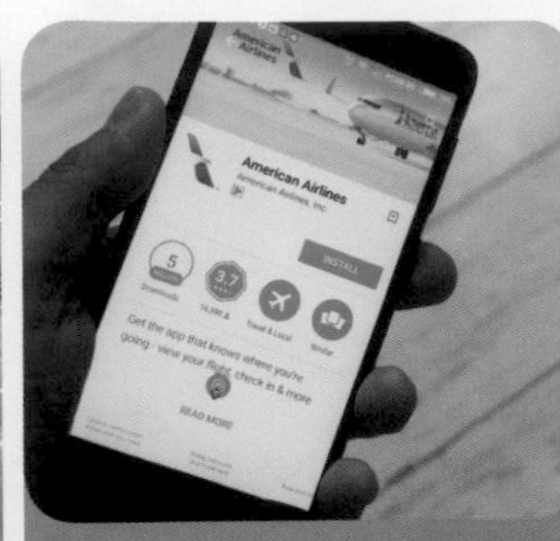

Mobile Check-in
手機報到

You spend most of your time and work on the mobile phone, and cannot live without it. As long as anything can fit into that mobile phone of yours, you'll do it!

Web Check-in
網路報到

You bring your laptop wherever you go. And, you prefer the good old computer to the mobile phone when doing your work.

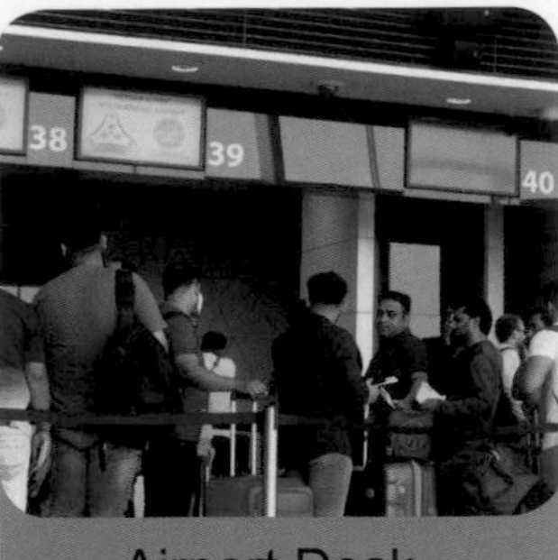

Airport Desk Check-in
機場現場報到

You like to do things the old-fashioned way. Using today's technology is a burden to you. You also like human interaction and love to socialize.

2. What are some ways of which your flight booking information can be retrieved at the self-service check-in kiosk?
   Example: scan passport.
3. What are some procedures involved at a self-service check-in kiosk?
   Example: scan passport → confirm flight information, etc.
4. Name some airports that have self-service check-in kiosks. You may surf the internet.
   Example: Australia-Brisbane Airport (BNE).

BASIC WORDS

self-service check-in kiosk
自助報到登機

screen 螢幕

Ways to retrieve your booking information
自行選擇多種報到方式

Retrieve your booking by selecting one of these options:

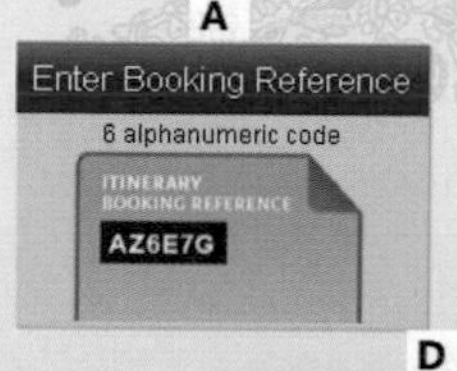

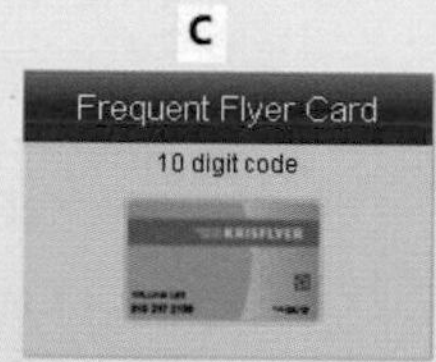

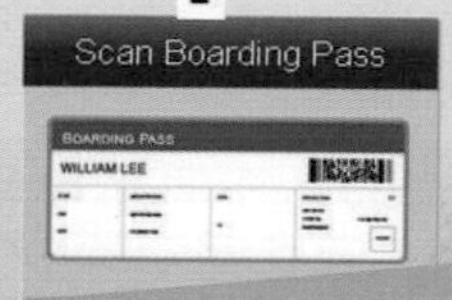

A. booking reference number 訂位代碼
B. E-ticket number 電子機票號碼
C. Frequent flyer card number / membership number 會員卡號
D. Passport 護照
E. Boarding pass 登機證

luggage tag / baggage tag
bag tag / luggage identification tag
行李標籤

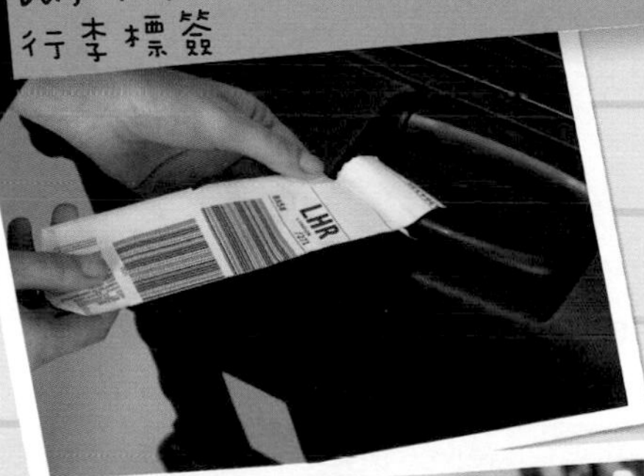

wait in line
排隊等候

customer representative
客戶服務代表

baggage drop counter
自助報到行李託運櫃台

Conversation Preview

Practice Phrases A

Practice the phrases below between a couple trying to check-in at a self-service check-in kiosk.

Ken	Michelle
★ *{It's their last day in Europe. Ken and Michelle are at the London Heathrow Airport1 heading back to Taipei.}*	★ Honey, it seems that the check-in system in London is rather different from Taipei.
★ Yes, I noticed that too. Everyone uses the self-service check-in kiosks.	★ Ok, I see one right there!
★ *{Michelle and Ken walked up to an open self-service check-in kiosk.}*	
★ The screen says, a "Scan your identification card or passport".	★ Whose should we scan first? ★ Let's scan my passport first.
★ Ok, here we go.	★ Now, it says "Enter booking reference number, e-ticket number or frequent flyer card number."
★ Why don't we use our booking reference number? I've got it right here with me.	★ Sure! What's our booking reference number?
★ It's AZ 98761820T.	★ Here's our names and travel itinerary.
★ Ok, press "CONFIRM". It's now asking how many checked baggage we have?	★ Enter "TWO". Now, we have to place our bags on the baggage scale.
★ *{Ken then placed their luggage, one by one onto the baggage scale.}*	★ Great! We are not overweight. Just below 25 kg each.
★ *{The self-service check-in kiosk starting printing…}*	
★ Look, it's printing our boarding passes and luggage tags now.	★ I'll attach our luggage tags onto our bags.

Practice Phrases B

Practice the phrases below between a customer service representative and a passenger at a self-check-in baggage drop counter.

Customer Service Representative	Passenger
★ Can I have your passports and boarding passes?	★ Sure, here you are.
★ How many bags are you checking in today?	★ One. ★ Just one. ★ Two.
★ Ok. You are all set to go! ★ Your boarding gate is at G77 and the boarding time is at 10:50 p.m. Have a great flight!	★ Thank you.

Test Yourself

a. baggage scale
b. attach
c. check-in
d. luggage tags
e. e-ticket

1. *Michelle and Ken are at the London Heathrow airport, heading back home to Taipei.*
   Michelle and Ken walked up to an open self-service ____ kiosk to check-in.
2. A: We can use our booking reference number, _____ number or frequent flyer card number.
   B: Let's use our booking reference number. I've got it right here with me.
3. A: We have to now place our bags on the ____ .
   B: Great! We are not overweight. Just below 25 kg each.
4. A: It's printing our boarding passes and _____ now.
   B: I'll ____ our luggage tags onto our bags.

track 71

Listening Practice

Listen to the audio. Listen to the conversation and then choose the correct answer.

( ) 1. (a) Michelle and Ken decided to scan their identification card at the self-service check-in kiosk.
(b) Michelle and Ken decided to scan their passports at the self-service check-in kiosk.

( ) 2. (a) Ken and Michelle entered their e-ticket number.
(b) Ken and Michelle entered their booking reference number.

( ) 3. (a) The customer service representative said that Ken's luggage is not overweight.
(b) The customer service representative said that Ken is overweight.

( ) 4. (a) Ken and Michelle waited in line to drop their bags.
(b) Ken and Michelle waited in line to check-in.

Conversation

track 72

It's their last day in Europe. Ken and Michelle are at the London Heathrow Airport[1] heading back to Taipei.

Michelle: Honey, it seems that the check-in system[2] in London is rather different from Taipei.

Ken: Yes, I noticed[3] that too. Everyone uses the self-service check-in kiosks[4].

Michelle: Ok, I see one right there!

Michelle and Ken walked up[5] to an open[6] self-service check-in kiosk.

Ken: The screen[7] says, [a] "Scan your identification card or passport".

Michelle: Whose should we scan first?

Michelle: Let's scan my passport first.

Ken: Ok, here we go.

Michelle: Now, it says [b] "Enter booking reference number[8], e-ticket number[9] or frequent flyer card number[10]."

Ken: Why don't we use our booking reference number? I've got it right here with me.

Michelle: Sure! What's our booking reference number?

Ken: It's AZ 98761820T.

Michelle: Here's our names and travel itinerary.

Ken: Ok, press "CONFIRM[11]". It's now asking how many checked baggage we have?

Michelle: Enter "TWO". Now, we have to place our bags on the baggage scale[12].

New Words & Phrases

track 73

1. London Heathrow Airport (n.) 倫敦希斯洛機場 (IATA 代碼)
2. check-in system (n.) 報到系統
3. noticed (v.) 注意到 反 unnoticed
4. self-service check-in kiosks (n.) 自助報到機 反 airport desk check-in
5. walk up (idiom) 走上前 反 walk away
6. open (adj.) 開放的 同 available 反 unavailable
7. screen (n.) 螢幕
8. booking reference number (n.) 訂位代號 (例如 : JV68HA)
9. e-ticket number (n.) 電子機票號碼
10. Frequent flyer card number (n.) 會員卡號 同 membership number
11. confirm (v.) 確認 反 unconfirmed 同 approve
12. baggage scale (n.) 行李磅秤 同 bag / luggage scale

Ken then placed their luggage, one by one onto the baggage scale.

Michelle: Great! We are not overweight[13]. Just below 25 kg each.

The self-service check-in kiosk starting printing...

Ken: Look, it's printing our boarding passes and luggage tags[14] now.
Michelle: I'll attach[15] our luggage tags onto our bags.

Ken and Michelle then waited in line[16] at the self-check-in baggage drop counter[17].

Customer service representative[18] : Next! [c] Can I have your passports and boarding passes?
Ken: Sure, here you are.
Customer service representative: [d] How many bags are you checking in today?
Ken: Two.

The customer service representative then placed their bags onto the conveyor belt.

Customer service representative: Ok. You are all set to go! [19] Your boarding gate is G77 and the boarding time is at 10:50 p.m. Have a great flight!

Q & A

1. How did Michelle and Ken check-in at the airport?

____

2. What did Ken and Michelle scan at the self-service check-in kiosk?

____

3. What is their booking reference number?

____

4. What two items does the self-service check-in kiosk print out?

____

5. What is their boarding gate number?

____

New Words & Phrases

13. overweight(adj.) 超重 反 underweight
14. luggage tag (n.) 行李識別標籤 同 baggage tag / bag tag / luggage identification tag
15. attach (+ to) (vt.) 繫上
16. wait in line (phrase) 排隊等候 同 stand in line / queue
17. self-check-in baggage drop counter (n.) 自助報到行李託運櫃台
18. customer service representative (n.) 客戶服務代表
19. You are all set to go! (phrase) 你一切都準備好了！同 You are ready!

Important Sentences

a. Scan your identification card or passport.
掃瞄您的身分證或護照。

b. Enter booking reference number, e-ticket number or frequent flyer card number.
輸入訂位代號、電子機票號碼或會員號碼。

c. Can I have your passports and boarding passes?
請給我您的護照及登機證。

d. How many bags are you checking in today?
你今天有託運幾件行李呢？

Conversation Review

Match the pictures with the answers given below

(a) Retrieving booking information
(b) Attaching luggage tag onto bag
(c) Printing boarding pass
(d) Confirming flight (destination).
(e) Placing luggage / bag onto a baggage scale
(f)Scanning passport
(g) Checking-in luggage at the airport counter

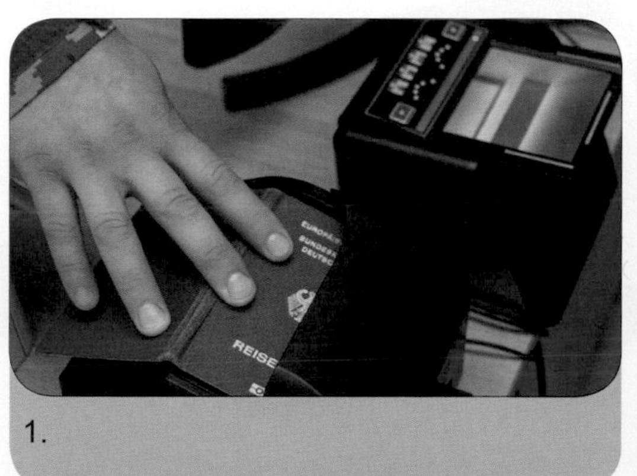

1.

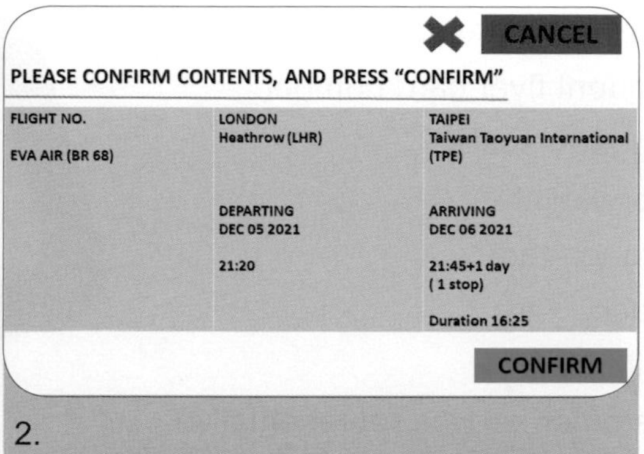

2.

3.

4.

5.

6.

 Match the English-Chinese translations

a. 行李識別標簽　　e. 自助報到行李託運櫃台　　i. 會員號碼
b. 繫上　　f. 行李託運櫃台　　j. 行李磅秤
c. 自助報到機　　g. 排隊等候　　k. 超重
d. 訂位代號　　h. 客戶服務代表

( ) 1. self-check-in baggage drop counter
( ) 2. self-service check-in kiosks
( ) 3. booking reference number
( ) 4. frequent flyer card number
( ) 5. baggage scale
( ) 6. overweight
( ) 7. luggage tag
( ) 8. attach (+ to)
( ) 9. wait in line
( ) 10. customer service representative

Listen and fill in the blanks

track 74

Listen to the conversation and fill in the blanks.

1. Ken and Michelle are at the London Heathrow Airport and are about to use a self-service ________-________ kiosk.
2. They scanned Michelle's ________ first.
3. They used their booking ________ reference number AZ98761820T.
4. Their luggage are below 25kg each, so they are not ________ .
5. The self-service check-in kiosk printed their boarding passes and ________

track 75

Listen and Pronounce

Listen to the audio first. Then, try pronouncing each one of the following airports.

Airport 機場	Location 地點	Country 國家
Beijing Capital International Airport 北京首都國際機場	Beijing 北京	China 中國
Dubai International Airport 杜拜國際機場	Dubai 杜拜	United Arab Emirates 阿拉伯聯合大公國
Tokyo Haneda Airport 東京羽田機場	Tokyo 東京	Japan 日本
Los Angeles International Airport 洛杉磯國際機場	Los Angeles 洛杉磯	United States 美國
O'Hare International Airport 歐海爾國際機場	Chicago 芝加哥	United States 美國
London Heathrow Airport 倫敦希思洛機場	London 倫敦	United Kingdom 英國
Hong Kong International Airport 香港國際機場	Hong Kong 香港	Hong Kong 香港
Shanghai Pudong International Airport 上海浦東國際機場	Pudong, Shanghai 上海浦東	China 中國

Choose the incorrect answer

( ) 1. Ways to check in your flight:
(a) self-service check-in kiosk
(b) mobile check-in
(c) spiderweb check-in
(d) airport desk check-in

( ) 2. Ways to retrieve your booking information:
(a) booking reference number
(b) E-ticket number
(c) frequent flyer card number
(d) airport ID

( ) 3. Ways to retrieve your booking information:
(a) passport
(b) identification card
(c) student ID
(d) boarding pass.

( ) 4. Items a self-service check-in kiosk prints out:
(a) boarding pass
(b) identification card
(c) luggage tag
(d) employee pass

( ) 5. Procedures involved in self-service check-in:
(a) Scan passport
(b) Place bag on scale
(c) Remove bag from conveyor belt
(d) Attach luggage tag onto bag

Photographs

Look at the pictures and then answer the questions:

1. Which statement best describes the picture?
   (a) The blue luggage is on a conveyor belt.
   (b) The blue luggage is on a baggage scale.
   (c) The blue luggage is at a self-service check-in kiosk.
   (d) The blue luggage is at a baggage drop counter.

Your answer: ( )

2. Which statement best describes the picture?
   (a) A person is scanning her e-ticket on a self-service check-in kiosk.
   (b) A person is entering her reference number on a self-service check-in kiosk.
   (c) A person is scanning Frequent flyer card on a self-service check-in kiosk.
   (d) A person is scanning her passport on a self-service check-in kiosk.

Your answer: ( )

Photo Sources

P.11

EVA AIR

https://www.evaair.com/en-us/index.html

IBERIA

https://www.iberia.com/?language=en

WIKIPEDIA

https://mwiki.upupming.now.sh/zh-hant/%E6%A9%9F%E7%A5%A8

FLIPBOARD

https://flipboard.com/@hassenalsaadjr/do-you-know-a02ggnjsz

P.51

Creditcards.com

https://www.creditcards.com/american-express/

GORDON RAMSAY RESTAURANTS

https://www.gordonramsayrestaurants.com/book-a-table/

OpenTable

https://www.opentable.com/

Reservation Genie

https://www.reservationgenie.com/

Michelin twitter

https://twitter.com/michelin

P.76

NYTIX

https://www.nytix.com/articles/broadway-tickets

Telecharge

https://www.telecharge.com/

Greenwood Festival Chorale

http://www.greenwoodfestivalchorale.org/?page_id=2843

BRITANNICA

https://www.britannica.com/biography/Hubert-Walter

P.116

El Cartel Del Gaming

https://www.elcarteldelgaming.com/2020/01/nerd/deja-vu-che-cose-analizziamo-il-mistero/

P.144

Wikiwand

http://www.wikiwand.com/de/Flight_(Wein)

P.172

THYSSEN-BORNEMISZA MUSEO NACIONAL

https://www.museothyssen.org/en/collection/artists/picasso-pablo/frugal-meal

其餘圖片皆爲全華提供。

國家圖書館出版品預行編目 (CIP) 資料

餐旅英文 / 鄭寶菁編著 . -- 初版 . -- 新北市 : 全華圖書 , 2020.06
面； 公分
ISBN 978-986-503-386-6（平裝）
1. 英語 2. 餐旅業 3. 會話
805.188 109005806

餐旅英文

作　　者 / 鄭寶菁
發 行 人 / 陳本源
執行編輯 / 黃艾家
封面設計 / 蕭暄蓉
出 版 者 / 全華圖書股份有限公司
郵政帳號 / 0100836-1號
印 刷 者 / 宏懋打字印刷股份有限公司
圖書編號 / 08296007
初版一刷 / 2020年6月
定　　價 / 450元
I S B N / 978-986-503-386-6
全華圖書 / www.chwa.com.tw
全華科技網 Open Tech / www.opentech.com.tw
若您對書籍內容、排版印刷有任何問題，歡迎來信指導book@chwa.com.tw

臺北總公司（北區營業處）
地址：23671新北市土城區忠義路21號
電話：(02) 2262-5666
傳真：(02) 6637-3695、6637-3696

南區營業處
地址：80769高雄市三民區應安街12號
電話：(07) 381-1377
傳真：(07) 862-5562

中區營業處
地址：40256臺中市南區樹義一巷26號
電話：(04) 2261-8485
傳真：(04) 3600-9806